MISSING CHILDREN

MISSING CHILDREN

GERALD LYNCH

Doug Whiteway, Editor

© 2015, Gerald Lynch

All rights reserved. No part of this book may be reproduced, for any reason, by any means, without the permission of the publisher.

Cover design by Doowah Design.
Photo of author by Maura Lynch, Crow Photography.

Acknowledgements
The editors of *The Puritan* magazine invited and published the short story "Child's Play" that, after lying fallow for a good spell, grew into this novel. I am most grateful to the staff of Signature Editions, and especially to publisher Karen Haughian for expertly guiding the novel through to publication and for tolerating, and pretending convincingly to welcome, my 'interventions' in that process. I owe the greatest debt of gratitude to editor Doug Whiteway—in my experience, a reader and editor nonpareil.

This book was printed on Ancient Forest Friendly paper.
Printed and bound in Canada by Hignell Book Printing Inc.

We acknowledge the support of the Canada Council for the Arts and the Manitoba Arts Council for our publishing program.

Library and Archives Canada Cataloguing in Publication

Lynch, Gerald, 1953–
    Missing children / Gerald Lynch.

Issued in print and electronic formats.
ISBN 9927426-79-1 (paperback).--ISBN 978-1-927426-80-7 (epub)

    I. Title.

PS8573.Y43M58 2015   C813'.54   C2015-905905-4
                                                      C2015-905997-6

Signature Editions
P.O. Box 206, RPO Corydon, Winnipeg, Manitoba, R3M 3S7
www.signature-editions.com

for
Mary Jo
and our adult children,
Bryan, Meghan, and Maura

Chapter 1

No matter a Saturday night, for a long time already we'd been going to bed earlier. No more staying up for the late local news and snacking away like teenagers. Getting older, sooner tired, even if a sound night's sleep was as long gone as the languorous passage of golden summer afternoons and endless evenings, when a night's sleep was all sweet dreams and restoration. Anyway, the only thing new under the TV sun was bad news. Even the local show increasingly blared crime: murder, muggings, break-ins, drugs, molesting of children in their schools and playgrounds and homes—anything to arrest your attention long enough to sell you snow tires for the SUV, if you really really love your loved ones. Such fare disturbed sleep like a bellyful of barbecue Fritos. So, early to bed. Which was also the only way we ever got any pleasure reading done. Or that was Veronica's idea of a bonus. I wasn't much of a reader for pleasure then.

For me the true bonus in going to bed at around ten was that both kids were still awake. Of course, Owen never slept regularly, prowling at all hours, sleeping in till shouted out of bed. I opened his door first.

On his back, with eyes closed and wearing earplugs, he couldn't have noticed me, yet something alerted him. A shift in the rank dimness? Paternal atmospheric pressure?

He pulled the left plug and made an irritated face. "Huh?"

I controlled myself. "I just saw something about that Rot-10 on CNN. Paternity suit. Looks like your rappin' rebel hero's about to become a daddy."

I'd meant only to mention the news item, and not in that voice.

"Anything about the Market Slasher?"

"Nope, not ready for the big show yet. He'll just have to try harder."

I hated Owen's sick interest in this, Ottawa's very own psychosexual serial killer, who'd already been dubbed with a CNN-friendly name and announced with percussive theme music. Three young girls' deaths so far, all hookers, two of them Natives, down in the ByWard Market. *MURDER IN THE MARKET*. That's what my son was asking after. The media had been instantly on it like starved sharks to a banquet of fat white thighs. I needed to redirect Owen's attention.

"Uh, seriously, you should listen to the remastered *Abbey Road* LP."

He closed his eyes. "Beatles again? Who gives a shit?" A dismissive puff. "How 'bout turnin' on the air?" He reinserted the earplug and dropped back his head like his throat had been incised. "*El-pee*," he wagged and smirked, which I liked.

It was hot but no call for A/C, as the temperature should moderate through the night. I had to fight a sudden urge to shake him by the shoulders and warn him against the tattoo he'd been threatening to get. So I shut his door and turned to my daughter Shawn's.

She was lying diagonally on the bed, facing away from me, on her stomach, legs together, in pyjama shorts that looked too small for her bum. From the back, her frizzy pale head made me think of a dandelion clock. She was growing, changed every time I looked at her, like when she was a baby and I was super-busy and hardly saw her at all. I suffered a hollowing pang of missing her.

Her curtains were still open, which I didn't like, and though gathered at the sides they were still moving in a light breeze, which I did like. But the window was a big black rectangle looking in on her.

"Goodnight, sweetheart. You should close your curtains."

She made a sound that was mere acknowledgement. I reminded myself to be careful, as she was moodier and moodier these days. I sometimes wondered if she was growing to hate me. Veronica said it was just normal girl growing up. I argued that Shawn was taking her cue from disrespectful Owen. Veronica said I had to make more of an effort with Owen, that we should be patient with those we love. So now I made an effort just to continue pleasantly with Shawn.

"What's Wy been up to lately?"

Wy's her favourite TV character, from the daily noon-hour show *Wy Knots* that was all the rage. Wy plays the ancient Chinese philosopher character in pillbox hat, half-foot-long moustache, and shining dragon-decorated robe that might have been cut from the curtains at our local Chinese restaurant. His low-production show couldn't be missed, even on Sundays, though it happened over the lunch hour. And the show's product line — all manner of stuffed animals with names like Hei and Wei and Meimei — must have been costing us fifty bucks a month. Supposedly, most of the money went to the Children's Wish Foundation. There must be a lot of kids out there wishing that Honourable Wy, as he styles himself, get filthy rich on Dishonourable Dad's hard-earned dosh.

Shawn went still, then spoke clearly: "Why *can't* we get a dog?"

"Owen's dander allergy, remember?"

"Owen says like you care about *him*." She moved her head only a bit to the side, but as she spoke she fluttered her lower legs, kicking the bed: "Wy says if we can't love our fellow creatures then we can't love anybody, including ourselves!"

She was rising, turning, so I was shutting the door when I said, "Goodnight, sweetheart, love *you*."

As I was pulling on my NOBODY KNOWS I'M ELVIS T-shirt (a gift from Owen, Veronica would have bought it), I said, "It did not go well with the kids again tonight."

She was reading in bed and closed the book on her finger, turned her big browns on me.

"That's because you argued with Owen about the tattoo again, didn't you? And all you do is make fun of Shawn's ideas…don't I know it."

She smiled forgivingly false, like *I* was the one needing forgiveness. Or maybe it was lovingly. I didn't want to argue. Her eyes in bedroom lighting were as lovely as the first day I saw her, some twenty years ago. I often thought so lately. I should tell her. If I could just manage the right tone.

In blue jockeys and T-shirt I lay beside her and knitted my fingers behind my head. "You're thinking of last night. Tonight I simply told Owen the story about the rapper Rot-10 we saw on TV. He grunted at me, spoke disrespectfully. Shawn's started that too now."

"I'll bet you told him *simply*. Anyway, Owen's embarrassed now about Rot-10. Didn't you notice the poster's gone? He's already on to something new. Let me just finish this chapter."

"What poster?" I grunted. "Something new, yeah. All our son cares about these days is that damned Market Slasher business. It's sick as sick can be." She was ignoring me. But I was spoiling… for something. "Have you been letting Shawn think it's up to me whether she gets a dog?"

I didn't have to look, she was pinching her lips. Then patiently: "No. Let's stay together on the dog thing, dear. Or we'll end up like Jack and Trixie using poor Jake as a bargaining chip. Okay?"

Jack and Trixie and Jake, our troubled and troubling next-door neighbours. Some new crisis with them, I forgot what, it's impossible to keep track. I could sense Veronica had returned full attention to her book. I moved my thigh against hers and she shifted away ever so slightly, made a knowing sound as if she were amused by something on the page. As long as Veronica was reading, I had the full back-cover photo of the female author staring at me. I think it was that Margaret Atwood character, looking like a mask from some Greek chorus accusing me of something I'd not even done yet.

I stared at the ceiling and wondered how I could get the lights turned out. I didn't really know why. I was restless. If Veronica turned away and slept, I'd probably lie in the dark again, my mind a wasp nest. Maybe I should be *on* something for sleep. I didn't really like this going to bed early and reading business. I'd been staring at the same book for months: a tome about water that Shawn had supposedly given me for Father's Day, whose author claimed that all future wars would be fought over fresh water. That's all I needed to know. The rest was all boring case studies and statistics about thirsty dirt and death, with enough footnotes to make a whole other book. Besides which, all future wars will be fought over the same things as all past wars: tribalism, religious hatred, revenge, territory, whether water's involved or not.

I said, "Did you know that all future wars will be fought underwater?"

"Uh-huh."

"It says so right here in my book." I pretended to read: "The ice caps will have melted by 2050 and antimatter submarines will rule! Aquaman will rally legions of giant squid and schools of piranha in defence of the American way! There's even a footnote citing *Entertainment Tonight*."

"Uh-huh." But her chest shook for me now, not for something in her book. "Funny, this novel's actually about the end of the world as we know it. Seems to be the new fad. Between the Apocalypse and sexual-abuse stories, there ain't much to laugh at no more."

I thought of a joke, but instead reapplied the thigh pressure, suppressing the beginnings of an urge to pee.

"Is there a world other than the one we know?"

"What? Are you getting weird on me?" She looked like she meant it.

Then she got excited, if not as I'd wanted. "Oh, yeah!" She clapped the book shut and rolled to place it on the night table. The pale flesh of her shoulders in the thin night dress, the curve of her cupped back to bottom, the bed perfumes… I forgot the piping up of my bladder. The next move was critical.

She hurried, "That Debbie Carswell phoned to remind you of a meeting of the Troutstream Community Association executive committee, something about our arsenic-contaminated playgrounds. She said it is absolutely essential that Dr. Thorpe attend." A fair imitation of the TCA's wonky chair. "This is connected with that same case you just had at work, right? Still the arsenic-poisoned little girl that Art Foster misdiagnosed? The lawsuit you starred in?"

I thought meanly about Debbie Carswell and yet another TCA meeting *and* that it was Veronica who'd roped me in with that crowd, but bit my tongue for once.

"Hmmm."

She put her hand on my thigh: "I was thinking—and don't say no right away—but why don't you take Shawn somewhere tomorrow, just you and her. She loves the Experimental Farm. *And she loves her father.*"

A negotiation. "In this heat?"

She removed the hand.

I said, "What about the Museum of Science and Technology? We've always had fun there, all of us."

She leaned on me, almost a snuggle-up. "Good idea, but just you and Shawn. Yeah, and that Carswell woman said"—and here she talked like a toff—"the necessitated emergency meeting is Monday, seven-ish."

"Necessitated emergency meeting my essential hairy ass. How did I ever get involved with those people? Oh yeah, it's all *your* fault."

She rolled away again, turned off her light, thumped onto her pillow sideways, flicked her hips, and that was that.

Hey, I was joking!

I pinched my mouth, shook my head and rose noisily to take a leak.

I didn't think I was sleeping a wink through yet another long night of wavering consciousness, but I must have, disturbed, angry, irrationally enraged. The most memorable image was my screaming after her retreating back: "All I want is something to eat! I'm starving!" And awoke from such uneasy dreams to find myself...well, myself.

Chapter 2

I was craning about for a parking spot, squinting against the glare and silently cursing the forgotten shades. Sweating as I manoeuvred Veronica's boxy little VW Golf through the rush of latecomers to the day's opening of the Museum of Science and Technology. Thanking God that at least it wasn't my white Caddy. But proceeding extra carefully because only the day before I'd driven her car into the wall while parking in my underground spot at work (bumping it only). I'd told Veronica my foot had slipped off the brake onto the gas pedal, but that's not really what had happened. Pulling into my space, at the last second I'd pressed harder on the accelerator—some jolt. No real damage to the car, but I'd been shaken, mostly from the shock at how suddenly it had happened. And the thought: what must a real accident be like?

Sitting beside me now, Shawn was searching the area on the right. "There's..." she trailed off, because there wasn't.

Such monster parking lots make me feel overexposed. No shade. It was early September, yet we were in another heat wave. Ottawa, Sunday, and an affordable air-conditioned museum for the season's late rush of tourists. The longer I cruised the choice lanes, the likelier I'd have to park even farther from the entrance. Just when I decided to give up and head for the Congo of tarmac, I spotted a space on the right. Shawn had missed it, as had all the others, a spot at the end of the row closest to the entrance!

I bellied widely at the end of the row and came nose to nose with a Jeep. Its steering wheel was topped by a big head of wild hair and bushy black beard, bared teeth in a biting smile. I thought: don't push me, suburban *bwana*, right now I'm game for a standoff.

Both vehicles rolled forward in pulling-in arcs, both stopped. He broke into an unhinged grin and gestured at the space with upturned left hand as if he were presenting me to an audience, then threw back his dwarf's head in a loud-mouthed laugh and gunned past me. Big of him, showing me up politely in front of my daughter like that.

It was a parking spot reserved for the handicapped, of course. I shook my pinched face at the freshly painted icon, the thermometer-like stick figure in the broken C of a wheelchair, the swastika-like legs. Ah yes, the dictatorship of the deprived.

Shawn whined, "You can't park here, Dad. This is for the physically challenged. Hurry up, find a spot!"

I didn't move. "Challenged? When they get the best spots and have to walk only a little ways?"

"But they can't even..." She got it—momentary shock—then giggled her guilt, the delightful Shawn, with her big green eyes and hated fair hair like that dandelion clock. Hated by her, adored by me.

I relaxed some and backed up. I must show her today how much I love her. I mustn't joke all the time. Resolved. But is such change even possible? Or would it have to be imposed, like smoking bans and designated parking for the afflicted—I jammed the brakes, almost having backed into a dad blinded by the toddler on his shoulders. Oblivious of his escape from disaster, he strolled on, his kid clutching his hair for dear life.

By the time I'd found a parking spot, way out beside the lot's lone school bus, and we'd walked to the entrance, there was a long lineup out the lobby. A stout woman in a tight grey uniform worked the door from inside, admitting a few at a time, quickly pulling it shut, enjoying her "empowerment." So we stood in the morning's mugginess, which thickened even as we waited, with the fat line extending behind us like a pale sunning snake.

The temperature was forecast to zoom again. Yet another "hottest summer on record" was refusing to die with dignity. Even the climate-change protesters were finding it too hot by high noon on Parliament Hill, while the politicians were promising what they couldn't do and really had no intention of trying (those would be my delusional boomer fellow travellers, whether demonstrating or promising to control the world's climate like that). A/C use was causing more brownouts than ever. At work we were spending over a million on emergency generators instead of the beds and nurses we sorely needed. A girl had suffered second-degree burns on her abdomen when a rad unit came back in a power surge. There's no malpractice suit as successful as one based on violation of the first principle of the Hippocratic oath, especially when it comes to kids, as my recent experience with the arsenic-poisoned girl, Marie LeBlanc, again testified.

Shawn was already watching a man and a dog standing some distance to the right along the ribbon of lawn that separated all the macadam from the cinder-block building. Man and man's best friend stood beside one of those spindly institutional trees that grow no bigger than the day they were planted. He wore a walking hat whose sloping brim was pulled down past his forehead, wrap-around shades, and sported a moustache and goatee. He was dressed way too warmly in a long-sleeved white shirt and black pants, like somebody suffering skin irritation. He stood ramrod straight. The dog, a golden retriever, slumped on its belly at his feet, panting out its body heat on that fat pink dog tongue like an incision.

The queue had stalled, permanently, it seemed, and I felt Shawn pulling toward the dog. I knew what she wanted: to kneel beside it, massage its scruff, learn its name, make a space of private play.

"Can I—"

"Yes, but keep an eye on me. I'm near the door, you hustle back. Don't make me step out of line. That happens, we go home." I love you.

She skipped off. I couldn't hear how she greeted the smiling man, but soon she was doing precisely as I'd predicted: on her knees and confiding to the dog. The man was grinning and talking straight ahead of himself like a blind man (I wanted his shades), looking at me, it seemed, though he had to be speaking to Shawn. There was something strangely familiar about him, but I knew no one who'd wear such a stagey outfit. Perhaps it was just that: that he looked like a disguised detective in a bad movie, a comedy even, a Clouseau or Austin Powers. One thing for sure: he looked like he'd bear watching.

As the line inched forward I turned sideways to keep my eye on them. Shawn glanced at me a few times — good girl — and each time I tapped my watch and wagged a finger at her. She scruffed up the dog, whose tail wagged.

I passed the time thinking of Veronica, of her turning away from me, at night, in our life together, of her growing refusal to understand my devotion to work, which she'd once admired so. Now she repeatedly joked in the presence of our idiot neighbours, the Kilborns, that *oncology* is the field of being *on call* all the time. Some joke. And it's pediatrics oncology. Though I guess it's not a bad joke.

I was at the door, Shawn cut it close.

"His name is Towser and he's dying of—"

"Mr. Towser to you, young lady." How lovely cool it was inside, like slipping through a membrane into a whole other dimension.

"Da-ad." Scarcely reaching, she slapped my shoulder. You've grown again, I thought. "Poor Towser, he can't keep his tongue in his head he's so hot. *So* thirsty. The man said he needs a drink bad—"

"He shouldn't be bothering you about his drinking problem."

"Da-ad." But no slap. "He *can't* get Towser a drink 'cause they're waiting for *his* daughter who had to go to the bathroom. She's ten, just like me, and Wy's her favourite too."

"That would make her *how* old in dog years?"

"You just won't listen. You never listen. You make everything I say a joke." Her mother's voice. She compressed her lips and exhaled noisily through her nose. Her mother's gesture.

"Sorry, I wasn't listening. What'd you say? Was it a joke?"

No deal, unless deals can be sealed by tighter pinch-lipped disgust.

I needed to get her off the plan to water the dog. She was emptying her account of compassion on that mutt. I knew the symptoms. Owen could walk into the family room missing an arm at the shoulder, squirting blood like a Supersoaker, and she'd scream at him to stop blocking the TV. Especially if *Wy Knots* was on, with the wise Wy mouthing his Confucius-for-tweens bunk. But a thirsty dog? Stop the world!

She relented: "*Can* I bring him a drink, Dad, can I, *please?*"

I was distracted negotiating the ticket purchase. "...No, Shawn, not now. As you can see, or should see, I'm..."

When I turned from retrieving the Visa receipt she wasn't there. I did a mildly heart-thumping visual search. Milling children, lots of girls who resembled Shawn. No big deal, I kept telling myself. It happened at least once per outing, Veronica had forewarned me. Don't panic, I told myself. Keep your wits about you. These things don't really happen, it's all media scaremongering, such crimes are actually down. *Purple tank top, pink shorts, purple tank top, pink shorts* — there. She's already at the concession counter? I moved towards her, temper rising.

I stopped. Took a deep, settling breath. No hurry. Veronica had also instructed me to take it easy on this one day at least, this day of rest. I was to squire Shawn to lunch at her preferred fast-food eatery. I forget which one. I was *not* on any account to check with oncology reception at work. "In fact," she'd said in the kitchen, "hand it over." She'd waited with her right hand flipped out for me to surrender my cell, like a cop confiscating a gun, performing for the kids. A standing joke with her nowadays, my devotion to my vocation.

Shawn was skipping towards me, swinging a large Styrofoam cup upside down at her side like a white bell. She was beaming her most irresistible smile of silver braces. I'd need to brace myself.

"It'll only take a sec, Dad! The bathroom's right there," she pointed. "*Please*, Dad. Towser's gonna suffer heatstroke! The man said he had one last week and his daughter had to save him by taking him into the bath!"

"He said *what?*"

I took her by the frailest of upper arms — no biceps to speak of, just bone and cords of sinew, hot skin still, and still smooth as a baby's — and began moving her towards the interior.

She resisted strongly: "No!"

Mothers and fathers glanced at me in irritation. *You cannot discipline your child in public, sir. That begins in the home.* To them I was a display labelled *Hurried Sunday Morning Outing for Another Deadbeat Dad Eager to Get to the Golf Course.* I even caught a few suspicious looks: *Who is that man forcing the little girl to go with him?* Foolishly I wanted to declare myself: She's my daughter! I'm happily married to her mother! We're as normal as your suburban neighbours!

I took her firmly by the shoulders, squatted and spoke through clenched teeth: "Look, sweetheart, we're not here to water the dog, okay? The dog will be fine. We're inside now and we don't want to waste time going back out."

"*I do.*"

"That man and his daughter have got the dog a drink already. Okay?"

We were far from okay. Her lower lip protruded, fat and glistening as an earthworm. She looked down at her chest, where breasts had recently begun to surface, plumping buds signalling gain and loss, hers and mine. But at ten? I'd read somewhere that the onset of puberty has been accelerating in developed nations. No time to lose.

With arm around her shoulders I ushered her onwards. I reached for the Styrofoam cup. She snatched it away with that same ferocious inwardness that would have let her brother pump out his life on the family room floor, away from the TV and the almighty animal-loving Wy.

I tried to jolly her along using my Fu Manchu voice: "This place cold as meat locker, and we, little lamb chop, are meat."

"Oh, shut up! Towser is so still out there and he's *dying* of thirst! The man *can't* get him a drink 'cause they are so still waiting for *his* daughter! And stop making fun of Wy! Wy says if we don't love our fellow creatures we can't love anything!"

"So I've heard."

That fucking Wy. I'd run him feet-first through one of those old-style roller wringers! If she kept this up, the day was ruined for me. My one day away from work in weeks. Even the gods get their day of rest, but not so Dr. Thorpe, it seemed.

I again squatted in front of Shawn. She jerked her pained face away, as she did when I snagged her hair the odd times I was charged with brushing it.

"Look, sweetheart, I'll make you a deal. After we've seen the chicks we'll go back, and if the dog is still there we'll bring him a drink. Okay? Deal?"

She pinched her mouth again, but she'd brought her face around. "Promise? No joke?"

"No joke. Did you forget the baby chicks already? I thought they were the *only thing* you wanted to see today, I mean now that you're all so grown-up and everything?" A flicker of smile for my mockery. "And let me know if you spot any bigger chicks for Dad."

"Da-ad, you are *so* gross. I'm telling Mom."

But deal. When she took my hand and pulled me along, I was in daddy heaven on our living leash.

Every display and interactive amusement was ignored now: the Krazy Kitchen that we couldn't get her to leave the other times we'd brought her and her brother to my favourite museum; the magenta lightning that comes to your finger on the bell jar, which she always had to be told not to hog from the other kids; the static electricity show where the demonstrator makes your hair look worse than Don King's (unnecessary in Shawn's case). All just obstacles now to the chick incubator and her eventual return to the thirsty...Towser.

Yes, children can be so single-minded. Though I would never admit as much to my colleague, flaky Art Foster, I sometimes believed that my patients were deciding whether or not to recover. I thought of little Lu-Ping, who surely was dying on me. She looked a little like Shawn around the eyes, even talked non-stop about the mighty Wy. But then, they all looked a little like Shawn when I was losing them.

I should call... I searched for my cell and found only absence.

I tried to slow her down: "Remember when you were little how you and Owen used to pretend *our* kitchen was the Krazy Kitchen, reeling around till you knocked something over and Mom had to shout at you to stop?"

She made her frowning-squint face back over her shoulder: "Huh?"

And forged on, dragging the dead weight of Dad and his *tempus fugit*. Or is it *memento mori*? In med school we'd learned just the catchy Latin phrases. *Ubi sunt?* was another. All meaning: remember remember remember. Life passes in a wink. Remember. But in reminding kids of what they did only months before, let alone years, you may as well be discoursing on the hereditary predisposition to foot tumours among Patagonian infants.

My heart ached, a growing pain of absence in my chest. I still had her by the hand and wanted so to hold her back. I actually had to fight the urge to pull her to me, touch her dandelion head, cup it to my chest, hug her forever...because such a display would only have made her mad at me again.

So I let her go.

She grinned back once like a kid allowed into deep water for the first time, then plunged ahead towards the farthest corner of the crowded museum, where the chick incubator waited. I could just make it out, a plastic-domed affair, like some illuminated bathysphere.

Shawn couldn't get close and I was comforted to see she still wanted to. The kids, most now younger than she, were pointing and squealing, four deep in their eagerness to see the chicks in various stages of hatching out. All around us were the wonders of science and technology — my gods, what I depended on to work my miracles — including an old NASA space capsule bearing the actual scorch marks of re-entry from the peaceful vacuum of space, yet the display the kids always crowded was as common as the nearest farm. One girl was half up on the dome, hugging the glass as if she were hanging on to the cone for dear life.

I was the only adult shuffling forward, as hulking as Dorothy among the Munchkins. The other parents kept their distance, forming a gallery in looming shadow. I tried to take Shawn's hand but she still held the Styrofoam cup in her right. She made an impatient

Shirley Temple face at the girl riding the incubator. I smiled, relaxed more. And as we inched toward the dome, I found my attention taken wholly by its display.

There were a few bedraggled chicks out of their shells, sticky wet. But unlike the lightning mechanism, these stunned newborns wouldn't come to the kiddie fingers pressed against the dome. Mostly the pathetic things stood catatonic in the shock of post-egg existence, or whatever dawning fowl-consciousness might be, looking perhaps for something or someone to blame or love, some mother hen to imprint... I was getting sentimental. After all, we eat these things, from eggs to roasters.

Only one of the chicks, which must have been near the end of its stay in the incubator, was moving confidently about, pecking at the slimy newborns. That upset the girls, while some boys hooted. Mostly, the dome was occupied by eggs in various stages of cracking. Chicks don't just hatch out instantly as we've been led to expect by cartoons and TV. You can spend forever watching an egg with a small star-shaped indentation, or even one with a fair-sized dark hole, before the unseen beak pecks again. Labour is labour is labour. So no cute yellow Easter chicks leaping fluff-feathered from split shells in a burst of light and cheep-cheeping to beat the clock. Besides which, the light at even the most minuscule crack would be flooding *into* the shell.

I beamed down at Shawn, who wasn't there. Gone missing twice in one outing! Too much. We're going home. No lunch.

As I waded through the swell of kids, I was periscoping the whole corner given over to the history of farming. Everything was freshly painted gleaming red and green and yellow, metallically toothed and tentacled, with glaringly lighted recessed displays as if for alien experiments on humans.

I broke through the periphery and stood searching. *Purple tank top, pink shorts, purple tank top, pink shorts.* She was nowhere.

I moved along the aisle we'd just hurried down as the quickest route. No sign. I couldn't conceive that she'd gone back outside without me. But obviously she had. In *her* mind that was the deal.

Already the stupid crowds appeared to be having loud ludicrous fun, the kids' screeching laughter was getting horrific, which was made worse by adults acting like children.

My cheekbones needled, I was aware of my esophagus just past my throat, its desiccated meatiness. I realized I was trotting. As a child I'd had a near-drowning experience, and that's what I was reliving—out of my element, plunging helplessness.

I forced myself to walk. I talked aloud: "This is silly. *You're being silly.*" It helped, hearing it spoken.

Veronica had mouthed over the unsolvable mystery of Shawn's hair: *Watch her.* She'd known I was out of practice. With Shawn ushered out the door, I'd said something like: *Those things don't really happen here, it's all media scaremongering. Such crimes are actually down. Besides, it's just about always a family member or friend.*

I again reached for my cellphone and felt its absence as a physical fact, a jolt, like thinking there's another step down at the bottom of a darkened stairs, or like driving into a wall. I touched my forehead and the fingertips came away wet. Before reaching the door, I'd again felt for my cell, twice.

The hot air outside stunned my lungs, because I'd gasped, because she wasn't there either and neither were the man and dog. Back inside.

I shouted her name into the women's washroom. I made a harried mother check for me. She understood immediately.

Security.

I tried to steel myself as I did when going in after a tumour behind a child's brain stem, praying that *my* exploration would prove the MRI wrong, that, miracle of miracles, the tumour would be encapsulated after all, not fibroid, so I could get it all, when we hardly ever could. But unlike when operating, my heart was thumping. The sweat that had been instantly produced outside continued in the cool interior.

In the end I gasped out the story to the lackadaisical security guard who'd taken forever to come to the front desk, where tickets were still being sold and children still whined for treats and parents tried to ignore them and all played out as if nothing were happening. For a moment the normality of it all let me think: *These things just don't happen to me.*

Then the whole scene began to look unreal, as if it were out of sync with the passing of time in my head. The bad movie was about to freeze, the frame crack…pieces of the bright world would fall and shatter, letting the darkness flood in. And no one else was aware of it, especially the stupid guard I was trying to alert. There was something Middle Eastern about him, dusky skinned and spicy smelling, overly precise articulation. I was sure he didn't fully understand me, or hated me. I wanted to throttle him: *You're not listening to me!*

But he was. I wasn't listening to him.

The search procedure was as slow as frustration nightmares where everybody is talking about meaningless details. You're a teenager lost in a vaguely familiar house full of relatives and your dead mother is alive and well and asking again why you're not going out with your friends, while with your hand behind your back you're failing to make your bedroom doorknob work: "But I have no friends, we move so much." Somewhere Dad laughs. "There's no getting away from that!"

We first had to look in all the places where in the past little kids had crawled in and fallen asleep: the old locomotives for boys, the polished wooden boats preferred by girls, and all along the monstrous green velour curtain that hid the rough cinder-block walls.

"She's ten years old! She'd not crawl in anywhere and sleep!"

"Yes, sir, but we have always been successful following procedure. Relax, please, sir. It always turns out to be just the child's play, sir."

After an interminable thirty minutes, I had to demand that he call in the police.

"But, sir—"

"*Now!*"

I didn't phone home for another half-hour of prickly hope. I borrowed the guard's phone. I calmly asked Veronica if, by any chance, Shawn had called… She faked composure for about ten seconds.

As I told the missing persons detective the story of the man and the dog and Shawn's determination to relieve its thirst, his pursed silence again raised needles all over my face and scalp. He was a lot taller than I, with a reddish brush cut that made his small head an aloof ginger ball. While I talked, he occasionally winced, as if he were suffering sinus irritation. No good at his job, I decided, especially if you judged by his skill at reassuring the victim, his curbside manner, as it were. I needed somebody else, somebody better, a second opinion or something, the very best detective Ottawa could provide! I would throw my weight around. Do you know who I am? Your life, or *your* child's, could be in *my* hands some day! This is *not* to be treated as routine!

Finally he removed his gaze from the green curtain and said, "You last saw your daughter…Shawn, right here, at the hatchery display?" Only then did I realize he'd walked me back to that far corner. "And you're certain she was still holding the…" He again checked his notes. "White Styrofoam cup?"

"For fuck's sake!" I shouted, it echoed, he winced. "Are you not listening to me? It was the man with the dog! Get moving on it!"

He looked down at me expressionlessly, as do I at the raging parents of unresponsive patients. "You think?"

"*Yes, I do think!*"

He resumed staring impassively. "Usually, Doctor, procedure makes us wait a bit before officially investigating a missing person. But you *are* Dr. Lorne Thorpe."

"Yes?"

"I too suspect it was the man with the dog, Dr. Thorpe. A man and his dog waiting outside a museum but not lining up? A dog wouldn't be admitted anyway. Somehow his daughter had bypassed the crushing crowd to use the bathroom?"

"Well, yes, I suspected as much my…"

And as he turned and walked away: "Had he come off the main road all the way into the crowded museum just to find a bathroom for his invisible daughter? Or was he leaving already? Waiting for his daughter with a dog, waiting to leave a museum that was just opening for the day? No, it doesn't look good, Dr. Thorpe."

In a panic that almost disabled me with its rising, I followed him back out into the heat to show him the spot where the man and dog had stood. As we neared the spindly tree, he turned and shoved me back and knelt right in the dirt, as careless of his pants as he'd been of me. He called commandingly to the two cops who'd suddenly appeared, signalling widely: "Cordon!"

Then I was disabled. It was his rude efficiency in pushing me away that did me in, his tunnel vision: my own style when death knocks on the operating room door. Only one thing matters.

And time was something else again. All the while I was standing there near where the man and dog had waited, the sun was interested only in burning away my thinning hair, melting my scalp and lasering my skull, to see if my dark brain matter could be made to bubble faster. I idly put two fingers on my wrist pulse. I tried to watch my watch. It made no sense, Salvador Dali time. I looked at the lettering on the glass doors of the museum. It may as well have been Cyrillic. I had gone to Russia. There was no law, no order, anywhere.

Ongoing searches of the vicinity were turning up nothing. At first I'd thought that good news.

The Museum of Science and Technology was closed for the rest of the day. Everyone was questioned before being dismissed, a procedure that took us into the late afternoon.

A dog was brought in, to sniff one of Shawn's unwashed T-shirts brought from home, to sniff about inside the cordon, to tear off into the empty parking lot, to stop and go nuts barking in the parking spot alongside my lonely car's passenger door—*of course, smart dog, Shawn's sleeping in the car!...which I'd locked.* The disobedient dog had to be dragged from the spot where the lone school bus had parked.

Veronica, careless of her wrinkled baby-blue sweat suit, and Owen, looking dressed from a sack of Rot-10 cast-offs, shuffled back to the car they'd borrowed from our next-door neighbours, holding onto each other like mourners from a grave. They'd hardly spoken a word to me. Veronica had whispered like a prayer: "She might be back home already."

The detective finally convinced me to leave. He said, "Go home now, Dr. Thorpe. I'll call as soon as something turns up. Comfort and give hope to your wife and son — that's your job for now. Your wife is right: Shawn *will* turn up."

Night was falling, that very worst time of day. Way out, far beyond the two mid-size police cruisers and the unmarked luxury car at the entrance, the little Golf was the only vehicle remaining, isolated in the expanse of dim black lot. Walking off into the growing darkness I was thinking madly. *Home?* I would drive the streets all night! I would find her. Anything else was impossible! Anything else and I *have* no home. These things just do not happen to me!

In the car I stared where Shawn had sat, looked out the passenger window. In the amber light of the parking lot something far off caught my eye. Tiny white tumbling, slow motion, like the simulation of an asteroid snowballing through space.

I got out and walked through the hot yellowish air, simultaneously dead to the world and alert to the moment, my operating-room consciousness again.

I picked up the white Styrofoam cup. No ants inside, no dirt, no stain of cola. Nothing but a few drops of clear liquid caught in a crevice at the bottom. Sprite looks like water. I inserted my finger into the crevice and the Styrofoam squeaked like dense snow. Praying for sweetness, I touched my tongue and tasted nothing.

I pinched the rim of the cup and turned towards the detective, who was already on his way with his hand out, like Veronica confiscating my cell that morning. He had made a note about the cup when I'd told him my story, and later he'd pointedly asked after it. The man might be good at his work after all.

Chapter 3

I went to work the next morning because I had to, if in a state of acute dissociation. The solid world looked more solid than ever, but somehow solidly apart from my fading self. I hardly knew which way to turn at familiar cross streets. But I had to go, I had to oversee some procedures that could not easily be rescheduled, and I couldn't very well delegate to the likes of Art Foster or Otto Fyshe.

Even at that, I'd been prepared to stay home. But I was compelled to go by Veronica herself. She insisted we follow Detective Beldon's urging to keep to our routines. Beldon hoped we'd not have to go public till that afternoon, and if I booked off work it could be seen to confirm some fast-flying rumour or other. He'd said there was already media buzz about the events at the Museum of Science and Technology. We'd be surprised, he'd said, how alert the media are to any hint of crime or scandal when a figure of my stature is involved. But we might get lucky and avoid it all. So Veronica, demonstrating a desperate faith in Detective Beldon's hunches and grasping that hope, had insisted I go to work.

Beldon had phoned again early that morning. At one point he'd said something that made Veronica smile. I couldn't imagine what. They seemed to be hitting it off. I always found that odd, when a visitor gravitated to Veronica as our house's centre of interest. Don't get me wrong, I know her attractions better than anyone. Veronica is easy to like. I'm not. I just find it odd, the snap judgments people make on first impressions. The great white doctor: *He's stiff, he's cold, he's arrogant*, etc. etc. *I can't relate to him, I could never warm to a character like that, what can his wife possibly see in him? And those jokes? I just don't like him, sorry!* (This last word with big Oprah-like inflection, that over-the-top way everyone acts all the time on any of Shawn's Disney Channel shows.) I've noticed, though, that people like me well enough when their child's life is at stake. Dr. Art Foster and his "Placebo Program for Pain" aren't quite as attractive then.

Veronica had moaned all night in a half-sleep on the den's couch (I'd not slept, I'd sat in the dark at the kitchen table, eventually watching the night pale to day like an oozing wound). In the morning she'd fuelled me with black coffee and, her eyes unfamiliar as a rubbed-raw mask, shoved me out the door, promising to call as soon as she heard from "Kevin," as she was already calling Detective Beldon. Owen would be staying home till we knew how things stood.

Things. *What things*?

In the hospital's cementy underground parking lot I checked the spot beside my name where on Friday I'd bumped the wall. I stayed bent over for a while with my hand hovering near the spot, wondering if I'd ever see Shawn again. That was too much to contemplate, as it fed anxiety towards panic attack. I straightened up and hurried off.

At reception for oncology, I answered Tamara's bright good-morning with my normal friendly nod, but kept my head bowed over the roster of procedures and consultations. I smelled something more acrid than usual, sniffed — human feces overlaid with disinfectant — and winced at Tamara.

"Accident," she said, giving her mouth a wry twist.

"Accident?"

"*It* happens, Doctor."

"Shit happens."

Tamara regularly played to racial stereotype for my benefit, and now she bugged her eyes like a comic minstrel and whispered, "Daz wad I means, Doctor, sir."

Though she was the most proficient receptionist I've ever encountered, I nonetheless still found something unreal about Tamara. Maybe it was just the simple fact of her shiny blackness, which I'd encountered regularly only later in my life (Philadelphia,

Johns Hopkins). Except for its biggest cities, the Great White North is still pretty white. Tamara and I worked well together, might even consider each other friends. But that day I wasn't up for her shtick.

She smiled normally and, as I made to turn away, touched the colourful neckerchief she always wore:

"We lost Lu-Ping last night."

I looked her in the eyes. She probably assumed it was her news that caused whatever was in mine. I'd never lost a child who was routine acute leukemia.

Without a word I wandered off along the garishly coloured hallway. Under the direction of some lame-brained marketer, we'd turned the Children's Hospital of Eastern Ontario (CHEO) into something like one of Shawn's fast-food places. Thick stripes of red and yellow and green and blue on the French-vanilla walls were supposed to make the hallway feel like a playground or something. The floor had matching colour-coded animal paw prints leading to all manner of fun places.

I had to stop.

With fingertips alongside my head I propped myself against the pimpled sweaty wall. I couldn't take it, couldn't face the day, I was not the pillar I'd always thought I was. All I could think of was Shawn and Veronica and home…and realized only then that I'd not even talked with Owen. I had to go back home. I couldn't work in this condition, I could be a hazard. Even if I might convincingly continue pretending it was Lu-Ping's death, I had to get home.

An echoing clack behind stiffened me and I patted the wall like I'd been doing something sane. I *must* function normally, for Shawn's sake. Detective's orders, wife's wishes. But again I recognized in myself the symptoms of rising anxiety. Or worse, panic attack.

I'm dead against doctors self-medicating, but I wanted a mild tranquilizer badly. Diazepam. And I knew where to get a handy vial of Valium.

I stood in our doctors' secret dispensary (an unused janitor's closet) clutching the smoky plastic container in my fist. I brought the other palm to my clammy forehead and tried unmedicated one final time to face up to the possible ruination of my life. *Our* life as a family. The world as I'd known it.

I went over my mistakes for the hundredth time already. How was it the man with the dog had a daughter exactly the same age as Shawn? That story about his daughter's taking the dog into the bathtub, I'd *known* there was something perverse in that! And what had been my big hurry anyway? What was I hurrying towards on my one day off? Why hadn't I gone back with Shawn and waited as she watered the dog? It had happened so easily, so normally. At the chick incubator, why hadn't I stood back and watched with the other parents instead of pushing right up with the kids to view the hatching?

The simple truth is there was nothing I would have done differently. There was simply no reason why this should have happened to me.

Yet my daughter, in my care, was missing.

I took a small blue tab. Another. Swallowing was nothing, but I knew that coffee would speed their effectiveness.

As I entered the clattering cafeteria I was waylaid by Dr. Otto Fyshe, as though he'd been waiting for me in the corner directly opposite the doorway. Otto was stout as a butcher, balding badly, with bristly tufts growing from his ears. He was a good ten years older than I and should have retired years ago. He was always in a lab coat with a raft of pens clipped to a cheap plastic pocket holder advertising some pharmaceutical company or other. Parents and kids loved Otto as though he were a grandfatherly hobbit, yet he was an incompetent pediatrician. *Everybody* loved Otto, so his sitting alone tipped me further that something was up.

He waved me over. As I approached, he dropped his head and pinched his chin in thumb and fingers, either puzzling over a chart or wanting to appear thoughtful. I didn't sit.

He looked up and handed me the chart, saying, "What do you make of this, Lorne?"

Nine-year-old boy, no history of health problems, a routine physical, everything within normal range.

I made a dismissive mouth: "Nothing. What's the complaint?" He retrieved the chart and slapped it with the back of his right hand. "No complaint, *that's* the problem. I was on emergency duty early this morning. The boy was brought in by the police for examination. And he's perfectly fine, not a scratch, not even a frown. Or traumatized only now from having some old doctor look close up at his asshole." Otto shook with phoney laughter.

"Yes?"

"The thing is, this kid wouldn't answer questions for anyone about what happened, even for his parents when they arrived in a panic. He went missing from the Silver City movie house last night, where he'd gone with his dad. There's a *huge* chunk of time missing."

I felt suddenly exposed in the steely bright cafeteria with its wall of windows and surgery lighting, that open-back hospital-gown feeling I always hear complaints about. Now I wanted to sit, but wouldn't.

"Where was he found?" I was keeping calm and thought gratefully that the unaided diazepam must already be tamping my receptors.

"That's what made me think of you just now, Lorne. He was picked up early this morning walking around those soccer fields near your neck of the woods."

"The Sharks Tank? Troutstream?"

"That's it."

My scalp prickled.

"Let me take a look at him, Otto. Second opinion."

"You can't. I discharged him. There was no need for further observation. But you ask this kid a question and he calls you a *dumb-dumb* and tells you to *ask again*. Every question, every time. I could have given him the back of my hand! And Mom and Dad just stand there grinning! What's with parents these days?"

The boy's routine sounded familiar. "I think that's from a kids' TV show, Otto, nothing disrespectful, just a game. My, uh, daughter watches it, too, it's called *Wy Knots*. The boy was probably overwrought, even in shock."

"No, he wasn't." Otto turned back to the chart, spoke testily: "Somebody sure did something. Children don't just go missing all night. I know kids, three of my own, seven grandkids. That boy is definitely hiding something. And it looks to me like no one gives a red rat's arsehole."

"Let me know if I can do anything."

I turned away. He'd meant me not caring. Time for a retirement party, my aged colleague. I must tell Detective Beldon about this. I had a lead. First things first though. I grabbed a coffee on the way out.

Human waste and disinfectant, the eternal odour war of hospitals, and my senses were chemically heightened already. Disinfectant may have lost the recent battle at reception but it had triumphed near the seventh-floor room where Lu-Ping had died on me. Absence now radiated from the door opening and drew me in. I needed to hide for a spell.

I'd last seen Lu-Ping Friday evening when I thought to check up on her before heading home, a thing I seldom do. Her room was one of our family rooms, furnished more like home than hospital. That area of the hallway was also dimly lit in an un-hospital manner. Before I knew I'd done so, I was intruding on an actual family's privacy. The moment I realized it, I heard the tinkling of tiny bells, which reminded me of something…TV…the show Shawn watched religiously, yes, *Wy Knots*.

The father and mother, who appeared exactly the same short height, were standing by the darkening windows. It was that very worst time of day, just before the lights come up everywhere. The mother noticed me first and waved me forward before I could retreat. Both parents were immigrants from Hong Kong and spoke English brokenly. Lu-Ping, twelve, had been wholly educated here.

She was propped on her cranked bed and smiling a frozen Cheshire-cat smile. She too waved me over, weakly, I thought.

"Doctor Thorpe," she called. "Come here, come here." She was childishly urgent and I knew she was acting. "Dad and Mom just finished the healing prayer I *told* you about!" When she exhaled there was an undertow of moan, though neither parent appeared to notice.

At the window ledge her father was packing the small bells into an ornately decorated wooden case like a very old-school pencil case, one of those whose lid slid into place like some coffin's. He looked ridiculous in a golden track suit and black high-top running shoes. He'd hardly ever spoken to me, though his daughter had been my patient for months. I don't think it was only the language thing.

I went and stood by the side of Lu-Ping's bed. She took my hand tightly in her own, which was unusual, though when alone we did sometimes hold hands and talk easily. I'd *never* lost a routine acute, but she'd been refusing to respond. I don't mean to imply that she had any choice in it. That's Art Foster's game, call it the *spiritual*, as he'd lately been telling me: "Lorne, you just don't pay any attention to these sick kids' *spiritual* needs."

Her mother, in a too-tight white pantsuit, had a face as round as a child's drawing of a happy moon. She said cheerily, "Lu-Ping better night now," and seemed to believe herself.

Lu-Ping smiled and smiled and squeezed more tightly. She didn't try to speak again.

The bronze-faced father said, "We pray for better or peace. Now we go." He was always gruff in his minimal speech. On his way to the door he flared at me: "You learn."

What?

The mother came forward to kiss Lu-Ping goodnight and I saw it then, the stark terror in Mom's liquid eyes, the downturn of tiny mouth. This was a goodbye kiss. She believed nothing. If she believed anything, it was that a great big nothing was coming to live with them in place of their beautiful daughter. She followed her husband out.

Lu-Ping exhaled as if giving up in some held-breath game, then grimaced and squeezed so hard that I felt pain. She turned her face to the darkening windows and cried as she'd never cried. In fact, she'd never cried.

I sat on the bed, still holding her hand tightly. Eventually her breathing regularized. She moaned more asleep than she ever had awake. It was time for Demerol, maybe morphine already, as she'd clearly been deceiving me. Why would a child conceal pain from her doctor? Why would anybody?

Yes, that very worst part of the day, the passage between light and dark. Most accidents happen at this time, they say. Suicides too, I would imagine. Darkness doesn't fall, darkness is everywhere, always. The sun doesn't set and the sun doesn't rise. Evening is a shunning, a wilful turning away from the pathetic sun. As the darkness had deepened in the room, it felt like black air.

And that is my job mostly. I mean, for the benefit of those who would get me wrong and hastily judge this character that enables me to do it well. This *bwana* me, the great white doctor, the patriarchal prick, whatever. If I mention Tamara's shiny blackness, I'm racist and probably misogynist to boot. If I prefer medical science to Art Foster's placebo voodoo, I'm an unfeeling machine, a shill for pharmaceutical companies dispensing drugs instead of providing spiritual care.

Now *my* beautiful daughter was missing. That one black hole of a thought was tearing apart my spinning mind and sucking it in with the rest of my world.

Unlike at my last visit to Lu-Ping's room, this time its big windows gave on nothing but washed-out, palest blue sky. The bed's dark privacy curtain was bunched to the wall, the bedside table was clear, and the bed... Even my breathing seemed to echo in the antiseptic emptiness.

Shit, piss, puke, and ammonia. Sterility. Death on a well-made hospital bed. Only the far side-rail was up. There is no worse sight than a freshly made hospital bed whose recent child occupant had not been discharged home. They might claim to have it worse in neonatal intensive care. Newborns die freighted with everybody's dreams and for the parents it's a waking nightmare. But neonates have negligible personality. They don't leave the consuming absence of a grown child who has died. They cannot command such defeat. It's like suicide, it kills everything.

I brushed the cool whiteness of the sheets with the back of my hand, then flattened both palms and rested there with chin on chest.

Why *had* Lu-Ping been hiding the severity of her suffering? The untreated pain would have been draining her depleted recuperative resources. Why would a child *do* that? Why would anybody hide pain from a doctor!

I sat on the bed. I swivelled and lay flat on my back. The rising chill seeped through my lab coat. I can't say how long I lay there. I was so weary, I dozed…

"Don't blame yourself, Lorne."

I was standing before I knew it. I kept my face averted.

"I don't blame myself, Dr. Foster. Why would you even think such a thing?"

"Sure, a more holistic approach to treatment might have kept…the girl—"

"Lu-Ping."

"Huh?"

"Her name: Lu-Ping."

"Whatever." He snorted lightly.

Is there anything else worth knowing about Dr. Art Foster?

"My point is that although a more holistic approach to treatment would likely have kept the girl alive longer, to what purpose? Don't do the guilt spiral, Lorne. I've read the charts, and it was too late for your looping girl the day her retarded parents finally brought her in."

"*Lu-Ping*, for *fuck's* sake! You make less sense every day, Foster! And it's never too late." I didn't like the subject of dead and missing children under my care, so I channelled my anger to the deal I'd made with him earlier in lending him my vintage car in exchange for his making an elusive contact for me. "You'd better be taking care of my Caddy, Foster."

"Easy, little man." He danced his eyebrows lasciviously: "Tomorrow's the big night. Sorry for the delay."

I reached for my vibrating cell and again turned my back on Foster.

"Yes, dear?... Right away."

On my way out I gave Foster a wide berth. I hurried along the sweetly acrid hall.

He shouted after, "I'm here to listen, Lorne... I told you so!"

I said to Tamara in passing, "Emergency. Triage and try to reschedule everything, please, give whatever you can to Dr. Foster on my orders, and thank you, you're the best, Tamara."

She called across her counter, "What's up, Doc?"

I pushed Veronica's little Golf and was soon back in Troutstream, slowing on our treed crescents. The continual run of dog-walkers paraded past — those decent suburbanites on retractable leashes — carrying tied-off plastic bags of dog shit, like some subspecies of human genetically designed to link a rich man's dog to its colostomy sack... That's right: the man at the museum had displayed no plastic bag, so was probably not the real dog owner. I must tell Detective Beldon that too.

As I rounded the bottom of our crescent, Piscator Drive, I had to slow further for a long parade of kiddies toting backpacks, like midget paratroopers marching off to war games at the playground. And as I bellied for the turn into my driveway, our aging East-Indian-looking neighbour came loping along the sidewalk and I had to wait for him to pass. He was an unsteady jogger who always had a white rag tied to his left knee and looked ready to pitch onto his face with each surrendering step. Unmindful of race distinctions, I'd christened him "the Tanzanian Marathoner." *There goes the Tanzanian Marathoner!* Shawn would call from the front window, with no idea of the reference to John Stephen Akhwari's incredible spectacle of plodding persistence at the 1968 Mexico Olympics. Injured earlier in the race, he'd finished dead last after the sun had set and the sated spectators were long gone. But would she ever call so again?

Stupidly, I waited to see if Veronica would come to the front door to greet me. Owen was probably still lying on his bed wearing earplugs. I regularly had to order him to turn off his music and come to a meal. Music? It's more rhythmic assault under a ground cover of woofer, the rhymed abuse of inner-city American blacks who rap as though they'd like nothing better than to use Owen's white suburban ass for target practice. But of course it's all really just "let's pretend." No real violence from those "gangstas," other than to melody-lovers' ears. Oh, once in a while someone named Fat Daddy will stick a fork in Big Mofo's ass and that will establish "cred" and satisfy violent cravings for another year. But mostly these hammock-crotched, genital-obsessed rich kids are capable of nothing more than a drive-by sneering.

Does saying *that* make me sound racist and old? As for the first, I've always thought racism the most dangerous form of false generalizing. And I was just old enough to remember peeling cellophane off the gift of *Abbey Road* and hearing Paul McCartney sing "Oh! Darling" for the first time. Top that, Sonny Jim, with your Bullwinkle rhymes of fantasy sex…and vio…lence…

Ah, I thought, sitting there in my driveway, so *this* is what it's like for a parent waiting for the diagnosis, the prognosis: frenetic, diverting thoughts, avoidance.

As if on cue, one of our big Troutstream crows cawed its mocking *caw…caw.*

I paused again inside the front door. My own house felt like a stranger's. It was too bright along the entrance hallway leading to the kitchen, glowing like the beginnings of a migraine. Could one… Okay, could two Valium do that?

They were in the living room to the left, Veronica on the couch with her hands twisting in her lap. She looked at me with a blankness I'd never seen, as if she didn't know me. She didn't come to me. I suddenly felt the breakfast I'd missed, on a stomach sloshing only with coffee and other chemicals.

Detective Beldon stood at the front bay window with his back to the room. He smiled a weak greeting over his shoulder and then, most oddly, turned back to the street, one hand holding the other wrist behind. His redheaded brush cut seemed almost to brush the stippled ceiling. He wore a shiny grey suit whose pants weren't quite long enough, and the shoes looked faux Oxfords. I'd not taken to him at the museum and the dislike continued. To him, I was just another missing-kid case, which his indifferent back was confirming for me.

I went and placed a hand on Veronica's shoulder and she briefly held my wrist. I cupped the crown of her head, kissed it and stepped back.

"Owen okay?"

"Hmm."

Detective Beldon turned. "Could we sit in your lovely family room back there?" He nodded through the archway to the adjoining room. "I for one would feel more comfortable."

He hadn't smiled. I liked that.

When we were seated—Veronica and I on the love seat, he in my green recliner—he said with a small grin, "Dr. Thorpe, your wife, Veronica, as she's asked me to call her—"

"Please call me Lorne. Yes, Detective?"

"Kevin, then. Veronica has answered my questions about the recent poisoning case at the hospital that got you all the publicity. But I'd like *you* to begin at the beginning and tell me the whole story, if you will please."

"What? The arsenic-poisoning case? What's *that* got to do with Shawn's kidnapping?"

Without changing expression he spoke directly: "Just tell the story, Doc—Lorne. Leave nothing out. Let me decide what's important. Okay?"

Puzzled, I glanced at Veronica, but her gaze had drifted to the French doors opening onto the patio and, beyond, the tall cedar hedge.

I took a deep breath, felt lightheaded as I exhaled slowly. "Sure, whatever you say."

But first I told him Otto Fyshe's story of the boy who went missing overnight. During the telling, Veronica swung towards me with a hand flat on her chest. Then my observation that the man at the museum had carried no plastic bag, so clearly was not a real—

He cut me short and prompted, "The poisoning case, it was a female child, right? A couple of weeks ago."

"Actually it began exactly two weeks ago Friday. A very sick five-year-old girl named Marie LeBlanc presented at emergency in a rapidly deteriorating condition, with severe symptoms bizarrely combined—respiration, renal, liver—what looked, in fact, like imminent total systems failure. She was drifting in and out of consciousness. Aggressive treatment was called for, but for what? Preliminary tests proved indeterminate and waiting for lab results would have been only to confirm the cause of death."

"*Dr.* Lorne Thorpe pulls emergency duty?"

"I was called in to consult because Dr. Art Foster suspected some variation of lymphoblastic leukemia. Foster, a heart-and-lungs man, acts on hunches a lot, though here he did have some symptoms support. Following my own examination of the girl, I was pursuing a different line of questioning with the parents—when Foster interrupted me.

"I intercepted a nurse and asked her to escort the parents to a privacy room. Over the past year we had decorated our privacy rooms in the iconography of the major religions, leaving some nondenominational. We also had accessorized our nurses to appear child-friendly, so that Nurse Louise's uniform, especially the top, looked like an advertisement for a carnival."

Detective Beldon interrupted: "Lorne, I know I said *everything*, but try to stick to the main story line, okay?" His face pinched: "Have you been drinking?"

I feared I was getting a buzz off the Valium, so I concentrated on the story.

"No. Dr. Foster looked at the father. 'Catholic?' '*Oui, certainement.*' The nurse said, 'We have a comfy Catholic room right this way, Mom and Dad.' The parents were confused. They looked to me with abandoned eyes, then followed the nurse.

"Foster and I remained in the wide smelly hall. Foster tented his hands on his breastbone and looked across my head. Tall Foster does that a lot, to signal you're only half-worthy of his lofty attention."

"Lorne," Beldon said flatly.

Veronica stood. "I'll make some coffee."

I watched her walk to the kitchen where, instead of preparing coffee, she first sat at the kitchen table and stared out its patio doors. I turned to Detective Beldon: "Foster smacked his lips and said, 'How do you explain it then?'

"'Explain what, Dr. Foster? I'm not telepathic.' '*Come on*, Lorne?' Like I'd missed the symptoms of full-blown leprosy. 'The blisters on the girl's palms?' Art Foster was always over-dramatizing, and now he was gesticulating with his own indecently padded palms.

"I smirked: 'I don't explain what I don't know, Dr. Foster. An accident at the stove? Abuse? Stigmata? You explain. What do blisters have to do with *any* leukemia?'

"He leaned down and whispered, 'For the good of the patient, Lorne, we must work as a *team* on this. We're losing that little girl.' He jabbed his forefinger down the hall, as if she were standing there waiting.

"I sipped air and said, 'You should not have questioned my method in front of the parents, Dr. Foster. You ever pull that stunt with me again, I'll break your bleached teeth.'

"'Lorne,' he pleaded, 'this anger! All I said was we'd be monitoring their little girl closely and running tests. Surely you concede that the symptoms could point to a leukemia. I mean, the anemia and all.' He again pointed down the hall. 'That little girl's lymphocyte count is in the cellar! I didn't know *where* you were going with your interview. You never consul...*share*. I was concerned we were confusing the parents further, and we both know where that leads—the malpractice team. Now, why don't you go see if we can stabilize the child while I talk further with Mom and Dad?'

"'Why don't *you* see to *your* patient, Dr. Foster? She is definitely *not* suffering from any leukemia. I'll continue my interview of the mother and father.'

"'Lorne, if I've overstepped my authority in any manner whatsoever—'

"'Fuck off, Foster.' That felt good. It even sounded good."

"Lorne," said Veronica as she drifted back to join us. I salivated at the smell of coffee dripping.

"Please," said Beldon. "Time in these cases is always critical. I don't want us to lose sight of *your* little girl. Just the essential story, please, Lorne."

Veronica inhaled sharply and returned her gaze to the backyard. I sped up the telling. "Okay, then. Ten minutes later I was still sitting with the father on a small blue couch beneath the colourful full-wall mural of Jesus with some children. Both parents were stupefied at the thought of not seeing their child alive again. I'd experienced it many times in my work, of course, the bereft, stunned silence. At best, a catatonic formality. Getting used to missing their child."

Veronica made a kicked-dog noise.

"I'd been patiently questioning the father, a broken-English-speaking French-speaker from Gatineau, when Foster barged in to announce that he'd stabilized 'their little girl' with a mild sedative — bad move — ordered blood and platelet transfusion and begun a course of antibiotics — 'prednisone,' he said to me out the side of his mouth like a gangster — all of which had produced an immediate favourable response, he claimed.

"The silent mother, shaped like a dark four-foot pillow with a perfectly round head, had to rock herself twice before she could lunge from her corner chair; she cupped Foster's right hand in both her own. She was so short she appeared to be kneeling and kissing the great healer's hand. And Foster permitted this display to continue!"

"Dear," said Veronica to the yard, "I'm sure Kevin means…"

But I saw that I held Beldon's attention, so I hurried on.

"I heaved to and, stretching, went eyeball-to-eyeball with Foster. 'I'm going to examine the patient again. Dr. Foster will wait with you till I return.'

"The five-year-old looked even smaller in the white hospital bed and glare of examination lighting. The covering sheet had been kicked off. Her dark hair was pasted to the side of her head, and closer I could see the sweat sliding from her temples and forming into beads alongside her ear. Her eyes were closed but her lips were moving, like the beak of an immature chick whose egg had fallen from the nest. Perhaps she was praying or silently protesting. I—"

"Doctor," Beldon said.

I expect I blushed. But I couldn't very well claim it was the Valium talking.

"I had to get closer to sniff her breath. Her lids flicked up and we too went eyeball-to-eyeball. She whispered, '*Suis-je dans le ciel?*' "What? The *sky*? No, *heaven*. No heaven. '*Pas le ciel, chère, pas ciel.*' I cupped her chin in my palm and it was as hot as a doorknob to a burning room. Her eyes closed and her face relaxed. '*Merci… papa…*'

"The latest ICU report confirmed my suspicion—very low BP, muscle spasms, tender abdomen, sheets they couldn't keep dry from sweat, those mysteriously seared palms. And the clinchers, which my closer examination had revealed—inflammation of the nasal and oral mucus membranes, garlicky breath.

"Since there's never any time to lose in my profession either, and as I *was* the consulting physician of record, I cancelled Foster's prescription and ordered an immediate course of chelation therapy, with injections of EDTA. I made a brief report to the chief resident and told him the patient was now officially his, or Foster's, I didn't care which, and that I was heading back to oncology.

"For the fun of it, though, I detoured back to the privacy room. Foster was sitting on the small couch, crammed between the parents with an arm around each, quite snug and smug. Per usual, Art was dressed to kill in a dark-blue three-piece suit. His lab coats are custom tailored, with big collars and bone buttons. His comb-over was perfect, probably held in place with spray or even pins. Art has handsome, chiselled features, chiselled from a bartering bargain he'd struck with a cosmetic surgeon. Parents immediately 'related' to Foster, warmed to him, liked him. To me, not so much, as you might suspect, Detective."

"I see."

It was obvious what obviously ironic Beldon meant: get on with it. But I'd tell the story my way or not at all.

"Savouring the moment, I looked over their heads at the mural of Jesus, who was sitting on a rock beside a tree, his arm loosely around a boy's waist, and smiling broadly at a little girl holding out a lily to him. Jesus's day off, I thought, taking a break from the halt and the lame. Jesus, fellow healer, hardly ever smiled. Dr. Lorne Thorpe needed a day off too, a smile, a flower from a child."

"Lorne!" That was Veronica again. She'd probably detected something different in me. "*Have* you been drinking?"

"I lowered my gaze at Foster. 'It's arsenic poisoning.' His eyes widened. 'What!' He pulled back his head and looked down his nose as if he'd just apprehended a pair Munchhausen's-by-proxy parents. I had to smirk. 'Not intentional, Dr. Foster, accidental poisoning.'

"There was the proverbial stunned silence. Then the father leapt to his feet and was pumping my hand: 'Since this, I am many thanks, Doctor! Oh very very manys *merci, merci, merci*!'

"'Well,' I said, leaning away, 'it's not exactly good news, arsenic poisoning, but better, I agree, than a misdiagnosis of leukemia.'

"Foster winced, shut his eyes. There was a more thoughtful silence. The father extended his face towards me. 'Mis…leuk…?' He puzzled for a spell, looking like a man trying to identify a bad smell. Then recognition: 'Ah! Mis-take! Mistake!'

"Both parents were all but dancing round me then. I looked at Foster's blank puss. He just managed, 'But how explain…?'

"How had I solved the medical mystery? As would any good detective. The model for Sherlock Holmes was a doctor, you know—"

"Jesus Christ, Thorpe," Beldon interrupted. "Your daughter *is* missing, you know."

"Okay, okay, I'm almost done. While sitting alone with the father, I'd coaxed him to retrace events of the previous forty-eight hours, again and again, stopping him frequently to make sure I'd understood his broken English and that he wasn't leaving anything out. Like a methodical dick, I was alert for variations in his repetitions. Finally, in telling again about his daughter's previous afternoon in the backyard kiddie pool, he said something he'd not mentioned before, something about smoke, *fumée*. I sensed fire.

Warily, he confessed that he'd had an illegal backyard fire to dispose of the rotting materials of his deck.

"It was instantly all there for me, rotting deck made of pressure-treated cedar, fire, the girl's blistered palms. I'd read about the toxins problem in the back pages of a Health Canada report. Foster had slid the brochure under my nose in the cafeteria because its cover featured him and his government-funded placebo research project.

"I held up a traffic cop's hand to the talkative father. 'The pool water soothed your daughter's burnt palms, *d'accord?*'

"He'd not tried to speak at first, just sat with bugging eyes and hanging jaw. Then, '*Mais, comment...?*'

"I immediately called Health Canada on my cell. Within a minute of their hearing who I was, I was talking to the chief investigator. She itemized the chemicals they'd found in pressure-treated cedar. Arsenic headed the list, both for quantity and toxicity.

"While helping Papa with his illegal fire, the short child would have inhaled the arsenic at more concentrated levels, the very worst means of intoxication, or the best, as in marijuana bonging, as I expect you know, Detective?... Okay, at one point she'd tripped and toppled into the embers on the fringe—the blisters on the palms, no facial burns or singed hair—which would have made her wail, whereby she'd sucked in who knows what concentration of the smouldering residue.

"Conclusion: the five-year-old patient was suffering from acute arsenic poisoning. Arsenic poisoning accounted for the low blood-cell count, the preliminary test result that had led Foster to suspect leukemia. That misdiagnosis was further confirmed, for Foster, by the low BP, the headaches and vomiting, the blood in the urine, the skin discolouration. I was confident in the course of treatment I'd ordered, the only method really, chelation to flush the system of toxic metals.

"But the episode had been a near-fatal blow to Marie LeBlanc's young system. The next day she remained in poor condition and I began to wonder if she would ever recover sufficiently to help Papa again. We ran the urine tests, sampling the hair follicles and fingernails for toxin levels, and were relieved to see the parts count return to normal range. Still, she malingered.

"CHEO's malpractice team and the instantaneous legal team of the poisoned girl's parents—"

"Thank you, Lorne. That's enough for now. You two need a rest and I need to look into some things now. Later this afternoon for the sequel, if that's all right with you two?"

With both hands pushing on his knees, Beldon stood, his small ginger head going way up in that room whose ceiling had always seemed high enough.

Veronica whispered to the patio doors, "Shawn. No one's even said her name."

Beldon pinched his mouth. "Rest assured, Veronica, this is all and only about Shawn. I will find her and the criminal who did this."

I took Veronica's elbow, but she jerked it away from me, stood, and we accompanied Beldon to the front door. It was like she'd dug that elbow into my liver.

Beldon turned on the stoop and adjusted his shoulders in the flimsy jacket. He looked only at my wife:

"I don't give false hope, Veronica, but I'd already known about Dr. Otto Fyshe's experience with the missing boy from last night. The boy is not talking, which is puzzling, but he was unharmed and that gives us real hope. I strongly suspect we are dealing with the same kidnapper. *And* there was also an eleven-year-old girl on Saturday."

Veronica gasped and returned the hand to her chest.

"Taken from Troutstream Arena, using the sick-kitty-in-the-car trick. She's also returned unharmed and not talking, or not much. She did tell us that none of her clothes were removed. Strange to say, she was asked to put *on* costumes *over* her clothes—a cape, wear a crown, hold a wand of some sort. Some harmless fetish. I mean, compared to other possible outcomes."

"What *can* it mean?" Veronica gasped, still posed as if restraining herself, or her heart. "Shawn…"

"What solid leads do you have?" I demanded.

He flicked me a frown. "I don't believe anything ugly happened between those kids and their abductor. Something sure happened, and is happening, and I'm going to find out what. Steady now, but all the kids are from Troutstream. And I suspect that others from here have been contacted or even taken by our man, but for one reason or another—shorter time missing, parents absent all day—the incidents were never reported. And I don't think we've seen the end of it."

"How can you be so sure of all that?" Veronica asked.

"It figures, and I have very strong gut feelings about these matters."

"So." I sneered, still smarting from Veronica's sharp refusal of my hand, "now we're relying on your hunches?"

He ignored me. "As is most often the case, Shawn may have known her abductor, who's most likely from Troutstream too. Anyone come to mind? Anybody at all?"

Neither of us had anything to offer.

"What about this Bob…" Beldon consulted his notepad. "This Bob Browne who unofficially treated your poisoned girl, Lorne?"

I was startled again. "Bob Browne? How do you come to know about him? Bob Browne couldn't have had anything to do with this. For one thing, the man with the dog was tall and slim. Bob's very short. I was going to tell you his part in the rest of my story."

"Okay, then. Before supper, I'll call."

"Supper… She must be getting very hungry." Turning back into the house Veronica knocked her knee hard on the aluminum door. She didn't react.

Detective Beldon strode to the maroon Crown Victoria at the curb, which I recognized from the museum. He drove off slowly.

Jack Kilborn's dishevelled self was standing at the end of his short front walk where it meets the driveway. He ran a hand through his hair and shook his head at me. I had no idea why. We'd have to explain events to the neighbours, what with Veronica having borrowed their car and all. I hoped the commotion hadn't excited their son, Jake, a powerfully energetic Down's Syndrome kid chronologically in his late teens, or Jack and Trixie would need Veronica to help out yet again. Nuisance neighbours, hopeless incompetents. But suspects? No.

I turned away. I was surprised again to find myself starving.

I didn't return to work after lunch (which I made for myself and ate alone, two cheese-and-onion sandwiches). I don't know why I didn't go back to CHEO after all the crowing about keeping to normal routines. Monday afternoon Veronica and I mostly avoided each other, trying not to look like we were doing so, hovering near the phones and monitoring texts and emails. We were waiting for contact, a call from Detective Beldon or the kidnapper himself, or a delivery of the hoped-for innocent photos—electronically or by courier—waiting and waiting for news. As I often say to distraught parents: *We're waiting for the pictures.* But nothing came, so the prognosis grew more desperate by the minute.

Except for no work, we made the day appear as normal as we could. Owen kept to his room. Veronica busied herself with laundry (the never-ending chore; she seemed to be forever running up and down stairs with the rose-coloured plastic basket). She used the outdoor line for drying, which entailed much conversation through the cedar hedge with next-door-neighbour Jack Kilborn. Jack wasn't snooping, she reported with a garish smile. Jack was upset about something of his own, per usual. I stopped listening to her once I'd heard what I wanted to know: she'd told him nothing.

I went and lay on the brown leather couch in my study, monitoring local radio too now, jumping when the email chimed. Nothing. Spam: "Dating services," sex enhancements, free money, a modicum of legit medical information, and a number of the usual conferences where I was invited to be keynote speaker for a sizeable fee too, me paying it to them. The World Wide Web had so quickly become the globe's exploding subconscious. Even on every useful screen the irrational mass pressed hard behind. We invited this thing into our homes, this demon that hated us and our…children…

Veronica cut the grass—I don't know how she did it—and the pleasant odour of chlorophyll inundated my brown study. I glided off on its green drafts. Other children had been abducted, and only for a brief period, and nothing horrible had been done to them, Kevin said so. I dozed. At times the gentler electric lawnmower was a distant plane somewhere over a northern lake. I snapped awake...dozed again...a small plane buzzing a pristine northern lake green as jade...far below, but coming closer as the plane spiralled downward, someone the size of an ant was circling the oblong dark lake's perimeter, someone was struggling in its black centre, drowning—snapped awake.

Chapter 4

This is the story, somewhat improved here, that I told Detective Beldon later that afternoon (*sans* his interruptions, especially as regards Bob Browne). Veronica had heard it all before, so she visited with the Kilborns next door.

The hospital's malpractice division and the instantaneous legal team of the poisoned girl's family were unable to reach a speedy out-of-court settlement. We had done nothing wrong; regardless, we, meaning Art Foster, had confused the parents with a misdiagnosis, and the silent girl continued to show malingering effects, mainly psychological, from the arsenic poisoning. The ambulance chasers determined to fight it out, first in the local media.

Our lawyers stressed that we continue not just to treat the girl but also to be seen to be treating her with the utmost compassion. But treating her for what? They'd also insisted on my continued involvement because I was the first consulting physician of record, and I *was* Dr. Lorne Thorpe (their emphasis). They said it didn't matter, legally speaking, that I'd been right in my speedy diagnosis of arsenic poisoning. The truth didn't matter. It was all public relations and minimizing what they'd already conceded would be the settlement against us. We were doing damage control, massaging the message, merely mitigating the cost.

The CHEO board made Foster and me take all the press conferences, assigning us a media coach who advised that we always wear freshly laundered lab coats and stethoscopes. Foster agreed to sniffle whenever the word *child* was spoken and to dab his eyes at *little girl*.

The situation deteriorated further. An enterprising reporter established that Ottawa's playgrounds were filled with equipment made of the same pressure-treated cedar. Soil samples were tested from a selection of playgrounds and it emerged that the sand and dirt surrounding the playground structures were also contaminated with arsenic. Manufacturers of the treated cedar were named in the suit, which was threatening to become class action and looked ready to go national. At the height of attention — CHEO TORTURING OUR KIDS IN WEIRD EXPERIMENTS, PARENTS CLAIM — we had crowded press conferences for five days running. Our media coach met with us privately beforehand each day for a wasteful half-hour, trying to force a clipboard on me, and with extra stethoscopes bunched in his fist like the guts of some machine.

Foster and I were thrown together too much, regularly having debriefing coffee after our press conferences. On the third day, he suggested that some friend of his be allowed to visit with the girl, Marie LeBlanc, who still had not spoken a word, though her vitals remained well within range. It was actually the friend of a friend of a friend, with the immediate friend being the mother of a patient and with the second friend being known only to that mother. Sometimes I wanted a lawyer present just to talk with Foster. This friend at the third remove wasn't a psychologist and not a *conventional* therapist. Foster called him a "holistic pediatric grief counsellor." I'm pretty sure he made that up on the spot for my sake. He claimed that his swami without accreditation had been known to work miracles with children.

"Known to whom, Pediatrician Foster?" I asked.

"Known to me, Lorne, personally."

"And the mother of your patient, the first unlicensed referrer, would I know her too?"

"Yes, in fact, I believe you do. But I'm sworn to keep her confidence. Why this attitude, Lorne?"

"Attitude?"

"Teamwork, Lorne, *remember*? Teamwork."

Apart from the perfect non sequitur, he couldn't simply have said *work together* on this. No, at CHEO we had become a *team*, from parking lot attendant to CEO, with every team member contributing to our winning… Well, I don't know how it plays out. Regardless, before becoming a team, we'd been *the CHEO family*. That designation had been dropped, perhaps because the CHEO family had begun to sound in some marketer's brain like a group of snacks or a sitcom about Italian immigrants. Whatever the reason, the CHEO family had donned the nattier uniform of a corporate team of "healthcare providers." That's what we'd remain till contract negotiations started up again. Then we'd become something of a family again, the Corleones, that differently organized collective of Italians, with their distinctive manner of making and refusing offers.

    I was weary of it all by then. "And your holistic quack, he gets results?"

    "Didn't I just *say* that I've seen the results with my own two eyes?" He pointed them out, his own two credulous orbs, just in case I'd forgotten the number he had or thought they were up his ass.

    I sighed melodramatically and said, "I'll tell you frankly, Art, it sounds to me like more mystic mumbo-jumbo. But what the hell, she's your patient, it's your call, and your funeral."

    He bristled: "You can be such a pri—so wastefully adversarial, Lorne."

    "Hey," I raised two John L. Sullivan fists, "wanna fight just for the fun of it?"

    He slid back in his chair. "You think my placebo research project is a joke too. Don't try to deny it."

    "I wouldn't dare."

    He fought to a smile, but he was actually coming to his old pre-anger-management-course Foster boil (the board had imposed the "re-education" as punishment for his behaviour in the operating theatre and with resistant nurses). "Such *a* prick!"

    I held up and shook both hands like an old-time Negro singing a spiritual: "Bring on da voodoo!… Do as you like, *Doctor* Foster, all the way from here to Gloucester, for all I care. I'm confident your juju man will be less wasteful, at least, than the tens of thousands of dollars Health Canada is throwing away on your placebo, so-called research, project."

He caught his breath. With teeth gritted he leaned over the table, halted. He licked his lips. With head slightly shaking he brushed nonexistent salt off the table with the sweeping edge of his right hand. Thought to speak. Didn't. Then: "You are going to learn a hard fucking lesson one of these days, Lorne Thorpe. And I may be just the man to teach you."

"Dr. Foster, *cher collègue*," sang I. "This anger? That even sounded like a...why, like a threat!"

"One hard, fucking, lesson."

He clamped his jaws, shoved back his chair, stomped off.

Victory.

Disturbing rumours began circulating about Foster's friend of a friend of a friend and the arsenic-poisoned girl. Out of professional responsibility I accompanied him to observe his non-credentialed therapist working with the depressed child in *our* care. We would watch through the two-way mirror on which both legal teams had insisted and which the juju man had resisted.

At first sight of the "holistic pediatric grief counsellor"—high-top red running shoes, billowing clothes, some huge amulet necklace, orange hair, near-midget height—I sputtered uncontrollably. He cocked his wild head with its considerable tonsure like he'd heard me. I looked around for the camera spying on *me*, suspecting I was the butt of some practical joke, that this was Foster's threatened revenge.

"Who, or what rather, is that, Art? Rumpelstiltskin?"

Foster continued smiling vaguely through the window: "Bob Browne."

Marie LeBlanc still wasn't talking and this Bob Browne was doing nothing. He just sat by her bed and twanged away on one of those ridiculous Jew's harps (the necklace). He never once glanced at the two-way mirror.

Was I in a state-of-the-art medical facility or Bizarro World behind this looking glass? What script were we following here? I thought the scene all too much like one of those bad TV stories about some eccentric traveller: the wandering charmer of lonely townsfolk, the converter of grumpy old folks, pal to daddy-damaged children, intimate of put-upon women, goat whisperer—the itinerant miracle-worker, whose original was probably Jesus Christ himself.

When the girl did talk—right out of the blue the next day, as though she and Bob Browne had been having a running conversation—I was the only witness present. Bob Browne let her speak in French at first, then led her to English. They chatted about mere nothings. He showed her how to get sound from the Jew's harp, without first using the available disinfectant wipes. She jumped off the bed and did a little jig with him, all the while twanging the thing (some instrument; there was no difference between her playing and his). Another time *she* sat in a chair while *he* lay on the bed. He may even have dozed, as I thought I heard snoring.

A TV was brought in and they began talking only about the kids' TV show *Wy Knots*. It could well have been from *Wy* that Bob Browne had learned the passive-aggressive style of echo, platitude, and challenge. Of course Wy himself was just another TV version of the wandering wizard.

The girl's spirits had become more buoyant between visits and were elated at each new visit, if you could go by her bouncing on the bed and clapping and squealing "Play, play, play!"

And I guess you could go by that.

My colleague Foster, strutting again after his potentially fatal, currently actionable malpractice, held me in the hall one day while Bob Browne was finishing up with the improving Marie. The three of us went for coffee together. Or I'd thought for coffee only. Bob Browne heaped his cafeteria tray, adding a second order of poutine. He wound his way to a table, scuttling more than walking on those un-legs of his.

Nodding at his tray as I approached the table, the first thing I said to him was, "Maybe we should ship you directly to the Heart Institute."

He stood glaring across the tray, beady green eyes unblinking from a ruff of orange hair. His first words to me were precise: "Just what the fuck is your problem, Dr. Thorpe?"

"Problem? *Moi*?"

Foster had been grinning absently at the wall of windows beyond Browne, and now he turned a rueful smile on me. "Oh, come on now, Lorne, lighten up. No need for professional jealousy!"

I could have cracked him over the head with Browne's tray. "And just what profession are we talking about here, Dr. Foster?"

Bob Browne slightly hefted his heaped tray and stared across it. "Look, I've not eaten since yesterday morning, okay? And I've just finished a lengthy session with poor little Marie…who, by the way, is fit to return home."

He sat and bowed over a plate mounded with poutine. "I don't buy all your medical crap about fat being bad for everybody. There are more serious threats to a person's well-being, which guys like you completely ignore. So, if you will please cram the sarcasm into a medicine ball and shove it up your ass, *Dok-tor*." He attacked the poutine without benefit of knife and fork.

Foster, too obviously enjoying his revenge, knocked the table once with his knuckles and stood.

Bob Browne stopped his slippery chops and, ignoring Foster, again trained those green eyes on me. "No real offence intended, Dr. Thorpe. It's just that I think you guys did as much harm as good to that kid when you completely ignored her spiritual needs." Back to his meal, fingers scooping.

Ah, so here was the mysterious source of Art's recent mystical bent.

"Well, I certainly wouldn't want to put you off *your* soul food."

He stopped and snorted a laugh, then said, with mouth masticating like a garburator: "I did say *as much* harm as good. I'm not denying that your quick action saved Marie's life, Dr. Thorpe. I'm not crazy. Medical science is its own form of miracle."

"We're flattered, I'm sure, all of us, from Hippocrates to Jonas Salk."

He hiccupped a laugh and blew a cheese-and-gravy bubble from his nostril; far from embarrassed, he pointed wide-eyed at the brownish balloon and tried to maintain it—till it popped. Nonchalantly he returned to his feed. Is it any wonder the child patient could "relate" to this man-child?

I was still shaking my head slightly when Foster slapped my back. "Well, I think I'll leave you two philosophers to get better acquainted." And walked away from the beginnings of my plea to remain.

Indicating his tray, Bob Browne called, "Art, I think the French lady at the cash register is waiting for you to sign for this! Mercy buckets!"

I swung back to the table. "Why haven't you eaten since yesterday morning?"

He didn't look up: "No dosh."

"What, OHIP put a cap on voodoo? It ain't fair."

He laughed, choked, but waved off my offer of Foster's half-empty cup of coffee. He thumped his sternum and was fine.

"Look, Dr. Thorpe—"

"Lorne will do fine, Bob, when we're alone. Catch your breath… Yes? I'm looking."

He smirked. "Look"—his voice was still pitched higher from the choking, and he seemed to enjoy the sound—"I'm not going to waste time explaining to you what I do." He was back in an adult register: "You're right, though, it doesn't pay, and it's not fair, but I continue to do it, as a favour to a dear old friend."

"Ah, yes, Foster's friend of a friend. Supposedly I know him or her, though my confidential colleague won't tell me who it is, which gives me no little cause for concern, let me tell you. Will *you* tell me?"

He pinched his lips and puffed out his cheeks for a thoughtful while. "Just an old friend of mine. We've been through a lot together, if that matters."

"It matters to me if you're treating our patients. Why all the mystery?" No response. I indicated the Jew's harp, which had been dipping into his messy fries: "If you need money, why not give music lessons?"

He ignored the joke, took the harp and licked it clean. Then posed with it reflectively:

"You know, Mesmer himself used one of these in his work."

"Why am I not surprised?"

He laughed lightly. "And Jew's harps were used as trade items to steal this land from the Indians. Bad from good, or good from bad, depending on your point of view." He looked straight at me: "It's no threat to anyone, what I do."

I let fire: "Just what *do* you do, Dr. Juju?"

He showed no offence. "You know, Lorne, I think you just might understand. Better than Dr. Foster anyway. But now's not the time."

"I thought you were Art Foster's friend?"

"I hardly know the man and don't want to. I've been here a few times before though at his behest, or my friend's, all on the q.t. I'll tell you this though—watch that guy. Very bad karma there, and between you two guys. Foster could be a crime looking for its victim. Maybe you. But what *about* you, Lorne Thorpe?"

I leisurely filled my lungs. Smiled to myself. What the hell. And he didn't like Foster.

"Happily married, two kids, seventeen and ten, boy and a girl."

He spoke without looking up from his feed: "I like a man who defines himself as a family, even in that wing-clipped way you have. That's a long time between children, the decision to again express your love that way. Who does Owen listen to? What's Shawn's favourite animal? TV show?"

I controlled myself. "Rap. Cats, I guess. *Wy Knots*, of course. You've been talking to Foster about me. Why?"

He glanced at me and I detected disappointment at my failure to be impressed. "Why? *Wy Knots*, eh? Marie's favourite TV show too. I asked *who* does Owen listen to, not what. Okay, smart guy—where does Wy ride off to on his donkey at the end of every show?"

"Is this a quiz show, Bob? Are rap and kids' TV that important to parent-child *spiritual* relations? My son, Owen, is obsessed with this psycho-fuck murderer the Market Slasher. That's real, and that worries me very much. My own father didn't know that I graduated at the top of my class at Johns Hopkins, the only Canadian ever to do so. So what?"

He smiled at me and turned down the voltage in those beady green eyes. "Thanks, Lorne. But I could have guessed something like that without you telling me. You're a good father. *Your* father *should* have known of your achievement. You believe your mother's love saved your life, right? Or your sanity anyway. Explain *that* medically or scientifically."

Now I was dumbstruck, and for too long. I'd certainly never said anything like that to Foster. Then hardly in control of what I said: "They both died last year, only months apart, him first. I think I hated him. I couldn't believe she'd loved him that much. I mean, to die for want of him. Yet I miss him more than her. I don't want to. She knew the nitty-gritty of me, every sin." I snickered like a fool. "Life and death, what's it all about, Bob Browne?"

He dropped his head. "Oh, this and that." And returned to eating, allowing me time to recover.

"And you, Bob? Are you a philosopher, like Foster said? A mind reader? Or just a clever simplifier?"

With his forefinger he marked the air three times: "Guilty, not guilty, and guilty. But it's really just paying attention, that and simple human compassion, a little imagination. And I know you were being sarcastic again, Lorne. You need to work on that. Why not just say what you mean, at least sometimes, eh?"

"Wy doesn't ride an ass. Wy's against exploiting our fellow creatures. His only companion is a goat. At the end of each show he walks the goat along the Noble Eightfold Path to a vanishing point, from which they emerge at the start of each show. For my prize, Mr. Trebek, I'll take the two-bit mystic's boxed set of Khalil Gibberish."

He startled me by rearing up and back, placing his hands on the small paunch that had popped out to accommodate his feed, throwing back his head and hooting so loudly that people—the colourfully smocked and weary, the coffee-guzzling and nicotine gum-chewing—looked over. A few acquaintances raised eyebrows at me, nodding in acknowledgement of Bob Browne, whose "work" with a few of our sick kids must already have inspired gossip.

He settled, wiping his eyes and mouth with a shirt sleeve that was as good as a big linen napkin.

"Wei," he said.

"Way?"

"Wy's goat, his name is Wei, must be a pun, eh? As in, *the* fourfold way. But too much—"

"I believe in Buddhism it's the Four Noble Truths and the Eightfold Path."

"*You* know that?" He didn't like being corrected, but the cringe passed quickly. "You know what's gold in this life, Lorne? I'm thinking you do. A good joke. Many of your fellow medical wizards now acknowledge it, that there's health benefit in laughter. You should try it in your practice, a little Robin Williams?"

I smiled without irony, it was a relief. "Tell me, Bob, how do you keep body and soul together, if your work doesn't pay? That's no joke."

"I knew I'd like you, Lorne. I knew it these past two days when you were standing behind the mirror all by your lonesome. Funny how quickly people lose interest, eh? The sound is two-way, you know. Or you don't. I know your way of coming in and shutting the door like you own the place. You sigh a lot. What idiot engineer forgot to soundproof the observation booth? And why's it called a two-way mirror anyway if you can see through only one way?"

"It wouldn't be a mirror otherwise."

"Man, that big brain!" He placed his right hand on top of his frizzled head and commenced flapping it at me à la Curly the Stooge.

"What did you fail at, Bob?"

The flapping hand came off his head and swung in a fist that struck his chest like an arrow to the heart—"*Schoop*"—and this time he mock-cringed: "Ouch. The notorious Clinical Director Thorpe's notorious clinical directness."

"Well, I need to be getting back—"

"You're right, of course. I did fail. I had my own business, a small landscaping company. I was good at it too. When I worked for other contractors, clients loved my stuff. When I struck out on my own, with a reputation and references glowing enough to secure big bank loans, no one would sign a contract with me. I was willing to ditch the contracts and still no one would deal. You know, I think it was something as simple as heightism. In case you hadn't noticed, I'm quite short."

"I noticed. It's really just paying attention, that and simple human compassion, imagination."

He startled me again the way he widened his eyes and pursed his mouth, this time clapping two hands to head as if to contain its orange jungle. He sputtered for a bit, as if afraid to unleash again the full force of his laughter. He wasn't play-acting.

There's nothing for beginning friendship like appreciation of one's wit. "But I wouldn't have thought height mattered in the gardening business."

He settled, continued eating and talked with his mouth full. "Landscaping. Anyhoo, I went belly up for good last spring. If you hear that the repo people are after me, it's because I've had to hide my combination backhoe-front-end-loader from creditors. It's all I have left. My friend and I are both getting pretty desperate for money. You don't happen to know anyone who wants landscaping done, do you?"

"I'll keep my ears open."

He reached for Foster's half-full coffee, downed it in one gulp and was looking inquisitively towards the stainless steel cafeteria kitchen.

"I've told you so much about myself, Lorne. How about telling me a little about Dr. Thorpe's rise to fame? You're a little god in this place."

"You've told me next to nothing about yourself, Bob, and there's no table service here. Where are you from? And this mysterious friend of a friend, a woman? Are you two romantically involved?"

"Here and there and nowhere. Yes and no…or not anymore, maybe never, I dunno."

"Well, that definitely answers those questions. Okay, how did you end up in Ottawa? You seem to speak sometimes with a German accent. Is that part of the act or are you Austrian or something? Other times I detect traces of a Southern twang."

"Good ear, Doc. I've been around ever since I was, uh, a boy… Really, Lorne, there's nothing to tell. I'd rather hear about you."

There was plenty to tell. But I did a singsong whisper: "Well, Dr. Phil, I was born at a very young age and nobody loves me enough."

He smiled into his empty cup. "Phil. It *means* love, you know. My one and only *phil*osophy."

So I gave him the thumbnail biography. I don't really know why. Only child. Father a diplomat. Family travelled the world a good deal. Parents always maintained a *pied-à-terre* in Ottawa. Decent cross-country runner, every year on a different school team. Just missed a Rhodes scholarship while doing a B.A. in history at Carleton U. Never looked to the humanities again. Pre-med at U Ottawa. Medical school at Johns Hopkins, specialized at Harvard. Could have stayed in U.S. for big bucks. Wanted to come home. CHEO's youngest ever director of clinical services. Met Veronica when she was doing a lab internship as part of a B.Sc. chemistry. Married right after her graduation.

He'd slowly pursed his lips and screwed up his face during that recital, bobbing more than nodding his head. His eyes seemed watery, sparkling aquamarine.

"That's it? What about your childhood? What about that *wanted to come home*? Elaborate, please."

I was perplexed. "Do you suffer from allergies, Bob? It *is* ragweed season, you know. You should let me…"

He shook his head and pushed off from the table. If the expression "stared daggers" has any real reference, my head was being haloed by Bob Browne's thrown knives. Yet he spoke with composure: "Your Market Slasher was a baby once, maybe a hated baby. Somebody sure hated him, and a lot, before you ever got to him, Dr. Thorpe. Do you think that baby wanted to be a serial killer of girls when he grew up? Talk to Owen."

"What?"

But without another word he walked away, suddenly a sad little clown shuffling offstage at the end of an unsatisfying performance. I'd been feeling buoyed and was suddenly let down. He could well be unstable, bipolar or something. And he *was* "treating" one of our patients, I reminded myself. And sympathy for the Market Slasher! Mixed with understanding for Owen! Bob Browne would bear close watching.

We met a few more times for coffee (me) and food (him, I paid), and, well, despite my misgivings I came to like him more and more. The last time we met, we talked about being middle-aged, which I'd never considered myself. He laughed that unless I was expecting to live to a hundred and fifty, I was long into my middle years. If I had any hidden dream, I'd better hop to it. Testily, I asked him when he'd started going bald. He grinned and said that already at thirty we're entering middle age.

I smirked. "So you'd say that Jesus Christ died a middle-aged man? Come on."

He peered into his coffee mug. "For a poor man of his time? Easily."

Whoever would have thought such a thing? So I relented, brushed the side of my head and pointed out how much grey I now had. "No delayed dreams, though," I snickered. "Just the same old nightmares."

He smiled up at me. "It's okay, Lorne. You're dying, that's all, but slowly."

"Yes, it seems to be a terminal condition with the living."

"Youth, hair, friends, children, it's loss after loss after loss. Until we accept that, every evening like a prayer, we can't begin to enjoy the trip. Death isn't the enemy, Doctor."

"Get invited to many christenings, Bob?"

He didn't smile. "Your persona is oh so serious, Thorpe, yet you refuse to take anything seriously. You could trivialize the Apocalypse."

"It ends with a whimper, remember? It's a wasteland out there, Bob, not Neverland."

"Why *not* a bang? It all began with a big bang. It could end with one too! In fact, now that I think of it, it will!"

"Bang-bang, we're all still dead forever. Your point?"

"I give up." He was rising.

"Do you have any idea what it's like dealing on a daily basis with dying children?"

He settled back and, strange to say, kind of leered into his coffee mug. "Yes, as a matter of sad fact, I do."

"But you're talking abstractly or poetically or something."

"Am I?"

He continued peering into his hugged mug as might a thirsty man a dry well. I watched his small gnarly hands massage the mug, noticed the old scars and fresher wounds, work-worn hands... I thought of my mother, who had read tea leaves for friends and neighbours, to my father's eternal shame. She'd had a talent for listening to other people's troubles. I don't know if she really believed in the mystical business, because even as a child I could see that she was clearly advising people based on what she'd heard from them in the tea-talk beforehand, not in the pattern of some clumped leaves. It was a form of free therapy for them and I'd witnessed it work wonders on a person's disposition. Her love really had saved my sanity more than once, even silently forgiven my sins. I felt a blow and suddenly missed her like a whole phantom body. I actually felt tears welling and fought them. I stopped fighting and the fear of humiliating myself disappeared with the gathered tears. I felt such relief, I can't explain.

"It's just too sad to speak of," I finally offered. "Even once seriously."

He still didn't look up. "I know. But Khalil Gibberish or not, it's death gives meaning to life and makes love essential, Dr. Phil."

"*The* paradox. Do you know the caduceus, Bob? Symbol of the medical profession?"

"The what?... Oh, yeah, but I thought it was pronounced ca-*doo*-sis." Don't ask me why, but as he said it he flapped his arms like a big bird. The man clearly maintained a certifiable side.

He settled. "But sure, snake on a pole, very ancient emblem. It's alchemical or something, right?"

"Well, symbols can be made to serve other interests. And it's two snakes on a winged standard. It's the symbol of my profession."

A bemused smile: "So you said. What do you think it means, Lorne?"

"What heals can hurt, what hurts can heal."

"I've learned something. Good medicine. And goodbye for now."

"Wait, where did *you* have experience of dying children?"

He wouldn't look back. "Uh... *big* childhood accident, like, a school bus. Some other time, Lorne. See you yesterday!"

A self-satisfied exit.

The following day, when Marie LeBlanc's parents came to pick her up, Bob Browne convinced them to drop their suit against CHEO and Foster and me and to accept a modest out-of-court settlement. How he did it, I do not know. Or I guess I do.

Chapter 5

A few days after Bob's disappearance I read in the abstract of an online medical journal that arsenic, while being the cause of various cancers, was being used in the *treatment* of some leukemias. A perfectly paradoxical caduceus. I realized with some surprise that I was dying to tell Bob Browne. But I didn't know how to find him — except through Foster — and would never bring myself to initiate contact anyway. I'd just have to continue dying to tell him, if slowly. Then a bit of luck came my way.

In the midst of my starring role in the arsenic case and the media frenzy over **OUR POISONED PLAYGROUNDS**, the Troutstream Community Association had turned to me for advice, as I was already its go-to guy on health issues and had recently agreed to be a member of its executive committee (thank you, pushy Veronica). I had to concur with Debbie Carswell, our over-eager chair, for whom a health-safety crisis was manna to a Munchausen's momma: all of Troutstream's treated-cedar playground equipment and the surrounding earth would have to be removed.

At the rare public meeting of the TCA executive, I first had to convince the committee that the appearance of conflict of interest was as damaging as the reality. I thereby earned the ire of Larry and Gary Lewis, owners of Troutstream's Twin Bros. Builders who, though on the executive committee, had assumed the contract to clean up the playgrounds was theirs, as per past practice. That was TCA reality, I was learning. Debbie hammered the table and pooh-poohed some trembling old guy's question about why the contract wasn't being put out to tender, as it was in wherever he'd just moved from. That gave me my opportunity to offer that I knew of someone who could clean up our contaminated playgrounds and would likely do so at a bargain-basement price, given the enormity of the job.

My offer had been received by the attending public like the announcement of a royal birth—Saved! Saved! Our children are saved—if not so by the old boy who'd questioned our questionable process, nor by the fuming, red-faced Lewis brothers; nor apparently were Chair Debbie and Treasurer Frank Baumhauser thrilled with the way matters were proceeding, though Secretary Alice Pepper-Pottersfield had applauded petitely, her fingertips tapping the heel of her other palm like she was merely miming applause. My immediate motion for us to consult with Bob was instantly seconded by Alice, and in the raucous applause that accompanied our procedure, intimidated Debbie forgot the necessity of a committee vote and simply hammered home the arrangement. I was only a bit ashamed that I'd made the crookedness of the crooked committee work in my favour, if all for Bob Browne's sake, of course. Or not *all*, to be honest.

Why had I done it, taken such trouble, exposing myself to official censure and future entanglement with, and maybe even indebtedness to, the TCA? What can I say? I liked him, I liked Bob Browne. I liked his radical difference from much of what I believed myself to be. I liked his eccentricity, his mysteriousness, his methods and his madness, his inability to threaten me even as he challenged most of what I held sacred: reason, science, proven methodology, etc. And this, the craziest of all: he reminded me of my mother, especially those beady green eyes of his (though hers were beady brown). I was in unfamiliar territory, and I can explain no more.

As I said, I didn't have a contact number for Bob Browne. I googled his name—and various versions and combinations of "landscaping" and his name—searched every online directory, clicked every link, but came up with nothing. In the end I had to go hat-in-hand to Art Foster, who had no number either.

"Listen," said Foster, "I'll contact my patient's mother and get her to get *her* friend to pass a message to Bob Browne, but only if I can borrow your vintage Cadillac for a weekend."

"Come again?" said I. "You'll put me in touch with Bob Browne only if I lend you my Caddy for a whole weekend? Look, Foster, I'm trying to do *your* friend Bob Browne a favour here. So no fucking way, my Caddy means more to me—"

"Have it your way. He's no concern of mine." He turned away.

"Okay, okay, wait!"

He turned back.

"Why do you want my Caddy?"

The hard bargainer left his face and something puerile grinned there. "A new lady friend of mine is absolutely crazy for Cadillacs, and the older the better."

"And she knows about *my* Caddy?"

"Everybody knows about Dr. Lorne Thorpe and his vintage white Cadillac."

"You told her."

He placed right hand over his heart. "On my mother's grave, I didn't."

I shook my head. "I might have known. *Lady friend*. More like cougar skank with a Caddy fetish. Where do you find them, Foster? Single moms of your patients? Or does *single* even come into it?"

"You won't believe it, but she found me, and she's definitely no cougar."

"You're right, Art." He grinned. "I *don't* believe it." He was turning away again. I hurried, "*Okay*. But only on these conditions: I hand over the keys down at my parking spot this Friday at six sharp. You return it on Sunday eve—"

He turned back. "Monday morning," he grinned, "and from Thursday. And not this weekend, next."

I hemmed and hawed but knew I'd comply.

"Okay, returned Monday morning, but at my house, at O-eight-hundred on the dot. I'll drive you to work or to a de-lousing clinic. But you have my Caddy at my house Monday morning at eight sharp. Absolutely no sex in the car. And the less Veronica knows about this, the better."

Foster continued the grin. "Don't worry about your precious back seats, I'm no randy teenage boy."

"Yes, you are, Foster."

"Do we have a deal, Lorne?"

"I'm not touching that hand. But, yes, deal. Don't make me regret it, which I already do."

But Bob Browne was as good as assured the contract, without a formal tendering process, and it would put a pretty penny or two in his pocket, and his special friend's.

Chapter 6

After Detective Beldon left, Veronica, Owen and I faked our way through Monday's supper, at which only Owen even pretended to nibble. His mother had responded with silence to his "any news?" I was hurt by his hurt look after I snapped, "About your sister or the Market Slasher?" He slouched away, with a more troubled look on his face than I'd thought him capable of.

I announced to Veronica that I was keeping my appointment with the TCA's executive committee that evening. No response. I said that my absence from the so-called *emergency session* could draw the sort of attention Detective Beldon had warned us against. But Veronica gave no sign of caring or even of hearing. Anyway, she could hardly object, as it had been her idea that I join the TCA in the first place, as I may have said already. The sad truth is I needed to get out, away from it all. And I owed it to Bob to go.

I'd already arranged the meeting between Bob and the TCA executive. We'd abused our power and exploited his need in order to arrive at a shameful deal, contrived chiefly by the Lewis brothers: no deposit, and Bob would be paid in cash only after he had shown that he could do the work to Larry and Gary Lewis's satisfaction. He did so in one park, proving up in what I expect was for him a most costly probation, and still he'd not been paid a penny, pretty or otherwise.

So off I went.

The new Troutstream Community Centre had failed as a gathering place for kids. Just why our youth preferred the dusky corners of playgrounds and baseball fields to the garishly lighted activity zones of the community centre still baffled Debbie Carswell, chair of the

Troutstream Community Association. "Like rats!" was how Debbie had described Troutstream's children during her campaign for a community centre. "These juvenile thugs and their molls congregate like *rats* in our parks at night! And you *know* what rats are always getting up to?" She'd nod round. But our children, those oversexed rodents, stayed away from the community centre in their randy packs. In point of fact, the only constituency still being served by the centre was the TCA's own proliferating committees, all chaired by Madam Chair Debbie.

Outside and inside it was painted white, with windows set too high in the booming space pointing to an A-frame ceiling. It felt like being trapped inside some big-rock candy mountain. When we took our seats at the long flimsy table, we were as shifty as movie gangsters meeting in a warehouse to plan a job. Which wasn't far from the truth, as we were welshers on a handshake contract with Bob Browne, met to reassure one another of our righteousness.

I sniffed twice. There was an acrid odour in the air, not hospital smell, but garage diesel, as if Debbie had parked her school bus inside.

She had brought along her own five kids, likely to proof the centre against charges of failure. In a show of discipline, she lined them all up to greet her school-bus assistant and TCA secretary, her lackey, Alice Pepper-Pottersfield, which the kids did in drawn-out singsong:

"Good afternoon, Miss Pepper-Pottersfield!"

Debbie dismissed them and hammered her gavel, then trilled her loonish Debbie laugh: "We do have work to do-oo!"

And as always with the TCA, I was back inside a bad TV sitcom, with irritating laugh track.

I sniffed again: "What's that smell?"

Across the table, Alice Pepper-Pottersfield's face came up from her intense recording and she levelled a blank gaze; her icy blues worked me over but good as a little blood came into her cheeks.

Good God, had Alice farted? I hurried (though as a pediatrician I have no trouble whatsoever with that human bodily function), "I mean, it smells like gasoline or something. Are we safe in here, haha?" I was failing to make it sound like a joke.

Alice flashed a shutter-speed smile and cranked her face round on Debbie Carswell.

Once when I'd forgotten never to make small talk with Debbie, I said, "Life must be a lot calmer on the school bus since calm Alice became your assistant." And Debbie had done her scrunching baffled face, like carpenter ants were a-building in her sinuses, and responded, "So one would have presumed so, Dr. Thorpe. But our Miss Pepper-Pottersfield is not what she appears, methinks. With the children she is *the* most *permissive* assistant I've ever had. Whereas with me, her hierarchical superior, she is become more and more… *familiar*, shall we say?" I had immediately warmed to Alice.

Debbie hammered the flimsy table again, actually stood and took two threatening steps towards the raucous children in the far corner, like some hippo making territorial display. Quite the sight, our chair in abrupt corporeal motion. Occasionally, as at the time, following one fad diet or another, Debbie rapidly lost weight, though it seemed actually to have dropped from her upper body to drape her pelvis like muffin tops. In sudden motion her rump and waist would shift vividly in mistaken Spandex and, when she twisted back suddenly, shimmy round her skeleton like hooped flesh.

Raising his hand like an effeminate traffic cop, Frank Baumhauser, treasurer, said, "Madam Chair, point of order."

"Oh, shut up, Frank! We're here for one reason and one reason only. To wit, how to finish the playgrounds apparatuses job that Mr. Bob Browne has apparently abandoned. Or should that be *apparatti*?… Alice?"

The anemic Alice, a regular rack of rigid bones, was a recent British immigrant, so automatically colonial Debbie's language authority. Alice always wore the same no-nonsense black pumps and plaid slacks, the same long-sleeved white blouses, the same pastel cardigans cinched round her shoulders. She had mousy hair lank as March drizzle and a wedge of a face as responsive as a snow-covered graveyard.

But meek Alice Pepper-Pottersfield nonetheless had a singular victory over mad Debbie Carswell. It had begun with Alice's timid suggestion that, perhaps, the proposed Troutstream Spring Masquerade should, "one hesitates to forward the notion," be changed to a Troutstream children's history fair. She volunteered to organize the whole thing; she would even, as a token of her immigrant's gratitude, operate a booth dealing with local history. Debbie had simply chortled as if humouring a child and begun assigning membership on the spring masquerade organizing committee. Alice cleared her throat and interrupted Debbie to raise the point again. A silence ensued. I broke it by suggesting that Alice make a formal motion, which I seconded. Without looking up, Frank Baumhauser, a high-school math teacher, voted with us and we carried the day, because Chair Debbie wasn't allowed a vote but to break a tie.

I'd been roped into taking Shawn to the children's history fair. Veronica had argued that I had to go, being on the TCA executive and having supported whatsherpepper's idea.

Inside the community centre, the four curved walls had been given over to the booths of organizations devoted to helping children victims and runaways: Child Find, Go Home Kids, Save the Children, the RCMP's Missing Persons Service, Amber Alert, Curb Appeal, and so on. Eoin McEwan, a lean and gruff Scotsman, chair of the Ottawa Children's Aid Society and my Piscator Drive neighbour, personally manned a booth that took the historical title literally. In paintings and photographs, his "The Child in Time" showed the ways in which children had been viewed through the ages, from medieval mini-adults, to romantic innocents, to labouring Victorian urchins and little savages, to the present day's confusion between the worship of eternal youth and opportunities for sex crimes. Impressive, but it couldn't hold a candle to Alice's whole corner display.

She was costumed in her usual schoolmarmish garb, but with her hair pulled into a bun that gave her pointy face a more penetrating look. Unlike the other booth hosts, Alice had gathered a sizeable audience of young and old and was holding them spellbound with her presentation of "Troutstream Through the Ages." Ancient maps were projected onto the white walls. She made the settlers of the land that would become Troutstream appear as pioneer giants. The construction of our 1960s suburb was the work of visionaries for its affordable, well-spaced family housing, child-friendly crescents and walkways, abundant playgrounds and park trails, and with the whole protected by encircling greenbelt. She'd made me reflect, see my familiar place differently. And when I thought about it, I remembered a disturbing truth: the much-maligned suburban dream of earlier decades was of an environment built for young families, for children. *That* dream now deserved the snobbish disdain of inner-city dwellers (the locale of nightmarish Market Slashers)?

Most enthralling had been Alice's slide show of life along the actual river that had given Troutstream its name. With the aid of an old map and a wooden pointer with pink rubber tip, she conjured for us how once upon a time a whole different world had existed along the busy river that was now the shrunken Troutstream creek. In the late nineteenth century a steamer had docked daily at a bustling landing near where the much-diminished stream now trickled under St. Joseph's Boulevard, ran on past the sewage treatment plant and eventually dripped into the Ottawa River. The former bucolic scene, I learned, had been called Dodgson's Landing, after the area's first settler, Blackburn Dodgson. To enter with Alice the vanished world of the sepia-toned slides, a community bustling with men in straw boaters and women in big hats and hooped skirts, with a side-wheeler steamship waiting to take passengers on trips along the placid Troutstream to small towns that no longer existed... Well, it was a transporting experience in every sense! Don't tell me about the Orient Express and the Giant's Causeway—take them away!

And children, of course; there were children everywhere in Alice's pictures: rolling big hoop wheels with sticks and playing on teeter-totters and tree swings, boys palming frogs and conspiring behind girls, girls chasing boys as if to hit or kiss them, and many eating ice cream or big lollipops or looking like they were about to swallow wedges of tiered cake—not a healthy food choice in sight!

Unlike Debbie's many fundraisers, Alice's Troutstream Children's History Fair had turned a profit. Debbie never referred to it again, or forgave Alice, I suspected from the increasing iciness in their relations. And I'd begun to hope that sylphish Alice Pepper-Pottersfield was the closest thing to an ally I had on the TCA. When push came to shove, as it was about to in the matter of paying Bob Browne the money owed him for the playground work, Frank Baumhauser would be a Debbie supporter. The only other committee members, the Lewis twins, were Debbie flunkies, certifiable, and probably my enemies now for depriving them of the clean-up contract.

"Oh, forget it," chirped Debbie when Alice didn't settle her mind about the plural of *apparatus*. "Here in the New World we have no time for the latitudes of proper grammar."

Frank Baumhauser winced as though a big cat under the table had swiped at his scrotum.

"What was that, Frank?"

To my surprise, Frank silently met Debbie's gaze, till Alice shot him a sideways look, which caused him to do a relenting *petite mal* with his eyes. I wondered if I'd been wrong about Frank too. Perhaps Alice and he and I could regularly make league against Debbie and the Lewis brothers. Then it struck me that maybe Frank and Miss Pepper-Pottersfield had a thing going on. Neither was married and the love of a good woman can embolden such a man.

The Lewis brothers always sat to left and right directly along the table from Debbie. Forty-something twins they were, Larry and Gary, the Tweedledum and Dumber of the TCA. Big beefy men with blond brush cuts, they may once have been close to identical but were now fleshy and fleshier, with differently evolved faces. Neither had married, and they lived together in Troutstream's only mansion. The Lewis brothers never opposed anything Debbie proposed.

At the previous meeting, which was only days before, after I'd again stated that we simply had to find the money to pay Bob Browne, even unto borrowing it, Larry Lewis had looked straight across at Gary and said my name like a joke: "*Lorne Thorpe.*" And Gary had slapped the table lightly, as he always did at one of Larry's poor jokes, which were always witless groaners. But this time they both smiled menacingly (they *were* big boys). Alice Pepper-Pottersfield had primped and squirmed on her seat as if transferring an impression of her bony bum to a soft mould. I'd taken that for another hopeful sign, glanced at Frank then back at her.

"Alice?" I'd prompted.

She'd compressed her lips, breathed audibly through her nose and said downwards, "All I know is that the children shall be *most* disappointed if Mr. Robert Browne does not keep his date with them, so to speak, in Shoal Park this coming weekend. His antics as he works are all they talk about on the bus."

Debbie had rapped the table. "Oh, Alice Pepper-Pottersfield, you are such a silly ducky!" But Debbie really did look unsure of herself with Alice now, anxious rather than assertive. And consequently the sylphish Alice appeared that much more a solid presence, and indeed my potential TCA ally.

Alice had raised her face to me, and those frozen-over eyes held me. "I *would* like to know how the repossession people came to know that Mr. Bob Browne was working for us?"

I'd blown a puff of air. "It certainly wasn't me, Alice, if that's what you're implying. I *was* contacted by the repo people at CHEO and I put them *off* the trail, just as Bob had instructed me to do. But they don't depend on informers anyway, those repo boys and girls. I don't know how it works in England, but here a lot of them are former cops, and they always get their man, recover the vehicle, if not any actual money."

"Yes, quite, the actual money." Alice hadn't budged. "If we didn't have the funds to contract with Mr. Browne, even informally, as I've only recently learned we didn't have, then *why* did we ever make the arrangement in the first place? Mr. Treasurer Baumhauser?"

Frank had dropped his chin and compressed his lips, mumbled, "Like I told you, Alice, usually Larry and Gary do our work, and, well, we have, like, a working arrangement with Twin Bros. It was Dr. Thorpe's fault. He brought Bob Browne in."

"Me? I didn't know how *your* finances work. I'd assumed we had the funds. I'm just your so-called community-health consultant, remember?"

The big Lewis boys had grinned at each other like the proverbial cat that ate the canary. Debbie had blushed deeply an uncelestial hue and quickly hammered back into place whatever group lie had suddenly floated free. Alice was relatively new to the TCA, if not as recent as I. She obviously wasn't privy to its history of suspect financial arrangements with the Lewis boys, though it certainly looked like she was beginning to wield some influence. Frank Baumhauser *had* snapped to at her remarks, and, as observed, even her "superior," Debbie, appeared more rattled by her than at earlier meetings. Perhaps it was the lingering effect of her success, both social and financial, with the children's history fair. But when we'd contracted with Bob for his work in the parks, neither I nor Alice had known that the TCA's money cupboard was bare because of the vast overspending on the Troutstream Community Centre, the monument to Debbie's madness in which we were again met to weave further our tangled web.

With a crack of her gavel, Debbie brought us to order.

"The minutes of the last meeting are approved and seconded by Larry and Gary respectively, no business arising from them, our only new business is continuing. To wit, how to proceed with cleaning up the playground apparatuses-usses...at Shoal Park."

I took a sharp breath. "But, Debbie, shouldn't our *first* order of business be to determine how we're going to find the funds to pay Bob Browne the money owed him for the work he's already done?"

"Indeed," mumbled Alice to the tabletop.

Larry again did his solemn percussive thing with my name: "*Lorne Thorpe*."

Gary was arrested with table-slapping hand poised—

"Indeed it should!"

And there he stood, in the twilight of the entranceway, Bob Browne himself, all five-foot-zero of him. In regular-size green rubber boots that on him came past his knees like swashbuckler legwear, sporting one of his many colourful flaring shirts (red-and-black checks, this one), with the whole ensemble topped by his wild pumpkin-coloured hair.

Debbie's kids immediately scampered from the far corner and came to caper about his legs (not much longer than a child's themselves). Since we'd contracted with him only a week or so before for the removal and replacement of all wood-and-metal apparatuses and surrounding earth in Troutstream's six playgrounds, Bob Browne had become a great favourite with the children.

He slid a few steps towards us but was unable to advance in the press of kids.

"*We had a deal!*" he declaimed, pointing a forefinger like a stunted parsnip at the vaulted ceiling. The kids, startled for an instant, squealed and clapped, the show had started. "A guarantee of service and a promise of payment! I was to receive thirty percent of the total hundred thousand when I'd shown that I could do the job in the first playground, Piscine Court. I showed that I could. Still I received nothing in recompense. Nothing, that is, but the smiles and laughter of children." He was serious, he smiled and touched a few heads. "Consequently, I have had to postpone entering the second playground, Shoal Park." The kids moaned. "So I put it to you yet again," he swept a hand towards us, "ladies and gentlemen of the Troutstream Community Association executive, *is* Bob Browne to be paid tonight, *as was promised*, or is he to leave here left to his own devices?"

"Pay him, pay him!" the children cried. To our eternal shame, they knew the whole sordid story of promises broken.

Debbie ignored his question. "Would you care to join us, Mr. Browne? We were just about to deliberate proposals for the completion of the work you've apparently decided to abandon forthwith."

"I would *not* care to join you, Mrs. Carswell. Nor have I abandoned any work. My part of the bargain has been kept. Now, I am going over to that corner where" — again he indicated with that root-like forefinger—"with the children to distract me, I will await payment."

The kids fought gently for his hands and pulled him to their end of the room—"Play! Play! Play!"

"As you wish it, so shall it be," murmured Debbie. Then mumbled aside, "But if you are *not* going to finish the work for which you were contracted for, well then, mayhap the police…"

Debbie frowned towards the corner, because Bob Browne was now standing amidst the seated children and playing his Jew's harp. Just what enthralled those high-tech kids was a mystery, because the "music" was something like the soundtrack to a cartoon flea bouncing around: *boing boing boing…*

"Lorne?" Debbie asked distractedly. "Can we have…your report?"

"*What* report?"

She performed that shiver of her big Debbie head, like someone had slipped a cold eel down the crack of her ass. Her bovine Debbie eyes bugged, her wattled chin dropped, and she didn't begin to stand so much as to stretch upwards with intent. We all turned toward the corner where she gaped.

The children were up and dancing in a growing frenzy. Bob Browne was leading them, twanging his Jew's harp and kicking out sideways in some devil's jig. One of the kids, Debbie's oldest I think, was coughing, asthmatic perhaps in the excitement or reacting at the height of the ragweed season. Suddenly his hacking was a whooping threat of respiratory seizure.

Still sitting, Debbie stretched her neck: "Why, that's my… that's Petey!"

But instead of rising and rushing to his aid, she flopped sideways and commenced rummaging in a white leather bag the size of something a hockey goalie might throw into a bus's undercarriage.

"Where *is* that blankety-blank inhaler? There—no, that's Stacey's insulin…Mickey's anti-anaphylactic…Barbie's bum-eczema cream…"

I pushed off from the table and was on my way to the corner—I stopped halfway. I touched my waist, my cellphone reassuring. Let Debbie pump *her* kid full of Ventolin. For the sake of my Hippocratic conscience, I'd call it in, if need be, then turn the case over to the paramedics. I had my own troubles, thank you. Suddenly, more than anything, I needed to be back home. What was I doing here?

Bob quit his playing. The children closed round as he took Petey by the upper arm. It was difficult to ascertain what happened next, but I think Bob put one hand on the small of the boy's back and the other flat on his chest and laid him into a bean-bag chair, like dunking a convert. The boy stopped whooping, though his wheezing still pierced the mountainous hall like a puncture. Bob quietly commanded, *Play!* And I heard the Jew's harp twang, but weakly. The other kids made *ee-yoo* sounds of disgust, some turned away, opening a space through which I could see better.

Bob was removing the Jew's harp from the child's mouth. He placed it in his own and twanged a few notes. Then he was handing it back to Petey, like two divers sharing an air supply. Again came the kids' *ee-yoo*, because the Jew's harp wasn't being wiped. Even from a distance I could see the saliva drip. This time Petey tried to block his mouth. Instead of shoving the harp into him, Bob took the blocking hand and, like someone forcing money on a proud relative, closed it on the harp. Nodding encouragement, he gestured for Petey to play again. Petey did, weakly plucking the small prong sticking out to the right of his mouth. The twanging grew stronger. Petey wasn't coughing. I looked back at the table, where they were all watching the hump of purse-rifling Debbie instead of the miraculous procedure taking place in our midst. Or all but Alice Pepper-Pottersfield, who was alternating between the corner scene and me with what I can only describe as an angelic expression on her normally dour face.

Petey took Bob Browne's hand and stood. He handed back the harp. He was breathing easily. He placed a hand flat on his chest, and the brightest amazement I'd ever seen on one of Debbie's kids beamed forth.

"Mom!" he called to the table. "Mom!" he shouted again, easily filling his lungs. "Call Dad! Get Dad!" He stopped trying to get his mother's attention and, looking down at himself, was enthralled by his own deep breathing.

Debbie's preoccupied voice idled past me: "I do seem to have misplaced your inhaler...Peter. Mayhap, just this one occasion, you can use Terrence's, if thereby abrogating my own edict about putting *any* other kids' thing in your mouth. Now where is..."

Bob Browne put an end to proceedings. He walked towards me, but instead of coming alongside, halted a couple of yards away, facing the committee. I turned sideways so as to watch both the TCA executive and Bob. He had their attention. He slid his left foot forward and made a sweeping bow like some Peter Pan doffing his cap to an unfriendly rabble of grown-ups. He straightened and merely flipped out his empty right hand, rubbing its fingers in the gimme-money gesture.

"Gotcha!" bellowed Debbie, straightening up from below the table with a flushed face and the blue inhaler of Ventolin pinched between thumb and forefinger. She saw that Pete was out of danger and, predictably unpredictable as ever, gave herself a puff. "Oh!" she piped. Then more seriously to expectant Bob: "Yes, Mr. Browne? You have changed your mind mayhap?"

He crossed his feet — he may even have hopped! — and flipped out both arms like some sort of court jester:

"What made the Big Bang bang?"

"Par...the big bang-bang?"

The children shouted in a mountain-ringing chorus: "*Don't be dumb-dumb! Ask again!*"

"Why is there something instead of nothing?"

"Why I—"

"*Don't be dumb-dumb! Ask again!*"

Bob smiled small at me: "What do the children mean?"

"*Don't be dumb-dumb! Ask again!*"

I recognized the routine from *Wy Knots* that had upset Otto Fyshe with the boy, the koan-ish questions followed by the string of dumb-dumbs and ask-agains till Wy got what he was getting at.

Bob gazed at me and mimed loudly with his mouth: *Love*.

Hey, fine by me! Though I said nothing.

Unsmiling then, Bob looked to the table and lighted on his most likely sympathizer.

"What do you think of that, Mizz Pepper-Pottersfield? What *do* the children mean?"

"*Don't be dumb-dumb! Ask again!*" chorused the kids.

Literally rising to the challenge, Alice Pepper-Pottersfield scraped back her chair and stood. She brushed away a strand of lank hair as though signing a tiny cross on her forehead. "Can we put an end to this charade?" *Shar-odd*. And snapped, "Debbie?"

Debbie, uncharacteristically cowed, harrumphed: "Yes, we must do as Alice says. Just what is it you want, Mr. Browne?"

Alice shivered as would a thin woman who'd stamped her foot. "Stop. As Dr. Thorpe said in a more generous frame of mind: *are we* or are we *not* going to pay Mr. Browne the money promised and now overdue?"

She looked at each of them, who in turn dropped their heads, then glanced at me, and came to rest on Bob. "What sort of example *are* we setting our children, Dr. Thorpe?" she asked, though she didn't take her eyes off Bob. She sat and stared straight ahead at nothing.

Bob Browne beamed at oblivious Alice: "Thank you for that ringing endorsement, dear Alice, if you will allow the endearment. Wy himself could not have composed a more appropriate question."

Bob swung round on the children and lifted his arms in shirking affirmation, I think, of the things he'd been telling them in the playground about their parents: *See? What's to be done with such grown-up liars?* He mimed brushing the children back, then turned away and, unaccompanied this time by their convoy, strode out the entranceway as well as those un-legs could stride.

I hurried after him outside and, as he pounded round the circular walk, called, "*Wait!*" He stopped, paused before turning.

"So," I said, arriving a bit breathless, "that went well."

In his eyes he wasn't himself, or at least not the Bob Browne I knew.

"What kind of stupid crack is that?"

"Uh, a stupid ironic crack, I guess."

"You and your fucking ironic cracks, Thorpe. I should crack you!" He actually made a fist.

"Me? Didn't you hear me pleading your case?"

"You're the man I dealt with, Dr. Thorpe, my primary contact."

"*Dr.* Thorpe? Look, Bob, I really wish—"

"Yeah, I have a wish list too." He leaned forward, his face fierce. "For starters, you could pay this fucking dwarf yourself and collect from *your* organization later."

"What? That much money?"

"Like *I* borrowed more against my equipment to show I could do this work, dumb-dumb?"

"Look, Bob, I'm really not part of all that," I gestured. "I'm sorry—"

"Sorry nothing! You will be sorry if I don't have a cheque in my hand by five o'clock tomorrow! Then we're blowing this fucking 'burb before something even worse happens! I can trust no one! No one!"

Excepting our first meeting in the cafeteria at CHEO, I'd never seen him utter an angry word, and here he was, fuming.

"Are you threatening me, Mr. Browne?" I snickered. "And who is this *we*? The mystery friend with whom you have the history? The anonymous one who brought us together?"

He smirked, shaking his head. "You think you're in a hole now, Thorpe? I'll put the whole fucking lot of you in a hole with a headstone on it!"

That certainly sounded serious. But this radical change in him, what really did I know about Bob Browne? Given the situation with Shawn, my mind ran madly and I could not collect my thoughts. Detective Beldon *had* asked about him specifically right off the bat after Veronica and I could come up with no suspects, and again throughout the second instalment of my story. And Beldon did seem to know his business. Now Browne stood with his mouth pinched, puffing heavily through his flaring nostrils, about to lose control. I thought of Jake, our neighbours' Down's child, and his legendary feats of superhuman strength.

Bob breathed deeply through his nose, exhaled slowly from puffed mouth. He looked up at me searchingly: "Don't worry, Lorne, no physical harm. But no idle threat either. I was promised and *someone* has to pay this fucking piper. Personally, you disappoint me. It may sound childish, but friends don't say insulting things about each other behind their backs."

"I don't know what you're talking about, Bob. But obviously you trust someone else enough to believe that I would do that. Was it Art Foster?"

He turned on his heels and walked away.

I called again: "Bob?" He slowed. "What happened in there? I mean, what you did to settle that boy who looked headed for respiratory seizure? Was it as simple as distracting him? Studies *have* shown there's a psychosomatic element to most childhood respiratory allergies."

"*Don't be dumb-dumb! Ask again!*"

"Tell me, Bob, please?"

He called ahead of himself as he scuttled off: "I did more than you were willing to do, Dok-tor!"

I returned to the TCA meeting and wearily took my seat. The kids were standing round the table again. A few were coughing. Not Pete though. I watched him till he noticed me doing so, then he coughed.

Debbie grinned around at us all. "Well, then, we are joined again then. And wasn't that a bit of jolly good fun!"

Larry Lewis said, "Mr. Bob Browne is a fun-guy. Plural of fun-*gus*, right, Lorne Thorpe? I expect Mr. Browne will be getting a lawyer and suing us, thank you again, Lorne Thorpe."

Across the way, Gary snorted and lightly slapped the table.

Frank Baumhauser smiled. "He has no contract, remember?" He looked at me. "And I too have heard that Mr. Browne's equipment isn't his any longer, legally speaking. The police are now involved, am I right, Dr. Thorpe?"

"Not that I know of, Frank. I'm aware only of some repo men." Some unsavoury sorts had contacted me at work, as Bob had forewarned, and I'd told them that I believed Mr. Browne had sold his combination backhoe-front-end-loader to a builder somewhere in Gatineau and moved back to Vienna. They were surprised, as they'd been sniffing along a trail that had them believing Bob was an American from the deep South. They were even more surprised when I called hospital security and requested they be escorted to the exit.

Without looking up, Alice articulated precisely to her writing pad, "How very honourable of you, gentlemen."

Debbie harrumphed again. "How positively medieval it's all been! But this puts an end to proceedings. The business of what to do with the remaining playgrounds will be put on the agenda for our next meeting. Motion to adjourn?" Gavel up. "Thank you, Larry Lewis. Seconded? Gary. All in favour?... Opposed? Meeting adjourned."

Crack.

Debbie, her children, and Frank Baumhauser filed out past Larry and Gary Lewis, or between them, actually, as they were standing sentinel either side of the doorway. As I approached they continued to look across only at each other and, smiling enigmatically, they said together, "Jolly good fun, eh, Lorne Thorpe?"

I was jumpy anyway, and that spooked me good. "Jesus Christ, you guys!"

Larry repeated alone: "Lorne Thorpe."

"Larry?" I said. The right one turned. "Why have you taken to saying my name like that?"

"Like what, Lorne Thorpe?"

"Like it's some kind of morbid joke? Surely it's not the playground contract still? As you know, as you've just *seen*, you'd never have been paid a cent for your work. I actually *saved* you guys money."

"Oh, we always get *our* money, Lorne Thorpe. We're just a couple of...what was it, Gary? A couple of *small-time suburban crooks?*"

"And what else, Larry?" Gary smiled. "*Sexual suspects?*"

"What?" I said loudly. "Listen, it doesn't matter to me how you two—"

Larry turned on me: "You listen up, you smug little prick, it ain't over till we say it's over. You're gonna pay big-time for fucking with the rep of Twin Bros. Builders."

"Pardon me?"

Larry, the fleshier one, continued, jabbing a fat forefinger at my chest: "Because, *Lorne Thorpe*, twins have twice the reason not to forget. And because you are one fucking snob of a prick who thinks he's better than everybody else in Troutstream."

"I apologize, Larry…Gary? I truly am sorry, gentlemen, if I have given that impression, but I really don't…"

They'd turned together and walked away, in their Hawaiian shirts, shorts to below the knees, black socks and sandals. They were big boys. They could put some serious hurt on me. The late-summer evening suddenly felt a lot muggier again. I'd wanted distraction and I'd got it, in spades.

I turned back to close the interior doors when Alice Pepper-Pottersfield stepped from the shadows of the foyer coat racks. I was startled yet again. She came into the light and, smiling weakly, touched my forearm.

"Alice?"

"Dr. Thorpe." Those ice-blue eyes shone like their own lamps in the twilight. Up close her skin was porcelain pale. She breathed a sigh of minty freshness as with her free hand she fingered a buttonhole of her cardigan. "Sorry if I startled you, Dr. Thorpe. I'm charged with locking up."

She met me eye-to-eye. "But I do wish those Lewis boys would just grow up and do the right thing. None of this needed to happen. *None* of it," she said, leaning toward me. "I know it looks like Debbie runs the show, but it's Larry and Gary Lewis who really call the shots. You didn't know that, did you, Dr. Thorpe?"

I pulled back my head, furrowed. "Are we talking about the same Larry and Gary?"

"Don't be fooled by appearances. Twin Bros. Builders has been stealing money from the TCA for years. I know. Frank has shown me the books. I was *so* pleased when you brought up the conflict of interest. At last, I thought, I have an ally on the committee."

I'd felt a tickle in my parts, the way she'd hissed *stealing* and drawn out *ally*. "Well, now I *am* shocked, Alice. But thanks for telling me. Was that, uh, all you wanted?"

"No. I've kept you from your lovely home and family because I need to intimate something to you, Dr. Thorpe."

"Lorne, please. Intimate away."

She removed her hand from my forearm. "Yes, well, *Lorne*, then. It's not the kind of thing into which one would normally stick her oar and one can never be sure of the proper protocol in such matters, can one?"

She needed encouraging. "No, Alice, one cannot. Or one can. I'm not at all sure what we're talking about. But, please, speak freely."

She made a thin determined smirk. "Well, then, I do believe that last Wednesday I saw a man in a white van pull over to the curb in front of the library and engage your daughter in conversation."

"What!" I couldn't believe I'd forgotten about Shawn for a nanosecond.

She drew breath. "For a good while too. Shawn didn't get into the van or I'd have run over. At first I thought there was already a child in the passenger's seat, but it was a dog, a golden-coated dog, I believe. The man and your daughter talked animatedly for a long time, and when it ended the van squealed off angrily, leaving Shawn looking quite perturbed."

I was blinking and shaking my head and making bewildered noises. Instead of slapping me back to my senses, Alice just waited and watched closely.

"Yes. And Shawn continued looking worried all the way back to the library doors. Now, I'm almost certain it was the same man I'd seen talking with Mr. Robert Browne at the playground a few days before when I was out for my constitutional, tallish, slim-ish. I apologize if that shocks you…Lorne. I've already discounted that any man would look tallish alongside Mr. Browne." She gently snorted a laugh, composed herself. "Still, I would say he was almost your height. Though I suppose you *are* a bit below average for a North American male."

It *was* like I'd been slapped back and forth. With an effort I gathered my wits. "Alice, are you certain of all this? Because if you are, I know a detective you must talk to."

She pulled back, then squeezed my forearm again. "I'm sorry, Lorne, but I can tell only you about this. My immigrant status is—how can I put this delicately?—not quite normative. Consequently, I cannot be involved in any police investigation. But even with that risk dangling over me, I had to do the right thing by you and my conscience. Besides, I do believe that you are at least as competent as any small-town detective insofar as knowing what to do with such information. After all, it was you who cracked the arsenic-poisoning case and started all…this."

"Thank you."

"Shawn may be afraid to tell you. Children, and especially girls Shawn's age, can be funny about things like this with their daddies, the attractiveness of the maturing female body and all. On the other hand, and what is by far the most likely scenario, the man in the white van is nothing to worry about. I'm sure you'll hear a perfectly simple explanation from Shawn. I just had to say something."

I was still distracted by careening thoughts. "I'm not so sure…"

She smiled sympathetically. "Lorne, I do apologize for unnecessarily alarming you. But there you have it, the paranoid ramblings of a spinster, I expect you're thinking… Regardless, I was concerned, justifiably so, what with this alarming Market Slasher business and all that has the media in such a tizzy."

"But Shawn's dis—Shawn has *nothing* to do with the Market Slasher! He's murdering teenage hookers!"

"Of course not, I didn't mean to imply otherwise, but one can never be too cautious, can one…Lorne? Did you hear that the police now suspect the monster is some form of a jihadist? And by the by, those young girls are innocent *victims*… Lorne?"

"...the kidnapper and Bob Browne? Kevin *had* asked about Bob... Or was the man in the white van and the playground *threatening* Bob, working for the Lewis brothers and trying to scare Bob off the job? And *that's* how I come into it? Scare Bob, punish me. But to take Shawn? That would have been a crazy revenge even for the mad Lewises... The *Market Slasher*? Dear God..."

"Pardon me, Lorne? I'm afraid I don't follow you. Somebody *took* Shawn?"

I hardly knew where I was anymore. My face must have shown my state, for Alice said, "Would you like to get an early nightcap at the Lighthouse Bar & Grill, Lorne? You don't have your Cadillac, I see. I mean, you always take the parking spot right in front of the door here. Or would you prefer to take a walk? Or would you rather not be seen anywhere in the company of such a silly old maid?"

"No...no." Where *is* my Caddy?... Foster. He was supposed to have had it back to me this morning! "Thanks, Alice. I walked here and I *prefer* to walk home, I need the air and exercise. See you around."

Normally, I'd have contradicted her self-deprecating remarks. Normally. But I was feeling none too chivalrous. I'd want to talk with her again, though. As would Detective Beldon.

Chapter 7

The three of us took Tuesday off, holing up at home, normal routines and media-prying be damned. Beldon said it was probably too late now anyway. When the school bus honked, I went to the curb and told Debbie through the driver's window that Shawn was sick. Standing on Debbie's other side, Alice Pepper-Pottersfield smiled sympathetically in her fluorescent orange vest, then nudged Debbie's shoulder. As the bus drove off, I was treated to a sideshow of kids' faces like an old movie's asylum scene: stuck-out tongues and thumbs in ears and fingers like wriggling antlers, cheeks and noses crushed sideways against the glass, eyes rolled up in zombie faces. At the rear a pillow fight seemed to be at full throttle. Pillows?... Backpacks then. Anyway, it would seem that Debbie was right about Alice's permissive ways as bus monitor. But who was running the show?

Back at our family breakfast (I'd secretly had only two Valiums), I did my best to distract them with tales of the previous night's TCA meeting. I featured Debbie and her duffel bag of medicines, fidgety Frank Baumhauser, and the dumb-and-dumber routines of Larry and Gary Lewis.

Veronica, sitting opposite, tilted back her head, eyeing Owen sideways: "What about the English woman with the funny name who helps Debbie on the bus? Ann Pepperpot?"

Owen shook his bowed head like *he'd* been asked to do something.

"*Alice*? You'd hardly even know she was there. She's got a talent for totally disappearing into the woodwork."

Veronica smiled weakly. "What? She's always been your showstopper. Last time you said a joke of yours had made her fart."

She leaned back, crossed her arms on her chest, closed her eyes for a spell.

"I did? Wait a minute…" I rifled my addled mind. Coincidence? The diesel smell, the fart? Was it Sherlock Holmes or Detective Freud who said there is no such thing? Probably that nutter Jung, an archetype for Art Foster if there ever was one. But I needed to keep a clear head.

"C'mon, give us Alice's constipated little-girl face taking the minutes." She'd opened her eyes but slid them only from Owen to the side door on my right.

The two of them felt far away. I thought I heard Owen sniffling and I couldn't even register my shock at the gangsta's breaking down.

I watched Veronica's face not watching me and reflected on the many times she'd saved me from the glare of a careless world, probably even shielded me from myself. She was no longer young and pretty, but lovely now for showing the wear of loving the three of us over time, refusing to dye her hair as it greyed, faking nothing…when a bar of sunlight shot through a tear in the awning that overhangs the kitchen's patio doors and, in some Stonehenge configuration, neatly crossed the midline part in Veronica's hair and spotted my right hand lying by the teaspoon, then instantly lit up the bowl of the spoon. *Why can't I just say out loud right here and now how beautiful she is and how much I love her?* I pinched the handle and rolled the spoon back and forth and stared, bedazzled, and the whole room was drenched in light. I checked squintingly to see if the others were experiencing the glare. They weren't. It was some rarity of canvas tear and Veronica's head and light and concave metal and optic nerve, for me only. I had enough presence of mind to know it was likely a delayed stress response to recent trials, perhaps even an ocular migraine or some such, simple optics, though I felt fine. In truth, I'd never felt better, and that realization was more shocking than anything.

Returning to the bowl of the radiant spoon, I had this flash: *Is it possible my family indulges me only because they love me, and Veronica especially? Looked at in a clinical light, I could well be the arrogant, snickering, witless shit others think me. Can love forgive so much?*

"Lorne?... You've never stooped to ugly faces before. Are you cramping? Or are you doing a new Alice Pepperpot?"

The earth must have shifted infinitesimally, for the sun slipped past the tear in the canvas and suddenly the light died. I was just staring at my pale surgeon's hand lying alongside a dull spoon.

Shawn.

I was washed by a tsunami of guilt for having left them and our family catastrophe. I pulled myself together.

"No...it's...Pepper-Pottersfield. And no, I'm not *doing* her."

She looked a bit quizzical: "Are you—"

"It's nothing, just..."

Then I lost my mind. I needed to test my hypothesis—that I wasn't funny at all, that my family indulged me out of love—so I went for Bob Browne, the easiest comic relief, still a fresh routine. I pulled in my neck, humped my shoulders and hunched down stiffly in my seat, gesticulating, exaggerating his Austrian accent, throwing in a few *zee doomb-doombs*, even a Nazi salute and some Hitlerian roaring about burying the TCA in a grave of debt.

I was rewarded with Owen's frowning face rising from his cereal bowl. Maybe he'd not been whimpering and needing distraction so much as lost in his own thoughts and trying to ignore me.

I poured it on, barking away unintelligibly with Adolphish ferocity. I was out of my chair, about to throw dignity to the wind and do a little *sieg heil* goose-stepping around the kitchen island—

"Lorne!" Veronica shouted, maybe screamed.

The scene froze.

The doorbell rang.

Veronica seemed too eager for an excuse to push away from the table.

"I'll bet that's Jack," she said worriedly to herself in passing. Then threw at me: "Are you still taking the...*ee-um*? You'd better watch that, some people react psychotically, especially if you're not under *a doctor's care*."

I deflated. "Jack? What the hell does he want this early?"

"I *told* you yesterday. Trixie's been gone for days and phoned home just yesterday. Jack's beside himself looking after Jake."

She disappeared down the hallway and I heard the aluminum front door's spring whine.

"Oh, yeah," I said to no one. I turned to Owen. "What's all this about tricky Trixie and good neighbour Jack?"

"Nothing," he snapped. "Fucking retards."

"Owen!"

He gripped the end of the table with both hands. "It's my body and I can get a tat if I wanna!"

"Son, is this really the time…"

He too pushed away from the table and, slouching past me, snapped, "You're cranked on Valium anyway. Where's that fucking detective with Shawn?"

"Owen!"

In nothing flat the woofer was thumping directly overhead and the white Tiffany lamp overhanging the breakfast table was jiggling as at a subterranean detonation at Troutstream's Mann Quarry.

Veronica began speaking before she reappeared: "Lorne, it's Detective Beldon."

Beldon was wearing the same shiny grey, poorly fitting suit. I shook his hand, anxious for his news.

"Apologies for not calling last night, Dr. Thorpe. Lorne. But I think you'll agree it's justified when you hear what brings me."

Veronica and I must have gasped, and I felt her knuckles dig into my back.

"Relax, please," he said, "it's not about Shawn, though I remain as hopeful there. Is Owen home?"

"Owen!" Veronica and I said together. "He's upstairs," I said, "the music."

Veronica pushed past us and up the stairs. The woofer thumping stopped.

"What'd he do?"

"No, no," Beldon said, appearing flustered for the first time. "I'm making a mess of this, I just wanted to know that he was home. I don't need to see Owen. This has nothing to do with him." He looked to where Owen had stopped in the hallway, with Veronica peeking from behind. "You can go back to your music, Owen, if you like, I'm not here to arrest you yet."

Owen smirked, turned and climbed the stairs. Veronica came and stood with us.

Beldon said, "Day off for everybody, eh? Good idea. Can we talk in the family room again?"

Veronica ushered us into the family room off the kitchen. Beldon paused and cocked his head, satisfying himself that Owen was occupied.

Rather than following us and sitting, he stood by the family room's patio doors and looked deadpan at me.

"Art Foster has been arrested."

"What! *Art?*" I don't know who of Veronica and I said what, but we both pressed back in the love seat.

"Take a deep breath. I don't enjoy playing the melodramatic detective. But no, not about Shawn's abduction, as I said, but for soliciting."

I was as confused as Veronica, who managed, "But I don't…"

Beldon delivered his next line calmly, though his eyes shifted rapidly between us: "Soliciting for sex."

I snorted. I may even have smiled: "Foster was caught picking up a hooker?"

He looked at me with little expression. "Not a hooker, Lorne. A teenager, a girl, with no history for solicitation. She says he used force."

He let that sink in.

Veronica put the tips of both hands to her temples, to blinker her gaze downwards. "Force? But that does mean that Art could be…"

I completed her thought: "The two incidents *are* related!"

Beldon shook his head slightly. "Where's your car, Lorne?"

Veronica dropped her hands. "His car?"

Beldon let me stare for another dawning moment, then said, "That's right, Foster had your Cadillac. Down in the ByWard Market, early hours of this morning. A young girl who was resident at the Curb Appeal home that rescues street kids. When they ran the plates and your name came up, the constable made the connection and I was contacted first, thank God. I've bought us some time, but we have little left before the story breaks. And I mean the whole story."

Veronica turned on me: "But you told me Art had a date with a Rockcliffe divorcee he was after for research funds? Lorne, you *gave* him your Caddy so he could pick up young girls!"

I wouldn't lie, not with Beldon there, it'd come out anyway. But I wouldn't plead either. "No. Yes, I mean. I lied about the Rockcliffe fundraiser. I was embarrassed, but I didn't know Foster had a thing for girls. It was arranged well over a week ago. It was the only way he'd help me contact Bob Browne for the job cleaning up the playgrounds. He took the car Friday, Detective Beldon, for the weekend. In all the, well, the excitement, I forgot it was due back yesterday morning. What on earth has Foster been up to?"

Beldon's voice was soothing. "Listen, we really don't have much time. Eventually you're going to have to give a statement downtown, Lorne. No one suspects you of anything and you don't need a lawyer. But you're involved and the reporters will be something else when they make the connections."

Veronica stood and breathed only one word: "Shawn."

"Yes," Beldon whispered loudly. "I wonder too about this development with Foster and Lorne's car happening incredibly at the same time as Shawn's abduction. I'm far from convinced that Foster himself had anything to do with Shawn's kidnapper, but it doesn't look good for him. And there's something else."

Veronica turned slightly towards me. She touched her lips, as if to stop what she would say: "Something else?" Above us the "music" thumped more loudly, like it would crack the ceiling.

Beldon had been watching Veronica only. When he glanced at me I said, "Not to worry, I've recently had practice handling the media."

He raised his eyebrows. "The girl claims that Dr. Foster not only forced her into the car but said he would pay her to go with him and dress up in some costume, and then he hurt her when she refused and tried to get out of the car. That, supposedly, is when she started screaming and the bike-patrol cop arrived."

Veronica's eyes widened: "A costume, same as with the other child here in Troutstream, the one lured by the sick-kitty-in-the-car trick!"

Kevin leaned towards her. "Listen. I've talked with Dr. Foster. He doesn't deny that he was with the girl, but he claims *she* lured *him* there and denies her version of the story, that he asked her to dress up in any costume, and especially that he hurt her in any way. Also, the girl's version doesn't jibe with the report of the patrol cop who called it in, not as regards any screaming and the girl's condition. He said she looked very surprised when he knocked on the car window and she saw who it was, even alarmed, like she'd been expecting someone other than the cops. I strongly suspect it was a set-up."

"And you believe Foster!" I startled them. "Why did he need my Caddy if not to implicate *me*? Maybe he was going to kill her and leave her *in* my Caddy! He's a psychopath! He threatened me!"

Veronica said, "Sh, Lorne, sh-sh."

Beldon turned towards me, clamping a hand to the crown of his ginger dome and rubbing down the back of his neck. He blew air. "Foster says their meeting was set up through an Internet chat room. The girl agreed to meet with him only if he picked her up in his friend's white Cadillac. He swears he doesn't know how she knew about you, Lorne. And then you surprised him by asking for a favour, and a quid pro quo was arranged, as he put it. The Curb Appeal people have got the girl back and are protecting her to the hilt. She's the victim, barely more than a child, et cetera et cetera, a sticky situation. We'll get more out of her, but it will take time, and I don't think we have time."

Veronica's fingers were slowly stroking the tip of her nose. She stopped. "But their stories should be traceable on their computers, and verifiable or not."

"They both used proxy servers and cloud chat rooms or something and, techno-illiterate though I am, I suspect such places are a jungle of aliases. Who knows what remains traceable. We've got Dr. Foster's and the girl's phones and our tech nerds are looking into it. But they say it too could take time."

"I don't believe it," Veronica said. "I simply refuse to believe any of this!" Her fingertips were now on either side of her head, palms just off the ears.

There was thumping on the stairway and Owen barged in as breathless as a little boy with news: "They arrested the Market Slasher last night! And now there's something about Dad's friend, Dr. Foster, being arrested for picking up a teenage hooker downtown! And they mentioned *your* name, Dad, it happened in *your* Caddy! Is *Dr. Foster* the Market Slasher! Or his partner! Holy shit!"

"Owen," Veronica snapped.

Beldon spoke seriously to him: "Hold on a minute, Owen. Dr. Foster *has* been accused of a crime while using your father's car. Only *accused*, mind you. Dr. Foster and the Market Slasher are *not* a team. But if Foster's arrest is on the radio already and the Slasher's been arrested—*damn*...uh, excuse me. But if that's now the situation, reporters are going to be swarming your lovely home, and soon. So, Owen, go through the house and shut all the windows, then turn on the air conditioning. It's going to be another scorcher anyway. Don't answer the doorbell till you know who it is."

Owen looked self-important for a moment, then took off.

Veronica led us back into the kitchen and shut the door to the front hall. She said, "Let's sit and gather our wits about us. There's still almost a full pot of coffee from breakfast. Detective?"

She set the pot on a coaster in the middle of the table and turned to the cupboard for mugs.

Kevin acknowledged with a nod the mug she set in front of him. She didn't fill it. He loosely held its handle and looked at me for too long, with the near-full pot steaming between us. He said, "Lorne, I want you to tell me everything you think relevant about Art Foster. For starters, what again did he say when you made fun of his research?"

"He said that I was going to learn a hard fucking lesson one of these days and that he was just the man to teach me."

He flipped the pages of a note pad I'd not noticed on his lap. "Before, you said that he said he *may* be just the man to teach you?"

"I'd say that constitutes a threat, wouldn't you, Detective Beldon? I'd say that moves Foster right to the head of the suspect line in Shawn's abduction." Still standing at the table, Veronica took a sharp breath. I forged on: "I'd say Foster could very well have been planning to implicate me with that teenage hooker in *my* Caddy, *and* I wouldn't rule out Foster being in cahoots with the Market Slasher!"

"Tch." Veronica removed the three dry mugs to the counter. "You're blinded by your hatred of Art, Lorne," she said into the quietly echoing metal sink. "It doesn't have to mean all that."

I didn't like her contradicting me at all. "I am not."

She continued staring into the sink. "What about this Bob Browne you're always going on about? What about those Lewis brothers you say hate you? Oh, what are we talking about! Where's Shawn? If two men have been arrested—one of them a sick sexual predator—where's Shawn!"

We both had the sense to let her cry quietly alone, shudderingly into her chest.

Beldon shook his head no at me and spoke more loudly than he needed: "Veronica's right, Lorne." I didn't like that either. His tone grew matter-of-fact. "Let's not jump to conclusions. Two men have been arrested, and the spotlight of high-glare media attention is on that story. Think—even we've hardly been talking about Shawn's disappearance."

I heard the breath leave Veronica, and I said, "So, a distraction to go with implicating me? Some distraction!"

"But, yes, this Browne character, no one knows where he comes from but Foster's friend of a friend? Who *are* these frien—"

The doorbell had rung, no one moved. Owen appeared too quickly from the front hall.

"I looked first, like Detective Beldon said. It's Mr. Kilborn. He wants to see you, Mom. I told him you couldn't come but he says it's an emergency. He has Jake with him, who's going nuts about watching Wy with Shawn or something. I can get rid of them if you want me to try harder."

Beldon said, "That'd be good, Owen."

Veronica clamped her forehead between left thumb and fingers and spoke as when exasperated with the kids: "Not now, Jack, not now." She looked at me: "Jack's beside himself, he's never known what to do with Jake. Not that Trixie did either."

My own head felt like it was shaking with Parkinson's: "I don't get it, I'm lost."

She clenched her jaw and a muscle popped high on her cheek. "I *told* you, Lorne. Trixie took off, days ago. She phoned yesterday, full of shit."

"Oh, yeah."

"Detective, I'd better go see what Jack wants or he'll be the next one arrested. Oh sorry." She turned to Owen: "Upstairs, you." He went reluctantly, saying, "What'd I do?" She continued, "May the gods have mercy on us all, and on that poor girl if Art Foster, *or* anyone, abused her. And on Art Foster too." She exited trailing her new mantra: "Shawn…"

As she disappeared down the hallway, I quickly moved to watch her. She paused at the hallway mirror to check herself, actually primped her hair. Gauze could have floored me. The back of my head was instantly aching something fierce. I would go to the bathroom, have another Valium.

Chapter 8

I said, "So, Detective Beldon, your case has widened significantly. You may make Homicide yet."

He shook his head in bemused disbelief. "The stereotype proves true, you surgeons *are* cool customers. But, yes, my missing person's investigation now includes two bigwig doctors, with one allegedly having solicited a minor for the purposes of sex, *and* on the very night they nab the Slasher! I don't believe Dr. Foster had anything to do with the abduction of Shawn but it doesn't look good for him. So far, he has no corroborated alibi for Sunday."

"No? Then how are the two cases related?"

"I tend to believe Foster when he says he was lured to the ByWard Market on Monday by the girl, who promised him who-knows-what delights, but only if he could get a Cadillac, and not just any Cadillac, *his friend's white* Caddy. *Some* condition."

"I'm not so ready to believe Art Foster had nothing to do with Shawn. He threatens me, Shawn gets abducted, then Foster gets arrested in my Caddy before he could finish framing me! And don't forget the dressing-up thing!"

Beldon smiled warily. "The thing is, the incident in the Caddy was phoned in by a cop who happened by at three in the morning and heard a ruckus from a big fancy car parked where it shouldn't be parked. As I said, I've talked with Foster, and it's possible the scene was meant to end differently. Or maybe not… Maybe that's *exactly* as it was meant to end, with Foster framed and the girl herself betrayed. I'm beginning to suspect that the *two* of you were being framed, or all three, and maybe primarily you, maybe for money, blackmailed. Someone must *really* want to mess with your life, Lorne."

He pinched the bridge of his nose and swiped it like a credit card. "I have a hunch that in this case one-plus-one adds up to three."

"An accomplice? *The Market Slasher*? Where's Foster now?"

"No, not the Slasher. Foster's at the regional detention centre just outside Troutstream, as you must know. I stopped off on my way here. He says he'd like to see you."

"I'd like to see him too—in hell!"

"Lorne, I need your help."

That stalled me. "My help?"

"I need you *not* to assume that Dr. Foster abducted your daughter. I need you to keep an open mind. What about those others Veronica mentioned?"

We were standing now at the kitchen island (he'd followed me as I'd edged towards the powder room's medicine cabinet), which I drummed once with my fingers. I came to a decision.

"Kevin, you were right in your hunch yesterday. Remember you asked me about Bob Browne and I pooh-poohed the idea? Well, I was wrong. I now think Mr. Browne should be high on the suspect list, though for me that list should still be headed by Art Foster's underlined name. But last night Bob Browne threatened me too, over money that's owed him for his work in Troutstream's playgrounds. He was irrational, livid. If we're looking for a likely suspect or an accomplice, Bob Browne could be our man."

"But you said he was very short? The abductor sounded closer to six feet."

He was leading me.

"True. But couldn't the abductor—*Foster*, say—have been Bob Browne's accomplice? They've both threatened me lately. In fact, when I think of it, physically, the man with the dog could well have been a disguised Foster. I'd thought there was something familiar about him, and he was a good distance away."

"Then why would Browne set up his own accomplice, Foster, in your Caddy?"

"Bob Browne may have wanted to discredit Foster, who could name him, and to implicate me through my Caddy. I still don't know why. But Browne could have used a teenage hooker to lure Art, just as Art claims. Bob Browne does have a way with kids. And he needs money."

Beldon again pinched the bridge of his nose, but this time held it thoughtfully. "Slow down, Lorne. What about," he checked his notes, "Frank Baumhauser? He also matches the abductor physically."

"Don't waste your time on Frank. Of that I am absolutely sure."

He cocked an eyebrow at me: "Deborah Carswell?"

"Debbie is capable of anything, except this. *She's* a physical meltdown. With the TCA committee, we're talking the *un*usual suspects." I laughed like a jackass.

"Forgive me for asking, but are you on medication?"

I wouldn't lie: "Just some Valium and just these past two days."

"I'm no doctor, but I think you need to watch that, Lorne."

"Hmm." I'd have told anyone else to fuck off.

"What about the other woman on the committee?" He was thumbing pages.

"Alice Pepper-Pottersfield? Same as Frank: don't waste your time. And a woman, of course."

"So much for the unusual suspects then. All the same, I'll have their alibis checked."

"You forgot Larry and Gary Lewis, owners of Troutstream's Twin Bros. Builders."

He smiled small. "In fact, Lorne, until Foster was arrested, and before you said that about Bob Browne just now, the Lewis brothers were my prime persons of interest."

"Really? You play things pretty close to the chest, Detective Beldon. Believe it or not, the Lewises also threatened me last night."

"Threatened you? How? Why?"

"Nothing specific, just vaguely, but seriously enough."

"Because of the playground contract?"

"No, but they definitely threatened me."

"Yes, but *why*?"

"Well, they sounded upset over some imagined insult I'd given them."

"And had you?"
"No."
"Well, who told them you had?"
"I don't know."
"…Okay then, that's all for now, I have to go."
"Are you going to interrogate Bob Browne and the Lewis brothers? At least that should make them back off."
"Interrogate?" Again he smiled, the prick. "Maybe. But backing off's not what's wanted, Lorne. If it turns out as I expect, that Dr. Foster is not our man, then more than ever we need the perpetrators to think themselves secure, so as to lure the abductor or abductors out into the open."
"I see."
He deliberated with himself for a moment, then: "I probably shouldn't be telling you this, but I think we may be onto something here even crazier than it looks. Some sort of extortion scam that got way out of hand, say between Twin Bros. Builders *and* Bob Browne, scamming money from your Deborah Carswell and the TCA. How Foster and you and the children would come into that, I do not know, yet. Other than that you interfered with the Lewis brothers' contract and seem to…well, Lorne, not to put too fine a point on it, you do seem to have a talent for pissing people off. But I want you to do me a favour, okay?"
"What can I do, Kevin?"
"Visit your colleague Foster."
"No way."
"Lorne, you are going to visit Art Foster and act as though you believe him. Talk and talk and talk, relax him and watch for slip-ups, just as you did with the father of the poisoned girl. And here's why you're going to do it: Foster's the connection to Bob Browne, and Browne is the link all the way from your poisoned girl to the TCA."
"The guy forces himself on a teenager in *my* car? He could well have abducted *my* daughter in some sick game? No way. Can't you monitor his phone calls or something?"

"Maybe, but for now the best way is you visit Foster. Not today, continue to lie low today. Screen any phone calls and don't go out. Tomorrow morning visit Foster. Find out what you can about this friend of a friend you told me about who contacts Bob Browne. That name could get us somewhere quickly."

He was turning again to leave. I said, "There's something else I should tell you, Kevin."

His shoulders hunched like he'd been poked between the blades. He turned and stared down at me: "Give."

I let my gaze drift towards the front door, wished I were taller. "Well, I've heard that Shawn was seen talking to a man in a white van about a week ago."

He looked quizzical for only an instant. "A white van?... Wait a minute, Lorne. Look at me. *I've heard, was seen.* Name names. This is your life, not some fucking mystery movie of the week!"

"I don't want to involve anyone else...especially Alice Pepper-Pottersfield. But she saw Shawn talking to a man in a white van."

"Is that all of it?" Cold now, the operator, in the zone.

"No. Alice thought she saw the same man talking with Bob Browne in one of the playgrounds. A tall slim man."

Yet more coldly, or so it sounded to me: "Why did she tell you this?"

"She inadvertently witnessed the Lewises threatening me last night."

He reflected for a moment, as his colour rose.

"Why the *fuck* would you keep that from me, Lorne? A stranger who matches the description? And Bob Browne involved again? For Christ's sake! We *are* investigating the abduction of *your* daughter here, you know!" He was near shouting, realized it, and whispered harshly, "This Alice could be a big help and you've been steering me away from her! Don't *do* that. These neurotic middle-aged women often see things, and somebody could be setting her up, using her as the go-between."

"Neurotic? Alice is not middle-aged."

He squinted. "Look, I'm not here doing dick-work on a cheating spouse."

"Whoa, nothing like that! I love my wife. I just promised Alice I wouldn't tell you."

"Jesus fucking Christ, Lorne, where are we, back in high school? Why would she make you promise that?"

"She's an illegal immigrant. She said she'd have gone directly to the police if not for that."

"She did, eh? And she hangs out in playgrounds to watch Bob Browne work?"

"No, she just happened to be walking in the park. Alice knows nothing about what happened with Shawn, if that's what you're thinking." I smirked. "When you meet her, you'll see how absurd your suspicion is. And when you do talk to her, as I know you will, reassure her that it has nothing to do with her immigrant status, uh, please."

"Of course," he said. And when he was satisfied I had no further revelations: "You'll visit Art Foster first thing tomorrow morning?"

"Yes."

He gave me a lingering look—bemused tolerance I did not like—closed his notepad and turned away.

I followed him to the front door, but before we could open it Owen startled us, shouting from the head of the stairs, "There's a picture of the Slasher on my phone, he looks like some surfer dude! They say he was a soldier, a Canadian soldier! They keep connecting him with Dr. Foster. Unreal! But, like, no talk of a girl or anything. That's good, right?"

Kevin said, "The Slasher has nothing to do with your sister, Owen. Shawn's going to be found just fine. What else on the Slasher? When was he arrested, before or after Dr. Foster?"

Why was Beldon looking disappointed?

"Before, it sounds," Owen answered. He straightened and was returning to his room as he called, "I'll, uh, monitor the feed, Detective. It'd be on the TV too down there, even CNN now, I'll bet! This is *good* news, right? I mean, now there's no way that sicko's been messing with Shawn."

"No way, Owen, not a chance!" Beldon twisted his mouth and turned away. I stepped behind him out onto the baking stoop. He stared off through the distorting heat waves rising from the dark roof across the street. "Owen's been worried sick about that possibility, you know."

I gestured small surprise with my open hands. "We could turn on the TV?"

"You do that, Lorne. But first you find a way to talk with your son." And as he strode to his car, "*Damn*," he said again.

Puzzled, I watched and waited. But he didn't wave from inside his big maroon Crown Vic. As he drove off, the distinctive yellow compact of an *Ottawa Citizen* reporter pulled up at the curb, as if it had been waiting for Beldon's departure. While shutting the aluminum door, I spotted a blue minivan with the CBC logo on it. Shouldn't they be hanging out at the detention centre or court or somewhere waiting for the Market Slasher?

Where was Veronica? I wanted to investigate developments next door but couldn't with the media alighting like this. Fucking Jack and Trixie and their mentally challenged son, Jake. Great timing on the abandonment, Trixie! *Per usual*.

I turned the deadbolt on the inside door. The house was cool and quiet. Early in the day though it was, I needed a drink, and a beer wouldn't cut it. My prized bottle of Macallan single malt, just a shot. No more Valium... My Caddy! How could I have forgotten it? Foster, you traitorous shit!... But I *would* visit him and I'd have to give an operating-theatre performance to hide my hatred.

The doorbell rang only a few times. Owen kept to his room. When I peeked out the front window, second drink in hand, I saw three vehicles along the curb with their reporters inside and windows rolled up. The Tanzanian Marathoner loped by, forever falling forward, head wagging back and forth between the media vehicles and my house.

Next time I looked, only two vehicles.

Then none.

Then three back slowly cruising, casing the place for signs of life. I guess, thanks to pervert Foster in *my* Caddy, I could still compete for local media attention with the Slasher. At least Art wasn't a serial killer.

Just one more Valium.

Chapter 9

To meet the media my way, I decided to wash Veronica's Golf. Feeling no pain, as they say. Veronica herself had still not returned from next door, so I might also get her favourable attention doing her the good turn.

The world was a bright doldrums, with the day's heat still brain-baking. At least I'd remembered my shades this time. But the whole neighbourhood was shut up, with A/C compressors humming their suburban song of themselves. These are the latter days of Alice Pepper-Pottersfield's Troutstream-through-the-ages dreamscape, the dream turned nightmare. An abandoned electromagnetic wasteland: as if everybody's been whisked off by aliens…to a planet where the children remain umbilically attached to both parents till they, the kids, begin to grow their own offspring; then the new grandparents behind the parents wither away and fall off like the old black cords they've become. Perfectly self-replicating families on the planet Suburbamor: Daddy grows the boy and Mommy grows the girl, only two per family. No one ever leaves home. Story of our suburban lives.

Yes indeed, the Scotch felt to be fizzling from my pores, the diazepam suffocating my most active synapses. Crazy time.

Only one reporter was a persistent nuisance, a spiffy lad in red bow tie and suspenders who introduced himself repeatedly as something called "videographer Donny Kynder from the A-Channel."

"What's the A-Channel channelling these days, *assholes*?"

I don't think he believed his ears, for he just kept insisting on "the public's right to know." I wetted him but good as I snaked the hose across the top of the car.

By four o'clock there were no more reporters and I was prepared for the sight of me on the evening news. After the arsenic-poisoning case I'd had more than enough of the fourth estate: distorters at best, falsifiers most often. The way they edit, my hose and bucket could be eliminated and I made to look like some Dr. Hyde, foaming from the mouth and flailing at the camera. (Voiceover): *Dr. Lorne Thorpe, distraught father of the abducted girl and friend of the accused, Dr. Art Foster, maintains his own innocence, though as can be seen here, he is rabid...*

I was on my knees buffing the wax off the front chrome of the Golf, working from driver's side to passenger's, enjoying the peace of mind car washing always delivers (though it's much more relaxing with my vintage Caddy). My shirt was pasted to my back from working in the lung-stuffing heat. But the chrome soon dazzled and even in shades I had to squint against the sun's reflected brilliance.

Then something felt wrong to my experienced hand: an imperceptible slope to the bumper, or what passes for a bumper these days. Earlier while washing I'd found a smudge of white paint on the passenger's corner, from bumping the wall at work last Friday. It had come off with just the soft brush attachment. Everything had looked perfectly normal then. But now the bumper appeared somehow... damaged. I compared the passenger's side with the driver's, rapidly back and forth, like a dog getting the scent. There wasn't even a scratch, yet I just knew in my heart that damage had been done.

I patted the little Golf and brought my hand to my streaming forehead. I made a fist and slammed the innocent bumper. I saw myself standing in my parking spot at CHEO, touching this very corner of the car, relieved that no damage had been done. The hairline crack in the wall must have been there before, surely. In my mind now I followed that crack up, saw it passing through the parking level above, widening ever so slightly as it went, through emergency, branching past reception, where Tamara stood in ironic command, through the Catholic quiet room and that mural of Jesus with the children, gaping...about to bring down the whole building!

Jake Kilborn burst from the neighbours' front door. He took off running, his elbows tucked and pumping, away from me. He was headed for the farther neighbours', I hoped, foolishly, because I knew Jake enjoyed nothing so much as running pointlessly in circles, always in the biggest allowable and most perfect circle, right back to where he'd begun. The amazing perfection of his circles was all poor Jake had been gifted of the savant.

Otherwise he was just your average Down's Syndrome boy-man who made himself at home everywhere in Troutstream. Young enough mentally to hog all the children's toys at the community centre, Jake was yet old enough to be allowed one beer at the Lighthouse Bar & Grill. He had been dubbed Troutstream's unofficial mayor, "Hizzoner Jake," and annually led the Troutstream Fun Fair parade.

Now, there are all sorts of Down's kids, as many different as normal kids, of course. I've encountered quite the range at work (Down's kids are susceptible to leukemia) and the majority are loveable human beings, needless to say. But not so Jake, which must be said. And as with most unlikeable children, this was not Jake's fault. His mother, Trixie Kilborn, had managed through a genius for system manipulation, special pleading, intimidation, and liberal bullying to turn Jake into what is best described as, unfortunately in the words of Troutsteam's parkland rats, "a stupid fucking retard." With her demands even for a high-school diploma for Jake (Jake could neither read nor write, Jake couldn't speak intelligibly) and well-paid employment upon "graduation," the statuesque Trixie had singlehandedly set the cause of inclusiveness back fifty years in Troutstream.

To take but one example (lest I be thought even worse than I am): Trixie had long insisted that Jake be allowed to serve as an altar boy at our church, Holy Family. Fine, the fittest place for a shining example of Catholic tolerance and inclusiveness. But Trixie would not budge when, despite a call from the bishop himself, participation at Communion fell sharply at those masses where Jake served. It tried the mettle of even the most Christly tolerant to see Jake picking his nose and eating it before, during, and after "helping" the priest serve the Communion feast (he invariably clipped communicants with the paten, though that *could* be tolerated). Jake would stand in the sanctuary facing the congregation and auger his nostrils for minutes at a time, head tilted back and face distorting like some corpulent dentist self-drilling. He would curiously examine what snot he got, then slurp it off his finger with a proficiency I've seen matched only in porn movies.

Completing the circle of his run, Jake swung towards me, leaning inward, in that skiing style he had of covering space rapidly on his stumps. Because Jake expected and received much loving attention, I dropped my head and pretended to busy myself with the finished task. I wouldn't look up but heard him halt a few feet from me. I could even smell him. I guess abandoned Jack was not used to caring for the grown boy's needs. I'll grant Trixie that.

He just stood there huffing adenoidal noises. Then: "Go see Wy, go see Wy, go see Wy!"

"What? Oh, *Wy*. But not now, Jake. Shawn's not home and Dr. Thorpe wants to be alone."

I could hear gurgling mucus in his breathing. Then: "Gonna tell Mom you made fun of me!"

That was Jake's one other gift. Instead of the Down's kid's legendary musical aptitude, Jake was not only "able" at running perfect circles but also something of a savant at sensing any weakening of tolerance and of correcting it with the threat of telling his fearsome mom that he'd been made fun of.

I glanced up: "Where's your dad, Jake? Is Mrs. Thorpe still in your house?"

He stood for a moment with that contemplative look on his face like he might swallow his nose. I reminded myself to be careful, Jake was notoriously powerful. But he did the other thing where he snorted and hugely pursed his mouth. Then enlightenment: "You're making fun of me! Go see Wy, go see Wy, go see Wy!"

What volume! "Nobody's making fun of you, Jake. Quiet down!... That's better. *Wy Knots* isn't on right now, Jake."

"Go see Wy with *Shawn*, dumb-dumb. Go see Wy, go see Wy, go see Wy!"

"Okay, Jake, that's enough now. Just go away, please."

"Making fun of me…"

"Jake, go back into your house and tell Mrs. Thorpe that Dr. Thorpe says it's time to come home."

"My dad and your mom are in love. They didn't see me take Oreos." He opened his bud of a mouth to show me the black lumps of cookie he'd been carrying through his run, dangerously so. He sniffled: "Nobody hugs me."

Still on my knees, I lowered my eyes. I had to. Jake's white thighs were bursting like uncooked links from the casings of his tight green gym shorts. Lately I'd liked his hanging around Shawn less and less. I resisted the urge to call Owen to rescue me.

Having remembered that he had an Oreo to work on, Jake grew somewhat mollified. Until: "Can I do that for you, Mr. Thorpe? Can I please please? You don't even have to pay me!" Oreo crumbs were bombarding me like black hail.

But I should clarify that I've been translating. I was fluent in the Troutstream idiom known as "Jake-speak." What he actually said just now was: *Aa eye oo aa oo, m-m or?*

"No, Jake."

He jigged from foot to foot: "Please, mister. I won't tell Mom you didn't pay me."

"No, Jake."

He flailed: "You made fun of me! I'm gonna tell Mom! You made fun of me!"

Jake's foremost teeth were as crooked as a crashed picket fence. Long ago I tried encouraging Jack to have the dental problem corrected before Jake got any older, suggesting the name of a good orthodontist. But Jack, a car mechanic who'd succeeded locally with a small chain of lube stations, suspected I was trying to drum up business for one of my brother medicine men. Wiry Jack, always dressed in worker fatigues, suspicious of his upper middle-class neighbours, thought himself far superior in matters of the real world of business and money.

I was distracted from Jake by a school bus bouncing slowly along from the left, passing in heat haze, the shaded driver—not Debbie Carswell—turning to look straight at me in a nightmare's extended moment. I stood, felt dizzy. The alcohol, the drugs. I steadied myself with my right hand on the hood. Then there was no bus. There'd been a school bus in the Museum of Science and Technology's parking lot on Sunday too. On Sunday?... Then there was no bus. I must remember to tell...Kevin.

I palmed my brow. "Work's *all* done, Jake," I drawled. "And you're getting yourself all worked up."

"Where's Shawn?" He was probably exasperated over Shawn's being absent the past couple of days. "Shawn said me go see Wy with her!"

"Shawn said you, eh? Maybe tomorrow, Jake."

He did his snort and purse, whipped up a fist and started smashing himself between the eyes. *"Now now now..."*

I grabbed his forearm and was fairly lifted off my feet. "Don't do that, Jake. You'll hurt yourself."

He covered his face and cried into both palms. I reached a hand to the top of his hot head of flaky scalp. Poor Jake. What a throwback, such a hulking no-neck brute. Not allowed to be the idiot he was born to be, he must play his role for the correct rest of us with our impossible dreams of perfectibility, our intolerance. If he'd lived only half a century ago, he'd have been truly tolerated—the neighbourhood idiot, running errands, walking dogs and such—protected from the worst cruelty. You could see Jake's potential for such repetitive occupations when he ran his perfect circles, as you could see he'd had to be trained by Trixie to take such wild offence. As things stood for Jake, though, his brainless mom was making his nasty, brutish and short life an even unhappier state. Oh, you are such a sad sad reminder to us all, Jake, of what *we* are: brutes too, brainier brutes, to be sure, but scarcely human, the lot of us, capable still of anything mindless, of every brutality. The more we think ourselves God's gift to dust, the more we can't tolerate the sight of you as you are. At least you'll never grow up, dear Jake, never go missing as the child you were. I guess that's one way to keep your children. I guess that's another perfectly paradoxical caduceus. And I guess my brain was sizzling and spitting in a cauldron of alcoh-chemical grease.

So I stood there with Jake in the desiccating heat, my throat further parched from the booze and drugs, stroking his head and holding him, Jake sobbing. I think I was crying too when Veronica spoke.

"Jake, your dad wants you in now for a snack. Oreos! Daddy's okay now, feeling much much better." For all her good nature, Veronica spoke to Jake as one does to lost foreigners. Maybe she was right, though Trixie hated it.

Jake swung up his fat bat of an arm and knocked my hand off his head. When I turned, Veronica was looking at me only and with no little puzzlement.

I said secretly to her, "What's up with Jake? Very agitated. He's already stolen Oreos, by the way."

She took in her shiny car, then back to me: "You washed the car?" She stepped closer, sniffed the air: "You've been drinking, Lorne, on top of the Valium?"

"Kevin wants me to go see Art Foster tomorrow. I'm helping with the investigation, dear. We're not accusing Foster of anything, though he's still a person of interest in the abduction case."

Jake pointed at Veronica and made a stuttering, teasing noise, like a winter engine struggling to start (I expect he'd heard that nagging whine a lot; I suspect that strictly corrected kids rebound aggressively from enforced tolerance). "I'm gonna tell Mom when she gets home that you and my dad are in love and you made fun of me sixty-eleven times!"

We watched him take off running a small circle counterclockwise—the breadth of bum on him like an appliance!—arriving at his own front stoop, where he tangled with the aluminum door.

I shook my head and smiled at Veronica. "Don't worry, dear, things haven't been so bad with the media here, though you'd better be prepared to see your devoted husband on the evening news washing *your* car! And yes, maybe even a little drunk!"

"…Lorne?"

"Jake is sure revved up. Jack's in bad shape too, eh? What's the story there?"

"I'll tell you about Jack inside, but it's Jake I'm more concerned about. And right now, you. You'd better get out of the sun. Come in now and drink some water? Maybe you should take a cold shower, have a nap."

"Me? I feel fan-tastic!"

She grabbed my wrists: "Have you heard something about Shawn?"

What a downer.

She was instantly crying and neither of us cared anymore.

She sucked it up and said, "Shawn must have promised Jake he could watch *Wy Knots* with her today. When Jake saw me he asked his dad if he could come over here, Jack shouted no and Jake went flying round the house, then out the door. When he gets like that, there's no stopping him. Then Jack just broke down."

"Trixie," I smirked.

"We can never know what she's been through with Jake, Lorne. And now Jack."

Surly Owen stuck his head out the front door: "Da-ad, that detective's been phoning for, like, an hour! He said he couldn't get you on your cell either."

I checked my cell. It had got turned off, probably from all the bending and crouching. I called Beldon from the front stoop. He wouldn't tell me on the phone what it was about but apologized and asked if he could return right away. "But it's not Shawn," he said. "Not yet."

We went inside. While we waited, too beat to be anxious about another visit from Beldon, Veronica tried to make me sympathize with the Kilborns' most recent woes.

"Jack really loves Jake so much, but he's lost without Trixie. They need our help, Lorne. How could Trixie leave them? She's *so* self—"

"We can never know what *they've* been through? For Christ's sake! Have you lost your fucking mind, Veronica? Look what *we're* going through!"

She set her unfinished iced tea on the kitchen island with little delicacy and fixed me with her determined browns: "It's been two days. We may need to get counselling for Owen. He may need to talk with a professional."

"What! Am I hearing things?"

"Lorne, think of your son, not your own crazy ideas for once. Owen's been traumatized and he won't let us help him get through it. He needs to talk with *someone*. I'd even settle for Jake!"

It was no easy matter recognizing disintegration in those deep browns, incipient madness. But I did and said sternly, "No."

She walked away in a self-consciously self-possessed manner. I again had to hear the front door strain its spring...

I shouted after her, "You don't walk like that!" Then to myself, "And I'm starving."

I sat at the table and propped my head in a crotch of thumb and fingers.

She'd lost it, was giving up. *Veronica?* I was dumbfounded. I'd been looking for an opening to tell her about the threats to me the night before, not to hear about wacky Jack's and tricky Trixie's tribulations.

Something made me look up. It was Owen standing in the doorway from the hall, just staring at me.

"What do *you* want? Counselling?"

I laughed. He left.

Chapter 10

Trixie Kilborn had been arrested some half-year before for half-drowning Jake in the bathtub. There was no question it was not the first time, as Jake was well known for his respiratory emergencies, which had been attributed to Down's Syndrome. Trixie was notorious for barrelling up to reception at CHEO's emergency and pushing everybody aside and demanding immediate attention for the inarticulate Jake. She often invoked my name and was Art Foster's biggest nightmare. When I asked Trixie to stop using me, she wouldn't even deign to reply, just smiled indulgently from her statuesque height. Then ever-suspicious Jack caught her on hidden bathroom video apparently trying to drown Jake.

Trixie's lawyer argued a recent innovation of the insanity defence. It turned out that Trixie wasn't a criminal mom trying repeatedly to suffocate her challenged child. *Trixie* was the victim, suffering from Munchausen's syndrome by proxy, which is criminal psychobabble for extreme parental attention-grabbing, up to and including killing one's own child. The more blatant were Trixie's crimes against Jake, the more certain the diagnosis of her raging Munchausen's-by-proxy affliction. As vicious a circle as was ever run, even by Jake, or in Dante's hell.

But would I ever like to have seen the video of the aquatic struggle between those two behemoths of the deep, Leviathan Trixie and Moby Jake! For how could even big Trixie have held down the powerful idiot? To Jake, such awkward items as bicycles were as Frisbees, as flingable as the bodies of teasing kids who couldn't avoid a lunging, surprisingly agile Jake. So the Munchausen's drowning must have been a churning contest to rival killer whales in a mating frenzy!

Despite the damning evidence of Trixie's damnable actions, spying Jack had been beside himself while she was incarcerated, split two ways to hell. Veronica had helped him out by looking after Jake while Jack managed his oil-and-lube franchises for the mere two weeks of Trixie's lock-up over at the very regional detention centre that borders Troutstream to the south and now held Art Foster. Jack and Trixie never wholly made it up when she was acquitted. In fact, life at the neighbours' deteriorated, audibly and visually, if mainly in the figure of unkempt Jake. Among Trixie's followers (and thanks to her lawyer's massaging of the media she had quite an entourage of the proactive, the neglected, and the vaguely victimized), Jack was to blame for her condition, which, thank the gods, was treatable with years of therapy. If patriarchal Jack hadn't spent all his time at business, leaving Trixie to look after Jake on her own, this near-tragedy could almost have been barely averted, pretty much. So the stories went.

And then, just days before our own troubles began, Trixie had disappeared. There would be talk from the fan club of suicide, of murder, of half a botched murder-suicide (Jack the incompetent coward), until the collect call for Jake from a resort in the Turks and Caicos. Trixie was taking a much-needed vacation with the lawyer who'd got her off (so to speak). On the advice of her paramour, she would not talk with Jack. On advice of same, Trixie instructed Veronica to inform all media that she was planning to sue the City of Ottawa, the police, paramedics, the fire department, Jack and his business, Veronica herself—if she didn't cease and desist meddling and execute these instructions to the letter—and Troutstream's Izaak Walton Pool, where Jake had received self-evidently inadequate swimming lessons (though I believed Trixie had insisted at the time that Jake be certified and employed as some new thing dubbed "Lifeguard Enabler").

A thought jolted me out of time-tripping reverie: How stable could the fairly tall, wiry Jack be? How envious of our normal family life next door? I must inform Kevin of that too.

Chapter 11

I said to Detective Beldon, "Want to hear a real suburban horror story involving my next-door neighbours? Could be relevant."

"No. I already know all about the Kilborns. Developments there have nothing to do with what's happened to your family."

"Uh, okay." Eyes front.

"You shouldn't be drinking at this time. I shouldn't be taking you along on this. Still taking the Valium?"

We were swooping round the crescents of Troutstream in Beldon's maroon Crown Vic, which was making me at once nauseous and nostalgic for my Caddy. As we slowed near the address on Rue Poisson, I observed Beldon signal the lone occupant of an unmarked car.

"The Asian guy is your backup, right?"

"All unofficially. Frank Thu. My only friend in the department. He's Homicide and officially he's off duty."

"Why's that?"

"Lorne, I have to ask you to shut up. We'll talk later."

We pulled into the shaded circular driveway of the mansion the Lewis brothers had literally built for themselves. Troutstream's only mansion, it bordered greenbelt land sloping to the stream that gave the place its name. Off to the south, about a kilometre distant, could be seen the regional detention centre's communications tower.

"Are they expecting us?"

"No. You say nothing more unless I ask, you hear? Then you answer simply and directly."

I shifted my jaw. I wanted to tell him to go fuck his badge. But Detective Beldon was *in the zone*, concentrated fiercely on the task at hand, my own surgery persona.

I stood behind him as he rang the doorbell, whose button centred a boat's tiny steering wheel. A sound from inside like an organ's bass key. He immediately rang again: yes, it *was* a two-tone foghorn sound. Kevin held the warrant in his left hand and now he smacked his right palm with it.

He fingered his cell and asked to speak to either of the Lewises. Waited. "No, I do *not* care to wait. Please inform Larry and Gary Lewis that the police are at their house, that we have a search warrant and that if they're not here within ten minutes we'll be forcibly entering."

"Who'd ever have thought the Lewises capable of kidnapping? Just because I got Bob Browne the playground work? Then setting up Foster in my Caddy! I'll have to apologize to Art for entertaining such thoughts about him. Bob, too. How'd you nail 'em, Kev?"

He didn't even look at me: "You don't know what you're talking about, Dr. Thorpe. Sober up fast. Not another word. Do you hear?" He said to himself, "*Big* mistake."

"Aye-aye, *mon capitaine*."

Then he looked at me all right. And I did sober up some.

Larry and Gary Lewis sped up a few minutes later in a white pickup with "Twin Bros. Builders" emblazoned on it. Their logo was a beaver in overalls atop a dam and nailing a shingle into place.

Larry didn't even look at me. He said to Kevin, "What's all this about? What's Lorne Thorpe doing here? Does Lorne Thorpe work for the police now?"

Gary stood behind him, looking ready to burst into tears.

Kevin held up his warrant: "Dr. Thorpe is here as an official police consultant on this investigation. Can we talk inside?"

With Gary alongside now, Larry stepped past us, saying, "What investigation? We, uh, fully intend to pay the import duty on the tower crane." He keyed a security pad on the door.

Kevin immediately showed disappointment, but said, "Relax about that, Mr. Lewis. I don't care where or how you buy your company's machines."

We paused in the foyer. The Lewis brothers were nothing if not true-blue Troutstreamers. Every item of décor participated in the community's nautical theme. The foyer itself was designed to resemble the bow of an old-fashioned sailing ship: a steering wheel was fixed to the railing of the stairway's first landing, a bowsprit lanced overhead. Everywhere the walls were covered with pictures of ships, a couple of lobster traps were upended here and there, and a huge fireplace in the living room off the foyer was topped by a monstrous arcing marlin. One wall of the living room was a bar meant to look like a ship's cabin, complete with portholes behind the colourful bottles of liquor, rum dominant, no doubt. I wanted a drink.

Larry moved towards the living room but stopped and turned on us. "Then what *is* this about?"

Kevin held up his traffic cop's hand: "We can make this unpleasant and official, if you like, Mr. Lewis. I can read you your rights and you can call your lawyer. Or you can answer a few questions for me. If I'm satisfied with your answers, this need go no further."

A standoff ensued, in which the brothers showed unexpected courage and discipline.

Kevin said to Larry, "Why did you and your brother threaten Dr. Thorpe last night?"

"Oh," Larry drawled mockingly. "So *that's* what this is all about? Big brave Lorne Thorpe ran to the police just because we told him to stop spreading dirty stories about Gary and me? Gimme a break, please."

Encouraged by Larry's bravado in the face of the law, Gary brightened. He rested a hand on his brother's shoulder and looked out at us: "A break, yeah."

"Who told you those, uh, dirty stories?" Kevin asked.

Larry's mouth was opening—

"You liars!" I cried. "You were ready to sic your thugs on me because I brought in Bob Browne to do the playground work! You two have been cheating Troutstream on construction projects for years!"

I just caught Kevin's half-turned pained face, as though he were dealing with his own Jake.

"Nobody calls my brother a liar!" shouted Gary.

"Oh, yeah? Well, I just did and he is and so are you!"

Larry had the presence of mind, I'm ashamed to say, to raise his arm as a restraining barrier to Gary.

Kevin held his hand up backwards, palm facing me. "Please, let's try to behave like reasonable men… Thank you. Okay, it wasn't the playground contract. Then what were the rumours? Who was their source? Those are the *only* things I need you to answer and then we'll be gone."

"*What?*" (That again was shameless I.)

Larry's face showed some rapid consideration of options, his eyes shifting, then settling. "Follow me into the mess."

"What mess?" Kevin said, his head pulling back. "Oh, yeah, sure."

We followed them into the darkly shining kitchen, where everything was black wood and brass polished to a mirroring sheen. Gary sat on a stool at the huge black-granite-topped island, but seeing that Larry wasn't going to take the other seat, he stood again.

Larry sneered at me past Kevin's shoulder and spoke normally: "Okay then, short and sweet. Your new partner there has been telling everybody that we stole money building the Troutstream Community Centre. If you want to come into our home office, Detective, I can show you that we did that job at a fairly large loss. Or, if you have to, you can ask Debbie Carswell, chair of the TCA. We'd rather not publicize our pro bono work, and that was part of our agreement with Debbie."

Kevin looked at me: "Dr. Thorpe?"

"I never said that about them embezzling TCA funds. I've heard the rumour, but I've never repeated it. Besides, Detective, *I'm* not the one who should be defending himself here!"

Larry looked at Gary, who was awkwardly trying to look casual, leaning on one hand on the island. "Tell the detective what else Lorne Thorpe's been saying, Gary."

Gary blushed. "That's right, Lorne Thorpe's been saying that we're a couple of homos with a taste for little boys. It sickens us, Larry and me, even to have to imagine dirty thoughts like that."

"*What*!" (I again.) "Who told you that? I've never said anything like that! It was Bob Browne told you, wasn't it?"

Larry looked smug. "Just like we thought. His little friend is in on it too. That dwarf has even been poisoning the children against us. And Gary and me love kids—in a perfectly healthy way, I mean."

"*Who* told you all this?" Kevin asked.

"We have our sources, Detective Beldon, which we don't care to…divulge, as I'm sure you as a detective can appreciate."

Kevin had taken out his notebook. "No, I cannot appreciate that. And you'd better reveal your source to me right fucking now, buddy, or I'm arresting you both for threatening Dr. Thorpe. And that's just the beginning. You've as much as confessed that a lot of your company's machinery is illegally imported from the States. On top of which, boys, what you're actually obstructing here is an investigation into child-abduction and soliciting a minor for the purposes of sex. You have the right to remain—"

Gary's voice quavered: "Larry?"

Larry tamped down Gary with air-patting palms: "Don't worry, my brother, we've done nothing wrong. We're not the ones spreading slanderous rumours. The duty on the crane is merely deferred. Our accountant can fix that. And *we* are not the ones lending our fancy-schmancy Cadillacs to coworkers so they can seduce and abuse helpless young girls! Oh yes, Detective, it's all the radio's talking about. What about *that*?"

Kevin tapped his notebook. "Settle down, Mr. Lewis." I could see he was disappointed. "Is that your final word on who told you that rumours were being spread about the Lewis brothers?"

"Yes," said brave Larry. "Are we under arrest?"

Kevin drew his left hand from forehead to crown—a bad sign with him, I already recognized—pinched his nose and held it for a moment. "Yes. You're going to have to go with my man for questioning."

"And if we refuse?"

"Refuse? It's not an offer." Kevin flapped his warrant: "And I have this. I call in the big boys and we take this love boat of yours apart till we find whatever you're hiding."

"Do we need a lawyer?"

"Be my guest."

Another standoff.

Kevin spoke into his cell: "Frank, take Mr. Larry and Gary Lewis down to the boiler room — I mean, down to HQ."

"The boiler room, Larry?" Gary again sounded on the verge of tears. "Can't we take our own truck?"

Kevin pursed his lips till he'd controlled himself, then shook his head: "No."

Frank, a husky Asian in a tight black suit, let himself in the front door. Kevin stepped alongside me and, concealed from the Lewises, exchanged murmurs and eyebrow-jigging looks with his partner.

Kevin turned back to the Lewises. "Would you please go and wait down by Sergeant Thu's unmarked police car? He'll be with you shortly."

Gary echoed, "Sergeant? Why is the car unmarked, Larry?"

When the door closed behind them, Kevin said, "Thanks, Frank. They'll be all right. I just hope I don't get busted off the force altogether for this put-on."

"Put-on?" I said. "What put-on?"

Frank Thu blew air, glanced at me disapprovingly, looked at the floor, shook his head. "Kevin, do you know what you're doing here? You'd better tie this all together or you *are* in deep shit. Wait, I don't care what you're doing here. What am *I* doing here?"

"Please, Frank. Just drive them around for a while, pass the detention centre slowly a couple of times. Be the good cop, see if you can find out who's been telling them rumours about Dr. Thorpe here. Pretend you have a call from me, then bring them back here and tell them not to leave town or something, that you'll try to fix it so they're kept out of it, *if* they keep quiet. No bad publicity for their business. I'll pray they don't call their lawyer. Let me know if you find out anything at all."

Frank spoke with drawled irony: "Oh, is *that* all?"

He drew himself up as he left the house. At his car he officiously clamped a hand on Gary's head as he put him in the back seat after Larry. He turned his back to the car and comically made big eyes. He got in and drove off.

Watching after them, Kevin absently tapped me on the shoulder with his warrant, handed it to me and walked ahead to his car. It was a brochure from the Museum of Science and Technology.

On the front walk he stared across his car.

"Lorne, I'm very disappointed in you. You were no help at all back there. It was a big mistake bringing you, *my* big mistake. But I believed they knew you and didn't like you, that they might just have feared you knew something about them. I'd wanted your presence to have a quietly intimidating effect, with the emphasis on *quietly*."

"I'm sorry, but what did I do wrong?"

He turned on me: "What'd you do wrong? You lost it. If you'd kept your big mouth shut like I ordered you and not got them all riled up, we might have learned something right off. My edge was surprise and you blew it!"

We sat in his car with its cold odour of cigarette...or cigar smoke. I let him settle.

"You *believe* that pair?"

He breathed deeply once and looked across the steering wheel. "I believe them. I've run quick checks on all your committee friends. Twin Bros. Builders does a lot a charity work in Troutstream. There never *was* any conflict of interest on their part. Bob Browne's not been paid because there *is* no money. It was all spent on the community centre, some labour but mostly materials. No one spent TCA money dishonestly, and certainly no one embezzled funds. *Why* that Debbie Carswell and the treasurer guy Baumhauser allowed you to bring Browne in to do work that couldn't be paid for is beyond me. Panicked over the arsenic scare, so ready to lie and cheat? Maybe. I'd hoped the Lewises could shed some light on what's going on."

"Then what the hell are we doing here?"

"I was wrong about the Lewises, but we need to know who told them you were spreading the stories that made them threaten you last night. Debbie Carswell? Maybe, but a long shot. Art Foster? A longer shot. Alice Pepper-Pottersfield? A pop gun. Frank Baumhauser? He will bear some further checking. But my hunch is Bob Browne, and I now strongly suspect that he's working with someone."

"You found out something about Bob?"

"Very little, and that makes me all the more suspicious. He's American, here less than a year. Worked for a few landscape outfits, got laid off. Started his own company only six months ago, a mess, receivership already, empty office at an industrial-park address, repo people hot after his one big piece of equipment. Has lived in a series of fleabags, Lowertown, but I don't know exactly where he's currently holed up. I have an idea how to find out though."

"The accent's faked."

"What accent?"

"He sounds, I dunno, German some times, other times like an American southerner, and once a touch British, Cockney I'd say."

"He *has* moved around a lot, but only three times outside the U.S., Germany briefly, yes, England for an even shorter time."

He fished a thin yellow tin from his shirt pocket and held it thoughtfully. The cover showed a big cat and the word "Panters." Small cigars.

Settled some, he mused: "Debbie Carswell has the profile of a shit-disturber from way back, though nothing criminal. And then there's your special friend, Alice Pepper-Pottersfield. But there's even less on her than on Bob Browne. I do wonder most about *your* Frank, the Baumhauser guy. He spends his every free minute surfing porno sites and emailing his mother."

"Frank Baumhauser? No. Alice? Don't forget—she's the one warned me about the Lewises and told me about the man in the van accosting Shawn."

"I remember."

"Debbie? I'd bet my own house she's got nothing to do with it."

"I'm ruling no one out, Lorne. Did Mizz P-P say if the white van had a logo?"

"No."

"Find out. Describe the Twin Bros. Builders' logo for her. Sometimes you have to, uh, enable a memory, but if she saw a truck, the picture's in her head somewhere." He tapped the cigar tin on the steering wheel and stared at it contemplatively for a while longer. "I'm not ready to give up on the Lewis boys just yet and I suspect they've used muscle before to get their way. They certainly don't like you." He smiled and returned the tin to his shirt pocket. "Though there does seem to be a long line forming under that banner."

"I'll have to ask Debbie Carswell how to get in touch with Alice. Like I said, it's the immigration thing with Alice Pepper-Pottersfield. But…Kevin, you've been acting awfully pissed about something, ever since Owen announced the arrest of the Market Slasher. Is it my interfering and bungling? What gives?"

"Never mind about that. I don't want to alarm you further, Lorne, but I'm worried our man has found that abducting children and returning them unharmed doesn't turn his crank anymore. Shawn's been missing longer than the others."

His cell played the "charge" tune of sports events. He snorted at its display — "HQ, big Slasher news" — and tossed it into the back seat, where it played "Charge" intermittently and persistently.

He said, "So his thrills need to escalate. Where *is* Bob Browne?"

"*You* don't seem too thrilled that a serial killer of defenceless women has been arrested?"

"None of my business." He was being resentfully breezy. "I never believed for an instant that Dr. Foster was the Market Slasher. *I* have not been assigned to that investigation. *I* need to know where Bob Browne lives."

"Foster knows, or could know from his contact, or the friend of his contact."

"And Foster's under arrest. How convenient for Mr. Browne. You're visiting Foster first thing tomorrow, Lorne, right?"

"I'll talk with Foster tomorrow morning. Okay, you could be right about Bob Browne. Bob could be the source of the lies told to the Lewises. He's pissed at me now because he's not been paid and he thinks I've been making fun of him, so he's turning the Lewises even more against me than they were."

"The Lewises don't seem to like him much either. But go on. How does Foster's arrest come into it?"

"Foster and I both know Bob more than he wants to be known. Bob figured out an ingenious way to discredit Foster with the girl *and* implicate me with my Caddy. I don't know, but if I'm right, we might never see Bob Browne again."

"Good. Keep that head clear, Lorne, you've got a good one and I need it. No more booze. We need Foster's contact for Bob Browne."

He squinted across the steering wheel, then frowned. "What a pair of creeps, those Lewises. They could be our bad boys yet, even in cahoots with Bob Browne or Art Foster, faking their dislike of Browne."

He started the car. By the time we were swooping along Piscator Drive again, to the tinny "Charge" tune continuously now from the rear seat, Detective Beldon was back in his professional zone. In my driveway he said, "Visit Art Foster in the morning. I'll meet you there. Keep it together, Dr. Thorpe. No more booze: for Shawn's sake, for your family's sake, for the sake of Troutstream's children, for your own sake and for my sake. Got it?"

I stood staring after the Crown Vic. Fuck you *and* your badge. I need a drink.

A crow cawed, strangely deepening the usual suburban silence.

The woofer thumped from on high. I'd take the stairs three at a time, pick up his player and smash it to smithereens on the floor!... But glancing down the hallway I noticed parts of Veronica showing disjointedly through the bevelled glass of the French door to the kitchen. I blinked hard. How would I manage my drink now?...

Enter ranting (thank you, Mr. Shakespeare): "I cannot take it any more!" I shouted bursting through the spring-hinged door.

"Hi, Dad."

Shawn smiled thinly at me from the table, her hair matted and face dust-streaked, with a big red tumbler of some drink before her.

Veronica didn't turn from the sink. She wasn't washing up, just staring out the window. I looked too: frantic squirrels hanging upside down trying to solve the latest bird feeders, birds frantically attacking them and other birds, chaos, the cedar hedge beyond, dull green, brown in patches, holes everywhere. The kitchen tilted like the Krazy Kitchen.

"She just walked in."

Chapter 12

As instructed by Detective Beldon on the phone—who couldn't desist cursing himself out for not having answered his cell in the car—we bundled Shawn off for the legally requisite physical exam at CHEO. When we pulled into my parking spot, I bumped the wall again, not joltingly as before, just gently, as often happens when gauging distance in such underground lighting. We were in Veronica's Golf, since my vintage Caddy was now impounded.

Otherwise, I knew what it meant to be overwhelmed by joy. As did Veronica, I was sure.

I glanced in the rear-view: "Are you all right, sweetheart?"

Sitting behind her mother, Shawn kept her face averted. "Nothing's *wrong* with me! I don't even know *why* we're here! I told you: *nothing happened*. I don't want a doctor looking at me! Mom?..."

"I meant only from the bumping of the car, sweetheart. Still, you won't tell us anything that happened. Your mother and I were worried sick. For starters, where did the man with the dog take you for the past two days?"

Only continuing silence. I was suddenly conscious of how buried we were down there in subterranean dimness, with the concrete mountain of the hospital on top of us. The most minor tectonic event and we could be crushed, buried alive.

Veronica was staring straight ahead. "Not now," she said through her teeth.

Instead of meeting the two of them at the rear of the car, I again went to the white wall where my name was printed boldly. I saw the hairline crack running up right from the spot where the

Golf had hit four days before, right between the *o* and *r* of THORPE. I bent to it.

Veronica was at my shoulder. "*What* are you doing now? We want to get this over with quickly and get home. Owen's alone and don't think he's not been worried sick too. This is no time to be buffing up your name plate."

My fingertips hovered at the crack, which I lost...then found again. "Fine by me. Achieve closure, let the healing process begin." I straightened.

"Leave it to you to joke at a time like this." She really was hissing.

"But I wasn't joking!"

"Bullshit."

Very un-Veronica-like. She was under a ton of stress, I guessed.

When Veronica and I returned to the small room, Shawn was dressed and perched on the high examination table, her dirty bare feet dangling way off the floor. Though it was typically cold in the hospital, her hair was still pasted to her head in places. She sniffled and snorted — not crying, her ragweed allergy — and looked down at herself dejectedly.

For the first time in a long time I took Veronica's warm hand as we heard the raw details reported: no blood, no bruising, no tearing — such words for a daughter's body! — nothing, in fact.

We actually said it together, we two proud atheists: "Thank God."

Veronica acted chirpy then, bustling about the room looking to pack things that weren't there, saying we had to hurry back home to Owen, now thanking "the gods" for small favours.

I lifted Shawn's warm chin in my hand — remembered my examination of the arsenic-poisoned Marie LeBlanc — and looked into her flat green eyes. *Mournful* is the word for this ugly new world occupied now by my beautiful daughter with her head like a rained-on dandelion clock.

She only mouthed the words to me, so as not to disturb her mother further: *Nothing happened.* Then jerked her chin out of my hand.

It was laughably mad, I knew, to dream of restoring the past in the present and securing the future. Because I saw as clearly as my empty hand that my darling daughter's spirit had shifted away—I actually felt its removal—and it would never return. And that maddened me like hell.

She hopped down and found her running shoes. Veronica draped an arm around her shoulders and they just walked off like nothing really *had* happened.

She was definitely hiding something from me. When the door closed behind them, I slammed my fist on the green leather table still bearing its protective paper, which had been scrunched and torn by my ten-year-old daughter's bared body. Don't tell *me* nothing happened!

Chapter 13

I decided mother and daughter needed some alone-time, so asked that the meeting with Detective Beldon be at the Lighthouse Bar & Grill. He was waiting outside the door and still cursing himself out for not having answered his cell earlier.

I said, "What difference would it have made, Detective?"

He looked me over, his irritation melting to bemusement. "What is it you wanted, Lorne?"

Good question. I couldn't remember. "Let's get out of this heat and have a drink."

He pleaded that he'd been cooped up all day, said he needed a walk more than a drink, and a smoke.

Reluctantly, I took him along Troutstream's winding paths to Shoal Park, our old family park. We sat on a brown-painted cedar bench. From the thin yellow tin he picked a small cigar, which he inserted into his mouth and withdrew moistened. With practised thumb he flipped the lid of an old-style silver lighter, ratcheted its wheel and fired the cigar, clicked shut. He puffed deeply once to get it going and let the smoke drift from his nose in blue ribbons. The aroma was lovely, redolent of burning autumn leaves and wise dads in bulky burgundy cardigans.

In the silence between us the small cigar dwindled to half an inch. He ground it out, gazed up into the trees.

"Lovely place you've got here. Listen to that silence."

He actually listened. I followed his gaze up into the leaf-laden maples, which were showing heat fatigue, curling inward. It had been a hell of a summer and the heat didn't look to be ending any time soon.

"It's far from pleasant valley here, Kevin. We have the sprawling regional detention centre to the south, as you know, and the Mann gravel quarry bordering us to the northeast. And at the end of the actual Troutstream further north, the sewage treatment facility. Wind blows from the north, you've got molecules of other people's shit up your nose."

"Ah, well, no suburb is an island. I should be heading back soon, lots of paper work. What was it you wanted to talk about again?"

My throat constricted. I felt my face flush and prayed he wouldn't notice.

"This isn't your burden to shoulder alone, Lorne."

We sat so still that a crow alighted in the massive cedar sandbox right in front of us. It began tugging at a mostly buried wrapper. Up close, Troutstream's crows are the size of roosters and this devil was keeping its beady black eye on me even as it worked at the hidden treasure. Just when it had dislodged what looked like a Golden Crunchie wrapper, an even larger crow came squawking down and tore the paper from its beak and flapped off with powerful wing strokes.

I'm the least superstitious person I know, but the injustice in that performance of pecking order moved me unaccountably. I buried my face in my hands and shook silently.

"I'm going to find him and kill him," I managed through my covering hands. "He's ruined everything."

I felt his fingers wrap my forearm, tighten, and he said, "Shit eventually gets up everybody's nose, Lorne. The miracle is that the sickos don't fuck with our orderly lives more often. If this is the worst of it, you'll adjust and it won't be so bad, in time. You've been violated, your entire family life, things will never be the same, but you already know that. What nobody knows is what's going on inside Shawn. That's your end of the *continuing* investigation, Dad. It's either you or the grief counsellors. Leave the criminal investigation to me. Okay?"

Unwilling to look at him, I spoke into my cupped palms: "Things had been going so well for us. No real problems to speak of. We'd been having fun together again. And now this."

"I won't lie to you, Lorne, innocent fun's over."

I managed, "What could be worse?"

I heard him sigh, and he said, "You know the Market Slasher?"

"Those were young *hookers* working the Market. I'm talking about my ten-year-old daughter! *I'm gonna find the animal that did this and kill him!*"

He stared at me for a long while, to let me settle some. He took a noisy breath, slowly, as if he were filling up for a plunge. "Okay. Do you know anything about developments in the forensic sciences?"

"What?... Yeah, that's when the lab downtown matches etchings on bullet casings to the suspect's gun barrel. I see it on TV all the time."

"Sure you do." He looked too smug. "Only there's forensic entomology now. Ever hear of that?"

I wouldn't be baited.

"Guns and shell casings aren't much involved in missing children cases. Maggots, now, they're a different story. Those hungry little buggers grow at a reliable pace. And the stages of their development are tied to local climate conditions and can be quite specific even to very limited territories. That's now one of the best ways of pinpointing the time of death, of ascertaining whether the body was moved, even how far."

"I get the point. We're lucky Shawn's returned safe and sound. But that's not *my* point."

"I've been studying the subject in evening criminology courses at the University of Ottawa."

"This is about what's been done to my family, and catching and punishing the animal who did it."

"Of course. That's what we all want. As for little girls who've been abducted and raped before being murdered, we've found an investigative ally in pubic lice. You know, *crabs*. The louse will contain the rapist's blood, no pun intended. And today's juries get a hard-on for DNA evidence."

"That is some sense of humour you've got there, Detective," I said through my teeth.

"Okay, but I had to turn your crank to make my point. I believe I can say this to you, Lorne, and it's strictly *entre nous*. But I'm going to find our abductor, I promise you that. I'm going to do it for two reasons that actually have little to do with Shawn's unsettling experience and your grief, I freely confess. One, *I* need to know just what the hell our man is up to, abducting kids, dressing them up and taking pictures, releasing them unharmed. And two, as *you* joked yesterday, I do indeed want to make Homicide."

I closed my eyes. "Since you haven't caught him yet, what makes you so sure you will now?"

"Stupidly, I didn't care as much before. In this business, with the things I see daily, comparatively harmless is comparatively harmless. The other kids weren't missing anymore, no foul play. I was hopeful, even confident, that Shawn would be showing up the same way. *And I was expecting to be taken off your case and moved to the Major Crimes Unit immediately.* They were feeling the heat on the Market Slasher and Homicide needed all the help they could get."

"What happened?"

He stood and looked at me silently till I joined him and stood.

"You know what happened. The Market Slasher was captured last night, not long before Dr. Foster — quite the night in sleepy Ottawa's ByWard Market, eh?" He deflated, pinched his mouth and shook his head as he had when castigating himself over not having answered his cell. He talked more to himself than to me:

"A big-time serial killer operating in my own backyard, national news, *inter*national, and there I was, still out looking for missing kids who weren't missing any longer. I was so pissed about it, I made a stupid mistake downtown yesterday morning. I butted in while my staff sergeant, who already hated my guts anyway, was giving the Major Crimes superintendent his thoughts on the Slasher, and I blabbed sarcastically for all the whole room to hear: *No way the guy's some punk gangbanger, not the way those hookers are sliced-and-diced right on the street. Check every guy in Ottawa who's had a tour in Kandahar or any other of those desert shitholes, and don't forget the mercenaries. Knife-work like that was copied from those Taliban boys.*

"As we now know, the Slasher's not long back from some *independent* work in Turkey. But the way my slack-jawed sergeant looked at me, then at our newly interested Super, then back and forth between us, I knew in my gut that my loud mouth had just killed my latest hope of reassignment. I tell you, Doctor, if something really good doesn't happen for me, and soon, I'll die in Missing Persons. I need to put our creep behind bars, and now."

"But the superintendent must have heard you and acted on what you said. They did catch the Slasher last night! They must have been watching guys who fit the profile you gave. Won't you get some credit?"

"No. Story of my life. Let's go."

Instead of heading home, I decided to accompany him back to his car at the Lighthouse. He wouldn't join me for a drink, so I had his as well.

When I entered the kitchen, Veronica said evenly, "Shawn's at Shoal Park with Jake and some friends. Maybe you should go get her. It'll be dark soon. And Jake needs a bath."

"You let Shawn go out! There are reporters lurking everywhere, and who knows what… Look at me! What's wrong with you?"

She didn't look. "Lots. Right now, you shouting at me. Are we going to keep Shawn indoors from now on, is that it? Do we want her to think there's something wrong with her that has to be hidden away? That what happened was *her* fault? She has to talk with someone. She won't open up to us. Jake could be a help there. But I don't want her staying out any longer."

She was speaking clearly, but without affect.

"I don't know about Jake being a help to Shawn. And by the way, that's the same prescription you had for Owen, the Dr. Phil talking cure. I just don't want anything else bad happening to us, love."

"I'm talking about Shawn. Will you go get her or do I have to? Were you visiting Art Foster?"

"Veronica, you are not making sense. I was, uh, consulting with Kevin."

"Sense?" She snorted lightly. "You'd better go. It's getting dark. Or don't, if you don't want to. Jack's not up to bathing Jake, who's afraid of baths now." Her voice was breaking, broke: "Won't *somebody* help me?"

That got me moving. I turned at the front door and shouted back, "Don't you go anywhere! You're experiencing post-traumatic stress! Let Jack look after his own kid and we'll look after ours!"

I hustled along the sidewalk and took the path back to Shoal Park. As I passed the schoolyard of Lampman Elementary, the outdoor lights came on in a *pop* and *fizz* of dim magenta glow, without much effect in the twilight. It remained dusky along the treed path between two rows of houses. No backyard lights were on and it got gloomier the deeper I went. The evening may still have been as warm as high summer, but the days had shortened already.

The golden-lighted playground was soon in sight like an oasis in the dark when a yowl made my heart trip. A bad-luck black cat came into view about twenty feet along, heading to cross my path. It was slow-moving and low-lying, it waddled, had a white patch... Skunk. I froze. It might turn and see me, it might spray me, it might dash suddenly and bite me! Skunks are often rabid and supposedly you can tell from a nonchalant manner. I waited nervously. It passed slowly...across my path, on to the left and under a large patch of shimmering hoya leaves, which rustled and glimmered dimly green.

There is something about the evening lighting of playgrounds that lends the space a golden aura. When the safety lights first come up, a dusky playground soon looks starkly different from its daytime appearance. And as the darkness deepens and the artificial light increases, the area transforms into something otherworldly. Shoal Park was now such a space, as silent as a brightly moonlit clearing in a woods, which in a way it was. The impression of a magically illuminated private space was enhanced because the playground, like so many of Troutstream's backyards, was enclosed by a storybook high-cedar hedge with shadowy gated arbours. A secret garden.

I picked out the children in the farthest corner. But the magical peace of the place had cast its spell on me, and rather than stopping and shouting for Shawn and Jake to come home, I moved onto the grass and shuffled toward them. The swing sets and slides and jungle gym had only a shadowy substance. I paused, some thirty feet distant, realizing in only mild shame that I was there to spy. I needed to hear Shawn talk.

A girl startled me with a squawk like a peachick in the night. Another girl's — Shawn's? — voice scolded, *Get your fat ass back here this instant, you stupid fucking retard!* That *couldn't* have been Shawn...could it? I'd not distinguished Jake among the children, but now I saw him huffing out of the darkness to my left and go thumping close by like some nocturnal buffalo.

Shawn seemed to materialize from the dark hedge itself, an apparition of shining daughter. Her fair bouncing hair carried the light. Jake passed the group and began running another circle, leaning inwards, elbows tucked and pumping. As he approached me again he uplifted to the night sky a radiant face like light made flesh. That was a whole new Jake for me, out of the darkness like that, transfigured in the radiant playground doing the thing he did best — a child at play.

I expect the booze and drugs had something to do with the vision, because that's what it felt like, a vision of one ecstatically happy kid, Down's be damned.

The others remained in their tight group by a corner arbour... five...four...maybe six children of about Shawn's age and size, which made it more difficult to distinguish them. Either they were slipping in and out through the arbour gateway or the strange lighting was making them disappear and reappear against the hedge. I strained even more to distinguish their speech:

No...swear... Why would never... You better not...you'll ruin it for everyone... Why says if we can't...

Wy, not *Why*. Silly kids' talk, that was all.

Mouth hanging speechless, Jake completed another circle where they stood. Huffing powerfully, he dwarfed the others like some tamed ogre. Shawn extended her arm fully and pointed at him, spoke clearly: "Remember, Jake, not even your dad, and *especially* your mom, if she ever comes back." Two of the figures disappeared through the hedge. Then they reappeared, but now it seemed there were far more than I'd originally thought, eight...no, seven...ten? And a couple were bigger boys now, much taller than Shawn.

Puffing Jake pointed at my approach and said something unintelligible. They all looked brightly toward me, and there were only five of them again, and no big boys.

Shawn's face changed first. "Da-ad! What are *you* doing here?"

I stopped. "You and Jake have to come home now." I didn't turn and leave, as normally I would have.

Jake took off like a startled cat out of the playground and along the path. I'd never seen him run anything but circles. I was impressed by his straightaway speed and I called, "Wait for us, Jake." But he didn't.

When I turned back, only Shawn was there. She walked towards me, somewhat regally, the nimbus of her hair absolutely fairy-like. She wouldn't deign to acknowledge me further. She wouldn't hurry, either. So I let her pass under my gaze and followed after.

I said, "Who were all those kids?"

"What?" She didn't look back.

"I counted at least eight at one time. And there were some big boys. Who were *they*, little lady?"

Nothing.

"Shawn, I'm dead serious now. What was going on there? I saw and heard some disturbing things back there. You shouldn't even be out at this time. I mean, right after what happened. Who *were* those big boys? I want their names."

"Friends," she tossed off. "We're making a *Wy Knots* fan club and we're not letting just anyone in." She couldn't help exciting herself as she proceeded, the normally chatty Shawn: "Not any of those big boys for sure. Or maybe just Pete Carswell. He's nice. And they don't want Jake to go, unless I really push because I'm president."

I grabbed her shoulder, more roughly than I'd intended, and spun her round. "*Go?* Go where? Who were you waiting for back there? You were expecting somebody else, weren't you, when you saw it was me?"

She looked surprised at first at the rough treatment, then quickly clammed up again, which only confirmed my suspicions. A cat cried in that baby-bashing way and Shawn leapt forward and threw her arms around me, pressing her face just under my chin. I cupped her head.

"What's going on, dear? That's all I want to know. Who were those big boys? Why Pete Carswell? What's so special about him? What's been happening with you, sweetheart?"

She pushed herself off and fixed me with one of her mother's fed-up looks.

"Nothing! I told you, nothing like *you* mean! No bad stuff! You are *not* ruining this for me!"

She turned and ran. She'd outgrown those shorts too. But ruining what? I jogged after, through the thick stink of skunk, powerfully concentrated, more suffocating than I'd ever experienced. I called, "Shawn, please, I just want to know what's happening."

Her reply came faintly on my echo as she rounded out of sight: "Don't be dumb-dumb…"

Approaching home, I saw her dash from our house and head to the Kilborns'. Inside there was no woofer thumping from above and no sign of Veronica. I fetched my bottle of Macallan single malt. I sat on the couch in the family room, poured myself a good two fingers and drank it straight off. It was instant ballast of hotter coals to a hot belly. I poured another and sat back. I wished Kevin were there. Men work their best over such…facilitating lubricant. I could make up for the fool I'd made of myself in the park.

The woofer started up. I heaved to my feet and bounded upstairs, opened Owen's door and shook a fist at him. His eyes widened and he twisted to turn down the volume.

From my room I phoned next door and, prepared for a nasty Jack, was taken aback when Veronica answered like she lived there.

"Order a pizza," she said. "You and Owen can manage that without me, can't you? Jack's still a mess. I'm needed here. Shawn's helping calm a pretty wild Jake."

"You're needed over here, dear."

"I have to go."

"Come home. Uh, I think Shawn's hiding something serious from us. We need to talk."

There was a shorter pause. "I can't handle that right now. Jake's all wound up about something and ready to have a seizure and Jack's verging on a total breakdown himself. I don't suppose you'd come over here and have a look at Jake?"

"Did you not *hear* what I said? You think Jack and his retarded son are more important than *our* family!"

She hung up.

Back downstairs, I phoned the private number Kevin had given me. "Any developments?"

"No, but then I only just saw you."

He sounded different. "Are you having a celebratory drink now too, Kevin?" I snickered.

I heard him smack his lips. "A hitherto hidden vice."

I carried the landline phone to the couch and picked up my glass: "You should come back here, I've been drinking alone too."

Yet another long pause.

He said, "No thanks, Lorne. Booze is a really bad vice of mine. I need to get some sleep, just a nap, then I'll be fine. Then I won't sleep again till I've solved this. You, too, big guy. Cap the bottle, get some sleep. We still need to apprehend the prick who did this, which is why you're doing something for me first thing in the morning, right?... And I need you clear-headed."

"Hey, I never drink, or very rarely, because I never know when I'll be called in on an emergency. It's this business with the prick has sent me to the bottle. But c'mon, we've both earned an exceptional drink. Take a cab." I hurried with what I hoped was an enticement: "By the way, I've just been talking to Shawn like you said I should and I think she's up to something with some of her friends."

I heard dry noises from his end. "Keep talking with her, Lorne. And here's why—I didn't want to say, but I believe this is still headed somewhere. Shawn and the other kids *are* hiding something from us, something they've surely been deceived about."

I felt the alcohol air go out of me. "Yes?"

"That's all. I have no proof, just a hunch that it all—the abductions and returns—points to something bigger that hasn't happened yet."

I was feeling bereft. "But it's only a hunch?"

"Logically, none of what's happened makes sense on its own, or not yet. But taken together, it has the feel of preparing for something else. Even Foster's arrest may be an attempt to distract attention from the perpetrator, *or* perps, to you. *Your* colleague, *your* Caddy, *your* daughter, Troutstream kids gone missing? And somebody up there, or down there, must really like our perp, because the arrest of the Market Slasher was a godsend...well, okay, not that. But what a lovely coincidence to thicken the shitty stew, eh? By the way, the Slasher is now Dr. Foster's cellmate, if not literally. It's a circus over at the regional detention centre."

"I don't like the sound of any of that. I mean, *some* distraction! You've been over to see Art? But come for a drink, Kevin, please. We need to talk this through."

The breath went out of him. "I have a drinking problem, Lorne. Binge drinker, which is another excuse they've used to keep me from Homicide. I now recognize the signs, though. One more drink and I'd be off to the races for days and this case could go to the devil for all I'd care. I've had just enough to test my resolve. You have one more on me, okay? You've earned it, but one more's the limit. Where's Veronica? Kids home?"

My pride kicked in. "Keep me informed, please, Detective?"

"Don't go off in a huff, Lorne. Remember, you're to visit Art Foster first thing tomorrow. And I want you sharp, as in *not hung over*. We need Foster's connection to Bob Browne. I'll meet you at the detention centre."

I drank half a tumbler of Scotch straight and lay back. Men drink and talk their best. Drink more and more, and forget what they talked about. Men...

I'm twelve years old. It's a steamy spring day and getting hotter by the minute. I'm working with my father at his father's house, spreading topsoil for Granddad's huge vegetable garden. Dad chuckles to himself as he piles the dirt higher and higher in the wheelbarrow each trip, so that gripping the bulky wooden arms and balancing the load is an incremental test. I'll die before I tip it. Granddad comes out onto the back porch and, shading his eyes with his hand, remarks what a worker I am. And my father snaps, *Go back inside*. Granddad looks around and says to the vague sky, *Inside where?* He's confused again since Granny died. Soon he will die too. I know when and why, I could tell him, from loneliness. As she dresses the broken blisters on my palms my mother scolds me for my bull-headed foolishness. I don't care. Then she just holds me for the longest time, in a place of regret we can do nothing about but share its suffocating futile misery. Since, only Veronica has held me so breathlessly close, say when I'd lost a child I'd let myself love. With just a *tch-tch* my father could leave me feeling afraid of everything, not knowing who I am anymore. Hollowed out. The wheelbarrow is empty, then overflowing with treats—Golden Crunchie bars, big bags of barbecue Fritos—I can feel it tipping, I can't hold it, my palms are tearing off—

I snapped to, poured a glass and drank my fill. My special bottle two-thirds empty. My Caddy.

I was going upstairs to talk to Owen when the woofer began thumping like a giant trying to pound our home to smithereens and the rapper commenced his Uzi rounds of brag and complaint. I turned back to the bottle, suddenly a chilled and shaking mess. The doctor in me knew it was still part of the delayed PTS response. My head was being pulped.

I found the smoky Valium vial where I'd hidden it and took one. Only one more, that would be it, no more. Careful, people died in their sleep. I took another. I collapsed on the small family-room couch.

I am walking along a raised road in the middle of nowhere, then running head-down and the road is sunken and endless, its diesel-smelling tarmac softening in the relentless sun. I'm parched and the flat gravel road just keeps coming at me, school buses pass me again and again or the same bus never completely passes. On its back is the sign DIESEL. *At the side of the sunken sandy road a man dressed like a desert dweller in Jesus garb crouches on his haunches. I realize I've been passing him for days and there is no road, only desert. I've been running in Jake-like circles on a black cinder track. It is Jesus. He holds out a glass of iced tea as I stumble by again and again, but I've not earned it yet, not worked hard enough, and the glass is dirty, take it away. The glass is cracked badly too, the glass is dangerously cracked and coming apart and diesel is running out, large shards pierce Jesus's hand and the baby he holds is crying now and there's a big bang of light—*

I awoke, or came to, raving in darkness, certain that there were strangely familiar people in the room with me. "Veronica? Shawn? Owen?…"

It took minutes to settle down and recognize where I was and that I was alone. I found the fridge and drank iced tea straight from the jug, washing down two Advil and a prophylactic Gravol. I climbed to bed, expecting to find comforting Veronica there. But she'd not come home yet. I checked. Neither had Shawn. Owen was snoring softly, his earphones in place. It was one in the morning, Wednesday morning.

Chapter 14

I'd not been aware of Veronica's coming to bed. I awakened facing her, our knees drawn up and touching. My right hand and her left, whose fingers had entangled in sleep, were resting on her hip. Our noses were nearly touching. Her eyes were closed.

So far, so good.

I did a systems check and was pleasantly surprised to realize I'd slept like a baby and didn't feel hungover at all. Morning in a master bedroom full of magic-sword sunlight, another indulgent day off work. The kids were still off school, with Owen asleep, as he would be till made to get up around noon. I could hear Shawn already at the TV downstairs, the sweetest sound in all the world. I felt a powerful presence in that master bedroom.

I considered: What a full and fortunate life have I made here. Why on earth am I always chasing after more happiness? Is this life of sleeping, dreaming and waking in the lap of family love not enough? How can I justify wanting more? The healthy, the comfortable, the well off, we so seldom acknowledge how lucky we are. And we should always be minding our good fortune, daily, like a prayer to that heathen god, Fortuna. We shouldn't be so stingy with our gratitude as to need the contrast of catastrophe to know how blessed we are in our life, liberty, and pursuit of happiness. On this part of the globe anyway, this narrowest wedge of the pie where all the choice fruit is packed. I'd just dodged the bullet of family tragedy. The media storm was being weathered well, with the Market Slasher its new eye. The luckiest man alive am I!

Veronica frowned and whispered like a hiss, "Glasses." Her eyes popped open.

We were still nose-to-nose. I squeezed her hand and said, "It's okay, dear, you were having a nightmare. Don't go near the Kilborns today."

She made a face but talked normally (her breath was foul): "It felt like it went on all night, the dream, or the nightmare. I was trapped in it. Just the one scene, a pair of plastic sunglasses sitting on a glass table in an empty room. It sounds like nothing, but it was unnerving, like all the glass was about to shatter or something. I couldn't look away or change the scene and I was in a panic that somebody had lost his glasses. Then I recognized them—Jake's prescription sunglasses. Remember them?"

I did. Jake had sported them proudly and forgotten them everywhere for about two weeks, and every day at our house, then never worn them again. It turned out his vision was fine, just more of Trixie's Munchausen's madness.

I said, "I wonder why you dreamt about that retard's so-called prescription sunglasses?"

I made it difficult for her to untangle her fingers, giving her hand one last squeeze and hurrying, "Things are back to normal now, dear. Or will be soon as Art Foster helps us out and Bob Browne's caught or somebody."

She snaked the freed hand round the back of my head and held me there eyeball-to-eyeball: "I'm leaving you." She let go.

I was starving. "Are you making a big breakfast? I saw some leftover potatoes in the fridge you could fry. Hmm, home fries." My Homer Simpson. "What time did you and Shawn come home last night anyway?"

She hoisted out of bed and with her back to me said, "I want a divorce."

"What new horse? Are you sleepwalking or something?"

"Stop joking for once in your fucking life! *A divorce.* I'm leaving you. This fucking marriage, this fucking house!" She was spitting mad. "I've had it! None of it—none of *this*—means anything anymore!"

I clued in. She was having a massive delayed-stress reaction, rampant PTSD. I could handle this.

"You're upset, Veronica. So am I. What with Shawn and hearing about Foster and the Market Slasher and teenage hookers, and what with asshole Jack making all these demands on you. But we're gonna be all right now. Lie back down and *I'll* make the big breakfast!"

She still looked pretty good in her underwear, a bit fleshy, but awfully sexy still in that strangely familiar way. She wasn't lying back down, though.

"What is it, honey?... Okay, I shouldn't say *retard*, I know, I apologize."

She spoke as she pulled on her baby-blue sweats: "Honey, my ass. You lied to me about lending your car to Art Foster. Now the police have the Cadillac and we have only my little Golf. What if we'd been planning to go somewhere all together today and had to take Jake with us?"

Uh-oh, hysteria. "Veronica, you are not making sense. Today would have been a regular work and school day. Besides, we haven't done anything like that in a long time. Try to hear yourself, what you're saying."

She flashed round on me: "That's right, Jack and Trixie and Jake did more together as a family than we ever do! And I don't want to listen to myself! *You* listen to me. Or try listening to *yourself* for once!"

"This old argument again? I've explained about work. It's still crazy there, like there's suddenly an epidemic of lymphocytic leukemias. And now all this shit with Foster, and me taking time off, I'll have to take a few catch-up shifts for a little while. That's all. Then we'll be back to normal, promise. Come on, be reasonable, dear."

She was near giddy suddenly. "Really, *do* listen to yourself, you're already making future excuses!"

"Be reasonable, Veronica. That's all I ever ask."

She snatched the matching sweatsuit top off the dresser. "Reasonable? But I am not a reasonable woman. I'm not very smart, either, as you keep reminding me *and* the children."

"What? But I haven't done that for a long time."

"Always, every day, every time I open my mouth. You have zero respect for me and you don't even try to hide it any more, not from the kids, not from me. Even Jack has noticed it."

"Good neighbour Jack? Oh, please. Jack and Trixie? Look at them, always publicly gushing with respect for each other and big displays of affection, *and* for that obnoxious re— son of theirs. Look where they are today. She's respectfully fucked off with her lawyer and respectful Jack doesn't know whether he's coming or going!"

She looked at me then, unemotionally at last. "*Listen* to yourself, Lorne. You make me sick, sick of us, sick of all…all *this*."

"Me? I make you sick? I do not get you this morning, dear."

"And don't *dear* me. You have no idea what the Kilborns have been through with Jake, every day, for years and years and years, every school, every teacher, every *thing* kids do that Jake wanted to do but couldn't. Sometimes I think you're incapable of empathy. You're like one of those functioning psychopaths. How can you *say* that about Jack?" She'd grown sad and quiet, as if she might cry.

"Jack again? What'd I say about Jack? I'm talking about Trixie and the monster she's made of poor, uh, mentally challenged Jake. Who gives a fuck about Jack?"

She paused, rethought something. "Okay then, why did you loan your car to Art Foster?"

"What is this, non-sequitur day? I mean—"

"I know what a non sequitur is. You wouldn't lend Foster your stethoscope to check your own heart. Why suddenly your precious Cadillac?"

I had to think. "Like I said, it was the only way he'd put me in touch with Bob Browne, so the Troutstream Community Association could get the playground equipment removed and replaced. So?"

"Oh," she laughed falsely. "You suddenly care *so much* about the TCA and its troubles, whose members you're always making fun of? What was the sudden fascination with Bob Browne that you were willing to risk your darling Caddy? You've never even let *me* drive it! And I've asked!" Worked up again, she snatched her white sweat socks and, putting one on, hopped ungracefully towards the door.

"You're blowing this all out of proportion, Veronica."

Again she looked for a moment like she might cry—good—but changed her mind again. Bad. That put the point of an icicle on my heart. Normally she'd cry at the drop of a sparrow.

"Yes, I am. I have no sense of proportion to go with my little intellect. So let me stupidly answer my own question. You were *attracted* to Bob Browne. You—"

"Oh, please. Not some two-bit psychologizing of my paradoxical latently gay homophobia."

She smiled small. "Stupid me."

"Well, you are if you're suggesting that I secretly lust after Bob Browne's dwarf bum! You've never even met him!"

She smirked, not at all humorously. "That's right, but I've heard, a lot… I'm not saying you're in love with that freak of arrested development, but you were strongly attracted to him all right and you couldn't have cared less about the danger signals."

"Bob is not like that."

She just stared at me for a while.

"Lorne, how many times have you been attracted to oddball men I couldn't stand? Big-talking phonies you think possess some wisdom you've been deprived of? It's your biggest blind spot. It's what your brute of a father did to you. Oh, but that would be more two-bit psychology, wouldn't it?"

"Yes, it is." I may have squirmed a bit down into the bedclothes. Or two bits' worth.

"Sit still for it. And these daddy-dearests always disappoint you…almost like it's part of a bargain you've made with yourself. Even Detective Beldon, your new best buddy, right? Except that I like him too. Of course, that dooms him in your eyes. But it always ends badly anyway, like this has ended, in the biggest disaster of all, *if* it is over, which I doubt, given Art Foster's arrest. You never listen to me, you never will. Because you've never had any respect for me and you never will. If you'd paid attention when I told you to watch Shawn closely—which meant paying attention *to her*—none of this would have happened. I'm leaving you. That's final."

It was the length and coherence of that very un-Veronica-like speech, the fact that it had obviously been rehearsed a few times, that put the icicle through my heart. All I could manage was, "That is so unfair." By then I was sitting up on the edge of the bed, in my Nobody-Knows-I'm-Elvis T-shirt and baggy blue jockeys. I'm sure I looked a bargain. "Veronica, really, it's everything that's happened. Let me get you something, get back into bed."

She smiled genuinely and shook her head. "You'd better watch that Valium."

I felt my head. It hurt differently from a hangover, hypersensitive everywhere, like my scalp had shrunk and been stapled to my skull.

She was still smiling. "Of course, it's never you. It's me or the kids or someone else. Even now, when you've been behaving half out of your mind, you won't seriously consider what I've said. Even with all the evidence, our little girl abducted, your precious Caddy sacrificed for Bob Browne, and Art Foster in jail for being with a teenage prostitute *in your car*, maybe even for assaulting a girl in *your* car. *In jail*, Lorne!"

"But you're not making coherent sense, Veronica!"

"When did you last talk sensibly with Owen, your son, who is obviously deeply depressed?"

"But I do respect you! I love you!"

She pinched her mouth and looked at me with those dead brown eyes.

"They're not the same thing. And by the way, that was a doozy of a non sequitur... Okay, at least *picture this*, Dr. Thorpe, which I witnessed from Jack's house. You drunk and high on who knows what, washing my car in a heat wave, chasing reporters down the driveway to the end of the hose—when we still didn't know where Shawn was!"

At the bedroom door she hopped into her other sock and turned her back to me. From the sound of her voice, she may finally have been crying: "I'm leaving you, and I want a divorce. Jack says I can use his lawyer."

I didn't believe her for a second, though I was alarmed at her playing such a card. But then she picked up the suitcase, which had been pre-packed. I couldn't speak. Nor did she try again.

Soon the air seal on the back door whooshed like the non-negotiable kiss-off it was.

Where were the kids? I shouted, "Shawn?... Owen?" Nothing. Nothing came back but the nothing sound of the TV, which no one must have been watching. What could be more nothing than a know-nothing TV playing to no one?

I lay back and pulled the sheet over my head. I was suddenly greasy with hangover sweat and felt biliously green. I rolled back and forth and back and forth till I was trapped in a winding sheet. Flailing and kicking the mattress, I tore the sheet off. I lay still for a time, getting my breath, or sort of whimpering, I guess.

I looked in on Owen. He'd slept the night with his earplugs in. He didn't look depressed to me. I turned off his CD player and he still didn't stir, so I left the plugs in place.

In the kitchen there was a note from Shawn: "Dad work phoned and they want you to call back right away, I could save myself time by making photocopies of this message! Next door. Love S."

Just like that, like all was back to normal. We'd come so close.

I stepped towards the side door, but turned back and phoned Tamara at CHEO. Little Marnee (congenital heart) had died during the night. In the absence of Dr. Foster, who'd been scheduled for the day, would I please cancel my unscheduled holiday and come in just to close some routine matters?

Foster. I'd promised Kevin I'd visit Foster first thing that morning. I would. Then to work. It was late already. We'd slept in, for the last time, it looked.

I stopped again on my way to the door, slipped the CD of *Abbey Road* from the Beatles' digitally remastered box set, hurried upstairs, slipped it into Owen's player, lowered the volume and hit play. I watched until he smiled in his sleep. "Come Together." For once the black rapper wasn't threatening to tear him a new A-hole. I could have cried. I touched his cheek, felt my own. What the hell!

Chapter 15

"Bring it, Thorpe, your best shot," he challenged half-heartedly. Crossing the floor towards him, I stopped and struck a pose, palms up and arms spread: "Foster, I come not to shoot you in your cell but to retrieve a pimpmobile."

He crossed his arms on his chest and deadpanned the two words, "Not funny."

"I'm, uh, sorry, Art. It's just that I'm nervous here."

"*You're* nervous here?" He dropped his head and wagged it, looking around surreptitiously. He was signalling me to see where he'd landed himself. And *landed* was the word for Foster in his ill-fitting orange jumpsuit — parachuted behind enemy lines, delivered into the camp of "the other."

I'd been able to walk right through the media congregated at the front because they were distracted surrounding some woman who'd just emerged. Only "A-Channel videographer Donny Kynder" had recognized me, but too late. It was past ten, yet I found Kevin nowhere. Then I was stalled for some two hours because I'd never visited before and I wasn't a relative of Art. It made no difference that I was Dr. Lorne Thorpe. No one in the long chain at Police HQ would authorize my visit and it took forever to locate Kevin, who vouched for me and had them pass the message that he was delayed. Luckily it was a day of "free-time visitation," which meant a relaxed approach to time, and signalled either administrative irony or cruelty, or both.

Walking into the "visitation pod," I'd thought first of a school's cafeteria, a Catholic school's, where big kids were being prepped for confession. The place breathed such an air of institutional normality, with open concept and lots of glass (or Plexiglas). The impression of normality was strong because I'd been expecting TV expressions of incarcerated evil: shanking relays at a cafeteria counter, raging homophobic panic, big Black men in bib overalls. Not these mostly white and brown and swarthy guys in orange jumpsuits.

Then a correct impression of the regional detention centre sank in. A couple of well-armed guards kept alert proximity to the dull action. The inmates seemed to be either short and powerful or all sinew in suits that were two sizes too large (perhaps a preference; Owen dressed similarly "gangsta"). And they all looked so young compared to Foster and me. All had some form of facial hair, with the beards and moustaches sparse (Owen again). Further bold examination discovered the tattoos: crosses and other insignias on cheeks, lines running from cuffs like black blood or rising up the neck like dark flames, even tattooed teardrops. (Owen would *never* be getting a tattoo.) Men looked away shifty-eyed from their earnest or upset female visitors…looked at me standing there casually dressed, taking it all in like a day at the Museum of Nature. The very man at whom I was staring kicked his chair over backwards, pointed at me and shouted: "Who the *fuck* does *he* think he is?"

Ah, yes, we were in jail, a Canadian jail, Ottawa, Ontario. I'd been the target of that question a few times in my life, if never during my American days.

A guard took a step, riot stick at his chest, hand on Taser like a quick-draw, but the well-conditioned prisoner was already striding out the interior door. Perhaps he'd merely exploited my bad manners to end his visit (his woman-child, who looked pregnant, was sobbing with face in hands).

From that point on I knew exactly where I was: deep in the land of unreason, a foreign country of perpetual conflict. That true impression went well with the tang of cleanser and the other odour that now insinuated and could never be masked: human waste. As I've said, in my place of work, disease and death also go well with the smell of disinfectant. So there was still that something familiar in the experience.

Without looking up, Foster said, "Don't stare so fucking obviously, Lorne."

Everything told me to come right to the point, my point, screw Beldon. "Art, where were you on Sunday morning?"

He looked up and took me in. "Lorne, you don't look well. You look worse than I feel."

"Answer the question."

"Lorne, I forgive you beforehand for asking it. But I've talked with Detective Beldon a couple of times. I know about Shawn and I can't tell you how relieved I am she's all right. But, Lorne, we have *both* been set up, though for the life me, I don't know why." He dropped his head again. "Why, oh why, did I let her lure me back out Monday night? She was much younger than she'd said, we'd only talked and had supper Sunday, I went again only for her sake, she was so young and mixed up—hand to God, Lorne. She'd insisted on meeting in the Market both nights. There are witnesses now who will say your vintage Caddy was cruising the Market all weekend. If the Market Slasher hadn't been arrested—thank God for small favours—they'd be saying I was him! Or you were! Why, why didn't I return your Caddy Monday morning like we'd agreed? It's this fucking cock of mine."

I believed him, who was too shallow to lie so convincingly. Foster was no child-molesting criminal, whatever else he was. Beldon had misled me when he'd said that Art had no corroborated alibi for Sunday when Shawn had been taken. Beldon had withheld the information that Foster had met with the girl Monday *and* Sunday—the teenage hooker was his Sunday alibi!—and Beldon had done so to control my visit with Art, to make me aggressive, interrogative, a better source of evidence. Some lawman, that Detective Kevin Beldon.

Foster deflated. "Look where I am, Lorne." He glanced past me. "Do you know who that is over there? Blond kid alone in the so-called 'containment corner'?"

I looked. Tousled blond hair, a well-fed momma's-boy face, in general appearance a clean cut above his fellow inmates. I said, "Charlie's Canadian cousin, Norman Manson?"

"A riot as usual, Thorpe. But not here. Nothing's funny here… including riot jokes. You're not far off the truth, though — the Market Slasher, that's who. Did you even know you lived close to a facility that deals with his likes?"

The boy-man in the lightly guarded "containment corner" was transformed. I turned my back on him, or it, for part of the transformation was his becoming nonhuman. "Who visits *him*? They let him sit out in the open like that, with these young women all around?"

"They have no choice, it's the law. He already has more people advocating for his rights since he's been caught than wanted him dead before, lawyers on the make, media types, sick *women*. He's our star attraction. But what do I care? I've got troubles enough of my own."

"When are they going to let you out of here, Art? How are you holding up?"

"They? Who are *they*? My fucking lawyer's been great on two costly divorces, but when it comes to finding me a good criminal lawyer, he's tit-fucking useless! CHEO's fucking *team* will have nothing to do with me! How am I holding up? I'm not holding up, that's how! I'm cracking up!"

He again dropped his head and pinched his forehead in his right hand. I'd never heard Foster swear so much. And I remembered: once upon a time we'd been friends, Art and I, young doctors starting out, building CHEO Oncology and Respiration together.

He spoke into his lap: "If it weren't for Bob…"

I could have been touched by a Taser. "Bob Browne? *He's* been here?"

"He's the only friend who visits me, right from yesterday morning."

"I really am sorry for not having come earlier, Art. But about Bob, will you tell me the contact you use for him, or an address would be even better."

"And every time after me, he visits with the Slasher there. Quite the man, that Bob Browne."

"What? What's *their* connection?"

Foster appeared to relax. "I asked Bob that very question. He said a lady friend had reminded him that it was his duty as a fellow human being to visit the sick and imprisoned, and he may as well since he's here visiting me anyway."

My scalp felt on fire. "What lady friend? What do Bob and the Slasher talk about? *Do* you have an address for Bob? Think, Art. Or tell me your contact for him? This is of extreme importance."

Foster frowned in the Slasher's direction. "Believe it or not, they talk about boxing mostly. There's a long lineup of weirdos wanting to visit with the Slasher, but so far only Bob and his lady friend have been permitted, also since yesterday. Supposedly she produced proof that she's the Slasher's American cousin, and she convinced the authorities that Bob was a relative too. You just missed her, by the way. But some cousin, some friend, some lady, one who dresses like a slut and talks like some Honey Booboo. Her visits always rile the Slasher, then Bob has to settle him. I don't like the look of any of it, but Bob won't tell me more. And I know what you're thinking, me slagging a slut." He hung a sheepish smirk.

"Art." I got his attention. "If you've overheard anything, *anything at all*, you have to tell me exactly what they said."

"Like I said, they're both big fight fans. At the first visitation this morning, a guard had to break up their argument over some Lennox guy's place in heavyweight history. It was quite the show. Can you believe—"

"Art, listen carefully, this is of life-and-death importance. Detective Beldon believes that Bob Browne may be the one who set you up, me too. And now Browne's chumming with the Market Slasher, who was conveniently arrested the same night as you? And *who* is this American cousin? Just who the hell's in charge here! Or, wait, forget all that. You *must* give me your contact for Bob Browne, *now*."

Foster grew irritated. "That's *all* Beldon cared about, contacting Bob, but I was having none of it."

I fought to control my eagerness and realized I should have taken another Valium. "Art, the next time Bob visits, you tell the guards to get on the phone right away..."

Foster had been frowning with increasing annoyance but suddenly beamed past me: "Say but his name and he shall appear!"

I was turning when Foster's hand shot out and grabbed my wrist. "You'd better be careful, Thorpe, Bob's no friend of yours anymore, that's for sure, not since you cheated him and spread all those insults. I've never heard Bob say an unkind word about anybody, but he hates your guts. Why *are* you spreading lies?"

"Art, I've said nothing, I've done nothing. It's complicated. He mistakenly blames me for not being paid for his work cleaning up Troutstream's playgrounds. He threatened me. He may even be in cahoots with these guys, the Lewis brothers, to frame both of us. And what about this new connection with the Slasher? Browne must be schizoid or something. Or somebody else is lying to *him* about *me*. Who's this American cousin? Trust me, Art, please, for old time's sake."

He was still gazing past me and speaking *sotto voce* through his grin: "Bob schizoid? I do not think so, my friend. The man's a magician of the soul."

I swung round — and came face-to-face with Bob (as best we could). He didn't even look up at me and didn't so much smile at Foster as irradiate him. Instantly my suspicions were scattering, just like that.

"Art, you're looking better today!"

"Thanks, Bob. I think I'm feeling a bit better already. Sit down, please."

"Since you already have a visitor, I think I'll talk first with Michael. I'll be back." He turned away talking: "One good thing about being short, the media don't even see you."

"Bob?" I said. He looked at me, radiating absolute zero. "Are you involved with the Lewis brothers in a plot against me?"

"Are you out of your fucking mind, Thorpe?" Foster said. "Bob, I'm sorry about this."

I held Bob's eyes. "I have been trying for a week to get the Troutstream Community Association to pay you what's owed. I swear on the heads of my children."

His face looked calm enough and when he spoke it was evenly, but I felt him vibrating: "That is a mighty oath for the great white doctor. But why would *Bwana* Thorpe fight to have a pygmy pederast paid for his, uh, *vastly substandard* work?"

I knew then that Bob Browne was not my enemy. I don't know how I knew, as I am the least superstitious person I know. I just knew, I felt it, in my heart, like I'd known one evening that I would love Veronica forever.

"Bob, I can't believe someone convinced you I said anything like that. Do you cut your friends so easily? Who told you that?"

He was moving off: "A little fucking bird," and flapping his arms.

"Bob, listen to me, please, for one minute, that's all I ask." He stopped. "Whoever told you those lies — and they are lies — is a danger to us all, probably mentally ill. It *was* the Lewis brothers, wasn't it?"

"Thorpe, what the fuck are you—"

"Shut up, Art. And, Bob, I will take my strongest oath again if it will convince you that I have never said anything against you. I swear by my family. I think you do know what my family means to me."

I waited and saw him relent a touch. I was aware of my breathing and didn't care that we were being watched with interest by those nearby. Now or never, go for it.

"I thought we were friends, Bob. I don't make friends easily, never have. And I'm not a very good friend when I do. Ask Art here. I should have visited him right away yesterday, I'm sorry to say. I was afraid of the mess of it all, coward that I am. And whatever you decide, Bob, I'm still your friend. I'm an asshole in more ways than even you could imagine, but I would never betray you. You said it was a shame about my father and me. *You* shouldn't just walk away now because it's become difficult for you. That's what he did, that's what I did with him, what I've always done, and I've always been wrong. I've always been a coward. But I never thought you were, that's what I first liked about you—your courage, your courage in your convictions, your belief in your own experiences, your true heart. Some very sick person is manipulating both of us, all of us. It's those Lewises, isn't it?"

He turned and slowly beamed forth the irradiating smile. He took a few steps and hugged me, his arms wrapping me about the upper arms, his cheek on my chest, his Jew's harp digging into my belly. I had the most incredible rush of good feeling. In my med-school days I'd sampled a snort of this and that (mostly to stay alert) and this was something like the initial rush, but more like pure light pouring through my veins. I'd come to the prison with raging feelings, ready to blame anybody and everybody for my troubles—Foster, Bob, the Lewises, even Veronica—with the sort of uncontrolled emotions that too easily find violent expression. And suddenly there I was, a sojourner in la-la land. If with benefit of residual Valium, true.

He stood back, struck a boxer's pose and bobbed and weaved a bit, dropped his guard and laughed. "Well, that was no chicken's speech!" Then seriously: "Listen, Lorne, I can't tell you right now who's spreading the stories, sowing all the conflict. And I expect there's more than even I—and certainly you—know about. But this is a personal matter between me and a dear old friend. That's *my* problem, and I'll take care of it. I will tell you some of it, though, because I know it's become your problem too. Shawn. And poor Art here. Let's you and me have a long talk after our visits, okay?"

Foster said from his seat, "Yoo-hoo, down here? Don't I get told the big secret?"

Bob laughed, "You will, Art, and I promise my news will have you out of this place later this afternoon. I'll be right back after my visit with Michael."

"Michael?" I asked.

"Him over there," Bob pointed to the Market Slasher. "Earlier I promised him a longer visit, the poor bugger. Looks like Adonis but dumb-dumb as an ox. He was unpredictable as hell this morning and transferring his anger onto me! We need to work through that shit. Sorry for the psychobabble. You two catch up. Then we'll call in the police."

I extended my hand, no longer surprised that Bob Browne had a relationship with the Market Slasher. "Okay, Bob, but first you and I talk. The detective who's been investigating this case is supposed to be meeting me here. You'll like him, I think, if he ever shows up. But I'm sure now that things are going to get better."

He walked away more jauntily than he'd arrived. At the containment corner for "special inmates" (there was actually a sign), he was thoroughly patted down. Then on to the Market Slasher, to Michael, whose shoulder Bob cupped before taking a seat. Foster and I watched in a kind of mesmerized silence. The Slasher knocked his hand away.

But Bob was soon talking boisterously about the recent so-called Fight of the Century. "Yeah, what you said this morning, are you sure Pacquiao didn't injure his shoulder *after* the fight hauling all those Yankee dollars to his Manila bank? Or maybe injured it on purpose, for a few million extra from Money Mayweather to set up a rematch? But they fight ten times, Mayweather beats Pacman at least nine? You're crazy, gimme a—"

When Michael slammed the table with his fist and got everybody's attention. He stuck the same fist's forefinger at Bob: "Fuck that bullshit! *You* been fuckin' me all this time. You been fuckin' little pepper on me!" he roared, his mouth throwing off toxic spittle.

He flung himself back in the chair and dangled his arms, breathing audibly, a bad body ready to spring into action. The blond boy-man was long gone: the hair appeared less golden and more like dirty straw; his skin seemed to have lost tone as shadows played across his transforming face; his look grew so intense that even from where I sat his eyes appeared to cross.

Alarmed Bob saw it too, of course. He dialled back the power of his playful argument. He straightened up and slid his ass back on the chair, removing himself by that much from the chemical dump that was the transforming Michael. His feet now dangling off the floor, Bob looked like a child waiting for reprimand or release. But he appeared confused too, even baffled, and I had to strain to hear what he said.

"Little...Pep... *Where* did you get that, Michael?"

The Slasher was now huffing and puffing, straightening from his slouch with his arms slowly rising and seeming to pump up, and with increased spittle beginning to look like actual foaming at the mouth.

In that charged interval, Bob casually placed his Jew's harp in his mouth, keeping his own gaze averted, avoiding any mistaken visual challenge to the Market Slasher. For the first time I heard that Jew's harp as music. Just a single tone to begin, a lone one-note tune unearthed from deepest hurt, from buried sorrow and loss, from pain. If it continued that plaintively it would be too much to bear. So he changed to a twang of hope, picked it up and mixed it with something buzzing high, dropped again but now less forlornly. There really was a music to tame the savage breast, or so I felt and for his sake hoped.

The Slasher stood and stepped behind Bob's chair. In one practised motion he wrapped his left arm around the face so that Bob's chin was held in the crook of the elbow, reached for the Jew's harp with his right hand, cocked back the head, stabbed the neck and dragged the prong from ear to ear. He dropped Bob, who bounced on his chair and toppled sideways to the floor. The Slasher walked calmly past the stunned guards and through an interior door.

A slo-mo dawning...then the room went wild, with coffee cups and other small items flung into the air and the visitors instantly coagulating in a rush for the exit as the inmates pushed towards the containment corner to get a look. Foster and I began shouting that we were doctors, but with their big batons the guards pushed me back on top of Art, while those behind kept shoving Art forward into me.

I grew frenzied as the critical first moments ticked away and Bob's blood pumped onto the floor like a plum halo. I realized that

Foster's shouting the same thing as I was made it impossible for me to be taken seriously, so I turned and grabbed his collar and flung him into the sickos behind. I was trying to make my case more sensibly and caught a stick broadside on the chest. "I *am* a doctor!" I managed to scream, flailing at the guards. I heard a hiss off to the left and my eyes stung fiercely.

My cry was taken up by those around me and screeched effeminately — *I am a doctor! I'm a doctor! I'm a doctor!* — until the whole room was screaming it. I was alarmed at the amount of blood pooling now around Bob's whole upper body. I lost it.

I remember only that the bigger of the guards had me in a chokehold much like the one the Slasher had used on Bob. I may have been Tasered. The room was crackling and flashing and I felt myself losing consciousness... Released just before blacking out, I sat hard on my ass on the polished concrete floor. Noise, muffled, drowned vision, medicinal smell...

In a clearing daze I looked around. Armoured reinforcements had arrived and all the prisoners, Foster among them, were being shoved out to an alarm like the nasal sound teasing kids make, and through it all a calming female voice over the PA: *Lock down, return to cells immediately, lock down, return to cells immediately, lock down...*

I got to my feet and, gulping air, coughed out my plea to go to Bob. Freed up, the two guards finally checked my identification and, without apology, let me go.

I knelt down in the pool of tepid blood and turned Bob over. I let him lie against me sideways, I held him. He might have survived the shallowly cut throat, but the harp's trigger had torn both carotid arteries. Knowing that no pressure anywhere could do any good, I fought my doctor's reflexes and simply smiled into his shocked face.

"Bob, relax, you're dying, that's all, but quickly."

His face eased and he smiled small at the memory. Whispered, "Some joke, Thorpe."

"What heals can hurt ..."

He weakly touched the harp on its intact cowhide necklace, spluttered blood.

"Bob, I'm sorry but you have to tell me now. Who told you I was making fun of you?"

I could feel the life ebbing with the pulse's slowing *thump... thump* pump of blood from his neck. He was rasping, cheyne-stoking. Yet he managed hoarsely:

"I'm the one who's sorry, Lorne. I should have faced it long before now. Before he cut me, Michael growled, '*She loves* me, *you sawed-off runt. That's what she called you.*' She learned how to make men love her a long time ago, as a child, the poor thing. Life could be lived only as a lie. I still love her. Will you tell her that for me, Lorne?"

A sharp intake of breath, his eyes stared, then an emptying exhalation and I was sure he was dead.

I let him slump away from me, grabbed a fistful of his orange hair and yanked: "Who, Bob? Who?"

He tried to grip my wrist but was without strength, his fingers trailed off and splashed down. "She wants...save children...lil... pep..."

There is nothing more dead than a human body at the moment of death. Life is radically an on-off condition. I began to feel Bob's draining life drain my own body, as I did whenever a child died on me. Bob's body was only about the size of a...child's...

That's right! Little Marnee's heart had given out in the night! I had work to do!... True, I was a bit sticky with Bob's blood, but I could change at the hospital.

Unchallenged by the guards even though my pants, especially from the knees down, were sopping with blood, I walked out of that place. Still in red bow tie and canary-yellow suspenders, only A-Channel videographer Donny Kynder had hung around through lunch, but I was past his lulled self before he roused and recognized me. "Dr. Thorpe," he called after, "given that Dr. Foster was apprehended in your car, do you not admit to any culpability... in..."

Speeding off in Veronica's little Golf I popped a friendly Val.

I couldn't face my underground spot, so parked at emergency and put my sign on the dashboard. The doctors' dressing room was empty. I cannot fathom why we doctors are required to change in a sub-basement room with clanging metal lockers and a green-painted cement floor like a... Hey! The CHEO Team suits up!

Otto Fyshe, our mascot, came in before I could escape.

"Lorne, how are... Lose something?"

"Otto, would you say that down here we're on a level with our parking spots?"

"Perhaps, maybe a bit above. What are *you* doing down there?"

"Look at this."

"How's Veronica? Is that blood? But you're not on the emergency-surgery roster?"

I traced the crack for Otto, from the floor drain to where it disappeared behind the lockers, and looked up at him. But the man really is thick as a brick. I stood, thinking how gratifying it would be to punch him right in the face. I would. But then I remembered one useful thing about Otto: he's a sucker for flattery.

As I shucked off my weighted clothes: "Otto, you're a better pediatrician than any two men half your age. Please don't ever retire. We couldn't run this place without you!"

He smiled warily and nodded as I pulled on the green surgery scrubs and took the lab coat from my locker.

"Would you do me a biggie, Dr. Fyshe, and look after the paperwork to close Marnee's file? She's Dr. Foster's patient and he's, uh, indisposed for the foreseeable."

"No problem, Lorne. I heard. Is that what's eating you? Hey, here," he barked after me, "take my hanky! There's no call for..."

From a corner of the ceiling I watched myself risk a first-ever Tamara with Tamara: "Sistah, you be da bestest bee-otch at da stee-otch fac-a-tory."

She didn't get it. Let's face it: I was having an abominably bad day with jokes. I'd bombed with Foster, with Bob, and now with Tamara. This latest bomb jolted me right out of my senses. I didn't know who I was or who was watching whom. I thought of Dad... that bastard!

"Dr. Thorpe?" Tamara said. "I will ignore…" Then whispered, "Wait, I'll call you a cab."

"No! Call me Jekyll! Or Heckle! You've always thought me some sort of racist albino crow anyway, haven't you? *Well*, haven't you? Just who do you think you're talking to?"

She stepped back from her high counter: "I honestly don't know…"

I knew it!

She held a phone at the ready: "Is Veronica home?"

Per usual, I wasn't da go-to man o' da house. I had to go up on tiptoe and lean way across to pinch her glowing ebony chin in thumb and forefinger: "Not when where what who and *Wy*, my Nubian princess. Don't be dumb-dumb. Who am I?"

She materialized a fistful of Kleenex and kept one for herself. I blew my nose and simply tossed the mess on the floor. Like it mattered in this waiting room for hell's toilet! The stink of death and cleanser! Have I mentioned those?

Suddenly everybody's treating *me* like shit. Wazzup wid dat? *Me*…Dr. Lorne Thorpe! There. It had just been the momentary post-traumatic stress disorder of always having to be such an uptight prick and saviour of children, not even allowed a joke! *You* just try that for a lifetime! I needed some time to be alone with me, some "me time," as the good Dr. Phil regularly prescribes. But where?… I remembered the scene of my most recent triumph over Foster in the case of the arsenic-poisoned girl (it could be a Conan Doyle story title!), the Catholic privacy room—perfect! And beat a hasty.

I stood before the mural of Christ sitting beside the tree on that big solid rock cupping his holier-than-thou ass like a Flintstone easy chair, his arm loosely around a boy's waist. (*Welcome* touching, we can assume? Productive only of *Yes* feelings?) He was not preaching or exposing the thorny organ of his bleeding heart, thank the gods, or thank *his* dad, just smiling away at the little girl still proffering the lily …

Ah-ha! I was right! A shadowy fold in a petal of the white calla lily aligned perfectly with a fold of Jesus' white-ish robe, which crack

I followed upwards, which just missed Jesus' ear before disappearing into the ceiling. *There was a crack in the wall.* I hadn't been imagining it. It came from behind the couch, and not a hairline crack either but an expanding fissure! The trajectory pointed perfectly to my parking spot way down there.

Note to self: *We are spending scarce funds on emergency generators because of power failures brought on by overuse of air conditioning brought on by global warming brought on by the scientific revolution of the Enlightenment that makes my medical miracles and the Krazy Kitchen possible and here the whole hospital is falling down around our ears!*

Bring it!
I bolted for the Golf.

Chapter 16

Veronica had gone next door permanently, *moving in* with that glorified, oh-so-respectful grease monkey, Jack Kilborn! It was inconceivable! My wife of twenty years *shacking up* with the worst neighbour in the whole neighbourhood!

Jack wouldn't let me in the door. I reasonably said, "Jack, I need to talk with my wife. Everybody's been asking after her, per usual. I don't even know where Shawn is. Is she in there too, Jack? Or has she been spirited off by aliens? I need to talk with my wife and daughter, Jack. Don't make me force the issue *or* your door!" (Good one.)

The sun was shining down brightly, well past the meridian by then. Jays were laughing in the big blue spruces that surrounded us and crows were mocking me from the peaks of my neighbours' roofs. Over Jack's shoulder I caught sight of Veronica fluttering about *his* kitchen, preparing lunch for *his* retarded son!... But I must have hallucinated that. The Veronica I knew would be off somewhere crying. Regardless, *my* wife should be crying only in *my* house.

The wiry Jack stepped outside and squared up to me as if better to block my way. "Lorne, I don't own Trixie and you don't own Veronica." That got no reaction but my wincing at the stink of booze off him. "Where exactly have you been *living* for the past fifty years, Thorpe?"

"What the fuck does that mean *exactly*, Jack? Just because Trixie left you doesn't give you the right to covet thy neighbour's wife and family. Where the fuck have you been living for the past four thousand years, you ape!"

I moved to step around him, but he shifted to his right and blocked me. I stepped back and gave him my best appraising look.

I smirked at his thin, pasted hair, greasy from spending so much time under cars. He fixed me with his squinty Jack look, like he was examining me with a mechanic's lamp.

"Lorne, have you been in an accident or something?"

"Oh, you are *so* fucking sensitive, Jack. Well, fuck you! Fuck Trixie, and fuck that fucking wife of mine! Do you hear me in there?"

I half-turned, as if leaving, then rushed him. In a blink he took my left wrist, turned me around, bent the arm up my back and tossed me off his stoop.

"Don't try that again, Lorne. For your own safety. I'm a third-degree black belt in Muay Thai. I'll kick the shit out of you."

Try what? What had happened? My left arm was raging at the shoulder. I could hardly prop myself on my knees. I shuffled round on all fours to face him or, rather, to look up at him. What *could* I do again? Ram him in the knees with my head? Had that been a fight? I'd been manhandled. His front door shut softly behind him.

Up there with the crows, I watched myself get up, dust myself off, turn and haul my pitiful carcass to my garage. I was looking down at a silly little man in a doll's house. For some reason of unreason, the sorry fellow was still wearing his doctor's costume. With the sort of smile that defines dissociation, I fondled his stethoscope. Or mine. At least I was back in my body.

I heard the noise of an aluminum door opening. My heart leapt—Veronica, Shawn and Owen come to hug me! Surprise! You're on America's Funniest Fuck-ups!

Jack called across the strip of yard between our two houses: "And, Lorne, if there is any more trouble whatsoever, this time I'm calling the police! Veronica agrees with me. I'm fond of you, neighbour, and very sorry for your troubles, but Veronica and me, well, we have some things to work out."

Veronica and me, spoken by the neighbourhood's number one asshole, who was drinking heavily in the middle of the day? I ran from my garage into the driveway shaking a rake in Jack's direction. There was no one there. I must have looked a sight to the crows. It was one of those rakes as big as a trellis!

So of course I went down to the curb and stood watch. The Tanzanian Marathoner approached on the sidewalk and scowled at me as he passed. For years he's been loping by on his bandaged knee with never so much as a grunt of recognition and now he scowls? But I wasn't doin' nothin'!

O, end of summer day of hopeless leaves of grass and desiccated red maples. O, the world is too much with us lately, the world is weary of us. Some of us anyway.

Or not so much *scowled* as smirked disdainfully. But what had I ever done to the Tanzanian Marathoner? Openly, I mean. Could some new conspirator have told him he's a running joke in my home repertoire? (*There's* a groaner for you, Gary Lewis!) I'd just been standing there with my rake upside down, doin' nothin', and he has the bold effrontery, the temerity...well, I never!

Or perhaps the intent Tanzanian Marathoner had simply been disgusted by the incongruous sight of me: in my hospital scrubs, with stethoscope pendant, posed with an upside-down rake like some Healthcare Gothic? That's a distinct possibility, or a vague one.

Oh, scowl away, my nut-brown familiar, if you will. Or smirk disdainfully, at your peril. Because, my self-deceived Tanzanian, I now see clearly for the very first time that there is more dignity in *refusing* to enter the stadium when you're dead last. When you're beaten so badly and running on empty, there is honour, my aged friend, in quitting. In saying: *That's it, no more, not another excruciatingly painful step, I'm through, all in. Point me to the graveyard and I'll save you the trouble, do a Marathon of Hop to my final resting place.* And just quit. Quit already!

So, I wasn't *just doin' nothin'* standing down there by the street. I was thinking of literally doing nothing ever again. What really is the point of raking fallen leaves that would only grow again the following spring to die and fall again the following fall? Oh, my dear Tanzanian Marathoner, *mon semblable*, there is indeed something in dying, repetitive nature that mocks our striving selves, our little lives...big time!

Home life has settled back into its cyclical routine following the near miss of a cruise missile? Comfortable once more, are we, following the wise-daddy handling of the explosive family crisis of a lifetime?

Bang! Boom! Kabloomski!

Why, my dear Tanzanian Marathoner, should I live on running retarded circles to my meaningless grave? If I'm going to die alone anyway, now's as good a time as any! That order of nuns, the Caesarean Sisters or whatever, the ones who go every day into their convent's back yard and remove a teaspoonful of dirt from their future graves—those holy Goth chicks have the right idea, let me tell you!

Okay, maybe I'd imagined it. The Tanzanian Marathoner scowling at me, I mean. Maybe—and here's a thought to conjure with—mayhap the lonely long-distance T-M had intended his ghastly rictus in fraternal sympathy? If so, take your mug away, loser! That be *my* will. Healthcare Gothic indeed!

And that's pretty well why I'd leered horribly at him as he approached and passed.

...Dear God, don't let me be mad.

At the very least...I was resolved to stand there forever, just so. When along came Shawn on her bike, entering the curve at the bottom of our crescent and slowing...stopping to have a long word with the Tanzanian Marathoner. I would have to be on my especial guard.

She arrived breathless in a way that biking never made her. Up to something, all right. For sure.

"Why are you dressed like work, Dad?"

"Your mom's *still* not home."

"What?" She was suddenly alert to the threat of yet more strangeness in her familiar world.

"*Your mother* is next door with Jake's father again. Where have you been, young lady? You can't be out riding if you're staying home sick from school."

"Today's a PD day, didn't Mom tell you? Duh, like no bus this morning? I was just talking to some kids over at Shoal Park. You should *see* the playground. It's all torn up and Bob Browne's machine is still there. Go look if you don't believe me!"

"I don't know." *No more lies.*

"What's Mom doing at the Kilborns' again? She's there all the time now."

"I don't know." *You tell me.*

But she wouldn't.

"What were you and the Tanzanian Marathoner talking about just now, young lady?"

"That's *not* his name, Dad. It's Mr. Singh Cahir."

It was his name only days ago, my little Judas.

She may have sniffled, she drew her bare forearm across her nose. "Why are you dressed in your doctor clothes and holding the rake upside down? Is that blood on your face?"

"I don't know. Why shouldn't it be? Have you taken your allergy meds?"

"Yes, first thing when I got…back, re-*mem*-ber?"

That was said a bit too brokenly for my liking. I pressed my advantage. "I thought so. Where did you go with the man and the dog? You had a severe allergic reaction. Was it to a trailer in a field somewhere outside the city? Was it to a farm? A barn with hay for kids to jump in? I'll bet that was fun!"

Then her eyes really got big. "Huh? Da-ad, I told you about all that. Nothing happened! It's just a…a game we're playing." Her brow furrowed: "Did Jake tell you something? That stupid re… But we didn't go anywhere far away like that. Are you imitating a zombie now, Dad? *Stop* that with your eyes. You're scaring me!"

I love you.

She turned away in disgust, walked her bike up the driveway and alongside the garage. The sound of the back door slamming snapped me out of it.

She was sitting in the lotus position with the TV remote in her hand. She had recorded *Wy Knots* in order to keep a secret appointment in the playground. The tinkling bells and there was Wy coming down the Eightfold Path with his goat…with Wei, to open the show.

Danger, danger: bells had tinkled just before Lu-Ping died. Wy keeps on coming, alarmingly so, right up close to the camera, and mimes opening a small door with pinching thumb and forefinger, smiles in at us in our family rooms. He looks down: "Wei, when is door not door?" Tight shot of Wei's goat face, which shows why a goat's strange mug—those perfectly symmetrical horns, those vertical pupils—has often inspired representations of the devil. A deep echoing voiceover gives Wei's thoughts: "Don't be dumb-dumb, ask again." Cut to close-up of wise Wy, whose forefinger comes up alongside his nose: "When is open crack! Ha-ha!" Shawn feigned a chuckle but didn't get it. How could she have? Wy, who did his shows live and often had comical trouble with the English language, had murdered the stupid old joke: When is a door not a door? When it's *a-jar*. I remembered it from an ancient Bazooka Joe bubblegum cartoon.

I went and stood by the patio doors, fingered a leaf of the jade tree that wouldn't thrive anywhere in that house. *Or...wise Wy knew of Honourable Dad's hundred-fold troubles and was sending a coded message. I mean: When is open crack?...* Dear God, don't let me be...

I spoke as if to our suffocating cedar hedge, "Where's Owen?"

"I dunno," she snapped. "Still sleeping probably, sh-sh."

"He didn't go for a tattoo, *did he?*" I didn't know why I sang it conspiratorially like that.

I went and stood close behind her. "You talked to a man in a white van beside the library, didn't you?"

"What?" She giggled. "Oh, he means *a-jar*! I know that riddle. A door can be ajar! Silly Wy. When is open crack, ha-ha!"

It was like a sledge to the back of my head. "A man in a white van with a dog. He pulled over and you went and talked with him. The dog may not have been feeling well, dehydration or perhaps something dyspeptic. So you already knew that man and his sick dog at the museum, didn't you? Who was it? One of the Lewis brothers? Frank Baumhauser? Tell me!"

I leaned over her, saw her thumb move to increase the volume. She was definitely hiding something from me. More bad things were going to happen imminently, worse things. Kevin said so. She'd been returned unharmed *this time*. She could be taken from me again in the wink of an eye if I wasn't vigilant as a harem eunuch. Wy knew. She *would* be taken away from me. It was inevitable. But why was she lying to me? All I'd ever done was love her.

She paused the show and looked up at me backwards, the face as inhuman as Wei's with its upside-down green eyes. "Da-ad, that white van story's a suburban legend, everybody knows that! Whoever told *you* that stupid story is a retarded liar." She frowned: "It wasn't Jake, was it? If he ruins it…"

She returned to the TV, her swirled dandelion hair sparking the air. Wy squeezed himself a small glass of red from a wineskin, smiled at it: "All God's gifts good in moderation." He stopped himself with the glass at his mouth, frowned at the camera: "Wine only for grown-up!" He exaggerated his frown, his Fu Manchu menacing: "Never drugs!" Cut to the goat, who nodded, his vertical pupils dead serious.

"Look at me when I'm talking to you, young lady!"

She turned her head to the left and looked up, her lower lip already protruding.

"Where did you go with that man and dog in the white van from the museum? Who was it? What are you hiding?"

"I *can't* tell or she won't—Wy won't…" She clamped her trembling mouth. Her lips made a dry parting sound when she spoke: "Don't be dumb-dumb, ask—"

It was no more than a singular instant out of time, stepping round her, dipping at the knees and cracking her across the face, stopping that dandelion clock dead. Then slow motion, the nimbus of hair whipping dreamily, throwing off a spray of light, lashing my shins on the recoil, her green eyes shocked, beautiful face contorting. Pain. Caused by me. The man who loved her most in all the world.

She was up and out the side door. I ran after. She went left—I froze—then went right. I had nowhere to go.

I hid among the trees, leaning against a trunk and spying on the few kids in Shoal Park. They were excited over the destruction of the playground. As the day waned, fathers and mothers came to fetch them. The parents took in the wasted playground—the toppled equipment, the smashed jungle gym, the gouged ground—in bewilderment, turned and hurried away as if shirking someone else's trouble.

I wrapped my arms around a trunk, pressed my cheek to the bark and inhaled its musty cork. And just held on for dear life for I didn't know how long.

Someone walking a dog somewhere behind me said my name: "Dr. Thorpe? Is that you…Lorne Thorpe?" I didn't turn, but it eventually brought me round from my reverse crucifixion.

Touching other trunks for support—stumbling, I guess, maybe even careening—I made my way to the rubble of what had been the jungle gym. I sat staring at the playground's only remaining recognizable feature: the small hill where once Owen, and for a while Owen and Shawn, had run up and tumbled down, Shawn in a hurry to catch up with her big brother. I'd regularly taken them to this playground after supper to give Veronica a break (after she'd cleaned up). I was always exhausted myself and milked the favour for all it was worth. But the truth was, I'd looked forward to the walk and play more than Veronica knew, because I never told her, and probably more than the children did. Too late now. Words to die by.

But really now, pondering the distinction more closely: what is the difference between a hit and a slap? Because I didn't hit her, I slapped her. That much we can establish incontrovertibly. Granted, *slap* would be a subcategory of *hit*. And *backhand* a subcategory of *slap*? And so on in descending order of severity to *gentle backhand* at the bottom?

The very bottom. That's where I was and where I belonged.

The nimbus of hair whipping dreamily, throwing off a spray of light, lashing my shins on the recoil, her green eyes popping, beautiful face contorting. Shock and pain.

I needed to lie down, just for a spell. I tripped onward. Where was *my* white rag?

Is *suicide* a subcategory of *murder*? Or of *death*? They say a suicide murders the world.

But does any of that shit even matter anymore? Am I simply finished? Not worth anyone's attention anymore?

I think so.

Chapter 17

It was seeing the groundhog gave me the idea. Maybe because my mind was as blank as that of a newborn chick looking to imprint on whatever's going: a moving finger, a dwarf trickster, a detective...a groundhog. Not the groundhog *emerging* from the mound in the playground, impressive as that was: the sudden brown head in dry grass, the ratty snout sniffing the wind, the surprisingly plump emergence (consider the rodents of the fields: one's entranceway should be as small as possible in the event big trouble comes calling), a circuit of his territory, the scurrying return at the alarm of some sixth sense (falling leaves? rapid shadows? destroyed world?).

No, it wasn't the emergence but the return that put the idea in my head, the beat *retreat*—the arse-end wiggling into the earth, the groundhog's going back to ground. *That* melted my muscles, softened my bones, made me want so to snuggle into earthy depression myself.

Not to die, just to lie down, in a hole in the ground, alone, quietly, for an eternal spell. Perhaps to dream a dream of tens of thousands of groundhogs overrunning Troutstream like Pied Piper rats, raiding the fat larders of the middle class, carrying off the excess babies of the Project poor, undermining the very foundations of our lying suburban world!

Was I nuts? Who knew anymore? All I knew was that I was lying in a hole in the devastated Shoal Park playground, still wearing my hospital scrubs and lab coat, still with my silly stethoscope round my stupid neck. More comfortable than I'd been in days. Maybe more than I'd ever been in my whole worried life above ground. So if I wasn't clinically certifiable, I was playing a pretty good game of Mad Hatter.

The air at ground zero was earth-moist and filled alternately with light and shadows. Way up above, low clouds in smoky clumps scudded a late summer's indigo sky. As the sun flashed aslant, the semi-translucent leaves seemed actually to increase the green light. Though that's impossible: obstruction, opacity, cannot increase illumination. Some things still are, you know. Impossible, I mean. Oh, not the destruction of the careful life one has constructed over decades. That is quite possible. That—flash destruction, cosmic mockery—is, in fact, highly probable. *In fact*, given the second law of thermodynamics, the entropic tendency of organized energy and the inevitable end of existence... Well, a word of warning, a word to the wise: destruction of the well-ordered world of groundhogs and men, instant and otherwise, is to be expected, is the natural and most likely outcome of this thing we call living. What is *im*possible is continued contentedness (see: Bob Browne above and Lorne Thorpe below).

I slept, or passed out, in a hole in a playground. What more can I say?

I came to more soberly to view close-up a few grains of earth crumbling on the wall of my hole; then more, like the beginning of a minuscule dam collapse. Was I to be buried alive?... No, my hole was too shallow for that. Instead I anticipated the welcome dark head of my brother hole-dweller, the groundhog, come a-calling with some *Wind in the Willows* notes on living well underground. But it proved to be only a lost earthworm, plumping out sideways as though my earthen hole were evolving a fat lip.

And how do you feel, Brother Worm, having come to the end of your world as you knew it?... Nothing? Put 'er there, pardner!

I sat up and took in the brave new childless world of Shoal Park playground.

It still looked as if some very unfriendly giant had stomped it. And it was pitted hugely, as from a bomb shelling. The litter of play equipment had been ripped out by a backhoe whose mechanical mouth still hung over its last hole like some masticating monster. Only toppled litter and holes now where just yesterday there had been a three-swing set, two slides, a geodesic affair called Rocket to the Moon, and the complex of poisoned cedar called jungle gym. Only yesterday, children and parents had played beneath these sheltering trees, with squeals, laughter, shouts, repeated parental cautions, and with the children unwittingly inhaling toxic levels of arsenic from the treated wood and saturated earth. Now, only this dappled brightness, this silence, this late summer's afternoon in a ruined playground. Holes, only holes, where once the missing children played.

And I, Lorne Thorpe, MD, alone in my personal hole, right where Bob Browne had lately promised to put me. Forlorn Lorne, as the traitorous Veronica sometimes sympathetically called me, when she'd still loved me. Soon it would be dark, but I couldn't move, let alone go home. Home? Don't make me laugh. Ha-ha. I didn't want to go anywhere anyway. I would sit here—I lay back down—lie here forever in this wasted playground. Don't bother telling me that the going's got tough and now the tough must get going. Go to hell. Been tough, done that. For me, it's game over—

"Fun's over, Lorne."

Detective Beldon? Kevin! Why, Kevin, you old mind reader! Was I hallucinating his small ginger head hovering up there like some competing sun? I needlessly shaded my eyes in a salute.

"Ah, a voice from on high! And the voice of the law to boot!"

"Out of that hole now, Lorne. We have work to do."

He didn't sound surprised to have found me situated so. He just extended a bony hand at the end of an elongated arm.

"We?" I flailed about till he clasped my hand. "But you've heard about Bob Browne?"

As he pulled me up, he grunted softly: "Yes, I've seen Bob Browne's body. You should have waited for me. And yes, *we*. I'm stumped, I need your help."

He took in the mess of the playground. "I'll tell you something else and for now it's strictly *entre nous*. Promise?"

"Promise." And I gave my best Boy Scout salute.

He looked like he already regretted telling me. "The Lewis brothers did this damage."

"Ah-ha! We have our boys! I knew it!"

"Put down your filthy finger, Doctor. They thought they were getting even with Bob Browne. They got his backhoe from where he'd been hiding it at your Troutstream Community Centre and did this, hoping to pin it on him."

I bit strenuously into my knuckle. Eureka! "*That* was the diesel smell! At first I'd thought Alice Pepper-Pottersfield thought I'd thought she'd farted. But it was Debbie Carswell had let Bob Browne hide his equipment from the repo men in the centre's big equipment room! Sympathetic Alice knew, of course. She may have thought my question about the smell was teasing her because I'd told the repo men where Bob's equipment was hidden!"

Beldon made his pained sinuses face. "And that, I regret to say, is exactly why I need your help, Lorne. You know more than you think you know, which is just about always the case. It's murder now with Bob Browne, so it won't be long before the case is taken away from me, if I don't solve it fast."

He smile-frowned at me with the professional curiosity I myself use with patients I may need to distance myself from. "But *are* you crazy now, Lorne? Is that what this is all about?" He tapped his left temple. "Because if this isn't a game and you really *are* cracked, you won't be a help to anyone, not to your family or your friends and neighbours or to me. *Or* to yourself, obviously." He grew a bit angry: "We'll just throw in the towel and admit you to the Royal Ottawa and you can spend the rest of your days playing handball with your own shit!"

"Ha! Perfect! But I *told* you those Lewis boys were out to get me! And get Bob Browne! And get *at* me through Foster!"

He softened, squinted at me: "Lorne, you really cracked? Or is it still the booze and drugs?"

"You tell me." I blinked hard, like something long and jagged was twirling around in my own sinuses.

He placed a hand on my shoulder: "I was by your house just now and Owen sent me to your neighbour's."

Going by his face, I must have responded physically to the psychic body blow.

"You have cause to be mad, Lorne. That Jack Kilborn, I recognized the type right away. All along everybody's thinking it's Trixie Kilborn who's the cause of all their troubles. And she is, of course. But it's the Jacks of the world who enable the Trixies to do their thing. In some sick way it satisfies *his* needs."

The cool accuracy of his analysis had the effect of smelling salts. That, and him, his voice and very presence.

"But you have to forget Jack Kilborn for now, Lorne. We're dealing with a sick criminal mind. And I need your help if we're going to catch him, or her."

He led me by the stethoscope to the smashed rubble of the jungle gym. We picked our seats with care. He lit a small cigar and let a dark cloud drift from his lips.

I shifted. "You don't suppose one could contract arsenic poisoning through the arse, do you?"

"Lorne, it's not unusual what Veronica has done. It's temporary, I'm sure. It's eminently forgivable, if you love her. And I'm also sure it doesn't mean what you fear it means."

"What about what I've done?"

"Sorry, I don't follow…?"

I looked away as I told him about hitting Shawn.

"You weren't yourself." He made a decision, a selfish one. "How do you feel now? Are you strong enough to help me?"

Grateful for the distraction, I did an internal systems check. I felt incredibly weary and weak, wanted badly just to lie down again and this time do a Rip Van Winkle. "I guess so. For a while there I felt great, energized, manic. Now I feel dry and shrunken. But I'm not crazy, if that's what you mean. I don't think I *was* crazy, except when I hit Shawn. You have news, you said?"

"More bad news, I'm afraid, though not as bad as Bob Browne's murder. The Market Slasher committed suicide this afternoon, just after you ran and I arrived to have a little talk with him. He tore up his own artery with a screw he'd been hiding."

I lowered my head and shook it, whistled air from my lungs. "Two deaths now, a homicide and a suicide."

He puffed on his cigar. "I had it all figured out. Sure Bob Browne was our man, a psychopath who believed he was Peter Pan, planning to teach Troutstream's promise-breaking grown-ups a lesson by kidnapping the children to his version of the magic mountain under the Laurier Street Bridge or somewhere." It was his turn to lower and shake his head.

"Don't be too hard on *yourself*, Detective. But are you saying there's *no* connection between the defaulted payments to Bob Browne and the missing children and Shawn? And so no connection to the Lewis brothers? And Foster's arrest? We're right back to square one?"

"No, I'm not saying that. I'm confident that everything's connected and I have a couple of hunches, but that's all. But I'm, uh, kinda stumped just where to turn next."

It cost him to say that. He sort of drooped.

"Fucking Lewises," I said. "I bet it is still them. Or they paid some thugs."

"At least by stealing the backhoe and wrecking the playground, they've justified my harassing them earlier. Idiots, the playground was slated to be cleared anyway. For all I know, it may yet be them. I don't think so, but one of my hunches involves paying them another little visit."

"Fucking Foster."

"Fucking Slasher."

"Fucking Jack Kilborn."

Kevin smiled small. "I still don't know where Bob Browne lives. Or lived, I guess. Foster doesn't know either. And he still won't divulge his first contact for Bob Browne. He says he took a solemn oath — not his regular oath, I guess — but I'm going to get him to change his mind on that, and pronto, or have him made an accessory to murder. If all else fails, there's the word on the street. He got around, your man Bob Browne, especially with the street kids. I'm gonna find out one way or another and when I do I want you with me, Lorne, later today, I hope, or first thing tomorrow. You knew Bob, he trusted you, you could be a help, notice something I miss. There *is* an accomplice still at large and he could get to Bob's place ahead of me and remove or destroy evidence. Or she could. Homicide is on Browne's case now and they could beat us to his place too."

I said leadingly, "This hoped-for someone could count on Bob Browne to visit the Slasher at the detention centre. And this someone would have had to visit the Slasher first to get him to kill Bob, and all in a short time, since Tuesday morning. Art Foster did talk about a slutty female claiming to be the Slasher's relative, who was also a friend of Bob's."

"I got that from Foster too. It's what I'd been hoping to get out of the Slasher: *who* set him up to murder Bob Browne? The list of petitioning visitors, all manner of whack-jobs, is too long to get through in time, that's what Homicide will be doing. The so-called American cousin is just a fake number and address in the visitors' register. The guards tell me you were present when it happened, Lorne, that you and Foster witnessed it all, that you were with Bob when he died. Foster remembers nothing helpful, but you must."

"They got in an argument, I couldn't hear clearly, something about boxing, somebody named...*Little Pep*, I think. It was done in an instant and Bob was dead."

Kevin considered, squinted: "Could it have been *Willie Pep*? He was featherweight champion in the 1940s."

I showed bemused incredulity.

"Yes, I'm a fight fan, a dying breed. But how could that lead to murder? The Slasher's psycho, okay, but an argument over Willie Pep's place in boxing history? What the hell."

"The Slasher did shout something unintelligible about Willie Pep, though it sounded like *Little* Pep to me. And then Bob Browne talked about this Willie Pep just before he died, his last words in fact. He wanted me to save Willie Pep. It was probably just some dying echo from the argument with the Slasher. All that blood, the brain depleted of oxygen, he wasn't making sense."

"And he said nothing else? Think. *Remember.*"

I'd let him down. He touched my right wrist, wrapped his lanky left hand around it and held. I didn't mind. I closed my eyes and pictured Bob dying in my arms.

"Just some incoherent words about saving children too."

He flung the butt of his cigar from his right hand. "Let's go. My car's back at your house. My day's not done, but yours is."

I hurried to keep up. "Bob's dying gibberish means something to you?"

"Maybe. I may not have been so far off seeing Bob as a deluded Peter Pan out to save Troutstream's children from their lying parents."

"No offence, Kevin, but you're confusing Peter Pan with the Pied Piper."

"I don't know what they mean yet, but Bob's dying words sure have the feel of a big puzzle piece. In my experience, people don't waste their dying breath."

"In mine too." I needed to win back his respect. "Here's something Shawn's not telling us: she was taken somewhere outside the city before being dropped off at the soccer fields."

He smiled quizzically at me, controlling his eagerness.

I said, "She's displaying the symptoms of a pretty severe exposure to ragweed, which you don't get around here."

"What about the soccer fields?"

"Not concentrated enough."

He was impressed. "That *could* prove helpful, Lorne."

"But what sort of sicko are we dealing with, Kevin? Two, three more kidnappings, Bob Browne sacrificed, even the Slasher's suicide?"

"Listen," he said across his shoulder, "I have a memory-regression technique I've sometimes used successfully. It could help you better remember the scene at the detention centre. Would you be up for it? It's a little weird."

"I'm up."

Once again only Owen was home: laid out on the couch in the family room, surrounded by two damaged soda cans, with his old

PlayStation console like dead flowers on his chest. Though prone, he was still wearing his cap backwards.

"Mom home yet?"

He didn't even look, just made a noise such as a bothered cow might make.

"Shawn with Mom?"

"Dunno."

"Owen, I asked you a question." I recognized my temper flashing in the way that had made me hit Shawn, and it chilled me. I was watching myself again and didn't like what I was seeing in my attitude with my son.

"No. And no to whatever else you ask."

Okay, maybe he'd been sleeping and I'd woken him. He'd not noticed that Kevin was with me.

"Owen, we have a guest."

He looked, wide awake now. What had he been looking at? The TV was off. The ceiling? Had I been missing signs of drug use? He didn't smile, but flapped a hand at Kevin off the PlayStation console.

"Owen?" I said sharply.

Kevin said, "It's all right, Lorne. Owen's got a lot on his mind."

Owen frowned at the ceiling: "Where the hell have *you* been?"

"Sit up and mind your manners or you'll wish you had." I heard my own father's voice and was drowning again, it happened that suddenly.

He not only sat up but got up and walked out of the house. He'd had his runners on! He was leaving!

Forlorn Lorne Thorpe hurried out the side door and commenced shouting from the porch: "Owen, get your ass back here this instant!" He kept walking, turned left. "Oh, all right, run to *Mommy*, you big sucky baby. See if I care! All of you!" I flung my arms at the invisible legions abandoning me. "Go be Jack's family now! The Kilborn fucking bunch! The perfect name for your reality show, ha! Be brother and sister and mother to Jake the retard! But no tattoo, do you hear me, Owen! No—"

Kevin had jerked me back into the house by the collar. I raised my fists *à la* John L. Sullivan and called the only thing I knew from boxing: "*Let's get ready to rum-ble!*" I lunged.

When I regained consciousness I was sitting on the kitchen floor's terracotta tiles. Then he was hauling me up from behind by the armpits.

"Sorry about that, Lorne. You were hys…overwrought. Are you okay?"

I touched my right cheekbone. It was tender and hot.

"Did you hit me?" I heard my prissily offended tone.

"You attacked me, Lorne. You're not cut, but you'll have a bruise there." He was amused, the prick. "Don't fret, it's just a delayed response to trauma. I see it a lot. That and the cocktail of whatever you've been taking."

I smiled painfully, but felt my spirits returning yet again, strange to say. Felt myself knocked back together some. It was Kevin.

"Thanks, I, uh, needed that. Would you believe I've actually lost *two* fights today? And I'd never had *one* fight in my entire life! Would you be willing to give me boxing lessons, Kevin?"

He made me fetch the special bottle I'd tried to entice him with on the phone. I didn't have to be told to have a double. He had a single himself. He said he knew I had sedative and told me to fetch it, all of it. He threatened me with arrest for assaulting an officer. So I took the smoky vial from my pocket and emptied it down the toilet. I reached for the Macallan and he allowed me another double.

"You get a good night's sleep, Lorne, which I expect you will now. As I said before, you're no good to anyone in this condition."

I was being moved along, as cops will the unruly, and I slurred, "Tomorrow we go…sleuthing, right?"

I do believe he laughed: "Tomorrow we go sleuthing."

"And…"

"Tomorrow, Lorne, okay?"

"O…kay."

I was lying where Owen had just lain. I remember thinking: *Beldon's using me. Thank the gods, someone still has use for Lorne Thorpe.*

No dreams. I would never dream again. Bob Browne was sleeping with saints and angels. Willie Pep had been featherweight champion of the world till Mike Tyson ate him. Veronica was dreaming about prescription sunglasses with somebody new. I saw that man hitting Shawn. I would kill him. If I could just get up. I'd get that old bottle of diazepam from when Veronica...babies...Shawn's hard birth... working round the clock... My own daddy was telling me to get up and take my medicine like a man. I really wanted to. But Kevin had ordered me to get a good night's sleep. Veronica was right about me. We had work to do...in the morning...sleuth...ing.

Chapter 18

I awoke to the sound of rustling paper in the kitchen. Through the doorway I saw two brown lunch bags standing like familiar flags on the kitchen island, Veronica's back... Veronica's back!

I'd fallen asleep on the family room couch. But I did that sometimes when home from work so late that going to bed would disturb her. I patted myself down: still in my lab coat...with stethoscope? Bad form, but even that too happened occasionally in normal life.

The phone was ringing, then it wasn't. I looked at my watch: eight o'clock. I'd slept close to twelve hours! I kept my eyes on Veronica as I came through the café doors. She pressed the phone over her heart, feigning obliviousness, then she saw my face.

"What happened to you? Did you get in *a fight*?"

"Yes, with Kevin Beldon. And before that, with lover-boy Jack. Didn't he tell you, I'm not much at fightin' for my woman?"

Her face returned to blank. "It's Detective Beldon." She pinched the end of the phone so as to avoid any contact with me on the handover.

Kevin was on his way. I hung up.

Looking sideways at her, I touched my tender cheekbone, cringed for pity, got none. I was piecing together the previous day. As it came back to me, I abandoned the project.

She spoke over folding the bag tops: "Owen and Shawn left without their lunches again. Shawn's in a state and so is Jake. I'm—"

"You slept here last night?"

"The kids did. I didn't sleep. I'm dropping these off at their schools."

"Then you're coming back here? Veronica…"

She was out the side door. I should have said *fightin' for the woman I love*. I shouldn't have joked at all. I should learn when to shut up.

I hurried to the front door and watched her get in the Golf. She looked around at the untidy state of the front seat, crinkling her nose. That was cute. I hoped she'd not recognized the stains and smell as blood. Instead of driving off, she got out and went back to Jack's.

I waited, but she didn't return to the car.

I missed her so. And the children already.

I wished them well, without me.

I changed out of my filthy hospital scrubs into suburban wear and waited for Kevin at the front door. The Golf was *still* in the driveway. The Crown Vic pulled up at the curb and didn't shut off. I went and got in.

Kevin slipped the yellow tin of Panters from his shirt pocket and lit up off the old car's lighter. Opening his window a crack, he blew out the side of his mouth. We shot from the curb. At Izaak Walton Road we turned north towards St. Joseph's, then onto the Queensway West. It was morning rush hour. Kevin was breathing hard.

I said, "How'd you find out where Bob Browne lived?"

Peering around for an opening to jump into the bus lane, he said, "Bob's something of a hero among the street kids. A few more stops late last night, and by early this morning under the Laurier Street Bridge I had his address, I'm pretty sure. I should have gone there right away, but I was dead tired and afraid I could mess something up, and I said I'd meet you, *and* I still need your help. Probably a mistake already, waiting, because I'd forgotten the accomplice. *That's* what deep fatigue does to the brain."

"What do you need me for?"

He looked at me and, satisfied, said, "Lorne, I'm pleased to see you're your old self. I believe we're still a step ahead of

Homicide—another reason I shouldn't have waited. But I need someone, and I won't risk Frank Thu's career again. You knew Bob Browne. He liked you. I'm expecting this could get ugly and I'm gonna need everything you know, even if you don't know you know it."

"Perfectly clear." I looked at his profile. He was...glinting. He was using me, all right, to make Homicide, which he would. If he wanted to, Kevin Beldon could one day own the police.

He opened his window farther and flicked out the cigar butt, took the cherry off the dash and fixed it to the roof. He didn't hit the siren but we sped up as he shifted into the bus lane on the right. Off the Queensway at King Edward and down into Lowertown, he made that big old boat perform. He slowed to read the house numbers and pulled up at a dilapidated complex on St. Patrick's Street.

The apartment door was open, though not broken in, like someone had heard us coming and run for it. The room spoke of compulsive ordering and hurried chaos. Its dominant feature was piles and stacks of things: ancient VHS video cassettes dominated, but also lots of newspapers, magazines, pamphlets, photo albums and loose photos, letters and postcards, with silver computer disks cascading like spilled treasure. Much of the print material was in big Ziploc bags, as though evidence had been pre-packaged. The magazines were bundled, though sliding off in places too.

Cobwebs with desiccated flies draped a window that had never been opened. One dumb-dumb fly wouldn't stop bumping its head softly against the dirt-coated glass. A few breezy shirts lay crumpled about. In a corner, dirty grey-and-red thermal socks half hid a pair of green rubber boots.

Shouting came continually like raving sickness through the walls and floor and ceiling.

A cursory inspection revealed that all the media was devoted to the same subject: child beauty pageants. And the show of fixation was always the same: *Our Little Miss*.

Had we really found our man? The late Bob Browne? I couldn't believe it.

OUR LITTLE MISS. The show's name was also the label on every video cassette, followed by tape number, the level of competition, place and time, all printed neatly in black marker. The first cassette Kevin inserted in the old VCR was titled OUR LITTLE MISS #11: STATE FINALS, ATLANTA, 1/5/79.

The third little girl to take the giant step up onto the platform and totter stiffly towards centre stage looks most like a high-gloss wooden doll from another time: painted eyes with raking lashes, brightly rouged, stiffly animated. The hair towers in a blonde bouffant three times the length of the tiny shining face. The smile, too, is as permanently fixed as a marionette's. The arms are stiff at the sides with the hands turned out at the wrists like thalidomide flippers. The crinoline dress suggests a debutante's coming-out party somewhere posh — Cape Cod, the Hamptons, Beverly Hills — those legendary locales mythologized for the trash moms.

The child on the small dusty screen is named Little Pepper. The event's hostess, Auntie Alice, singsongs: "Little Pepper says she enjoys making mud pies and watching *Face the Nation*."

No one laughs.

When the shot cuts to Little Pepper's mother, who looks eerily like Auntie Alice, Mom is grittily beaming and nodding approval, even as she keeps her own arms tight to her sides and turns stiffly. And when the song portion commences ("You Light Up My Life"), she sings in mimicry of the cute tongue-tied mimicry that is Little Pepper.

Little Pepper completes a full circuit of the stage, like a mechanized baby bride atop a musical wedding cake, and curtsies. She exits somewhat less petitely (stompingly, in fact, gleeful that it's over). Her turn is followed by some dozen others. This is the "Not Tots" portion of competition, we've been informed, ages four to six.

Not Tots ends with the one boy in the competition: "Here he is, our perennial King…King Robbie!" And as King Robbie struts out in his little tux, complete with frill-fronted mauve shirt and crimson cummerbund, Auntie Alice gushes in hushed tones:

"Robbie is learning to play the harmonica and says he'd like to make the *whole world* sing a fun song!"

The shots of the backstage moms show a number of other child contestants awaiting their call ("backstage" meaning crowded behind grey bifold room dividers). The kids, whose competition days would be spent waiting on folding chairs in overly heated or cold rooms, are the picture of sullenness. Chins on hands, feet not reaching the floor, intermittently being pulled and pinched and hissed at with last-minute instructions, they mostly wait and keep neat.

The only activity from the waiting children is their group response to Auntie Alice's tagline. The mistress of ceremonies intermittently startles the room with a shouted question:

"What's that smell?"

"Money!" the kids and adults shout back.

"Let them hear you over in Dallas, Austin! What's that smell?"

"Money!" the whole room erupts.

Kevin switched tapes. OUR LITTLE MISS #12: STATE FINALS, MEMPHIS, 1/6/79. More of the same. Fast-forward. More of the same. Skip a couple of months. More of the same.

OUR LITTLE MISS #15: STATE FINALS, LITTLE ROCK, 1/9/79. Little Pepper likes boys who know how to treat a girl of any age like a lady and watching *Kung Fu*, her bestest friend Robbie's favourite show too. King Robbie has learned to play "Over the Rainbow" on the harmonica and Mom is his hero. We listen to him play it in a low register, incredibly well for any age, and neither of us can speak.

More months and more state finals. Little Pepper and King Robbie are regularly crowned together, they make a cute couple.

Flip through tapes and *years* of this... It's enough—the costumes getting tighter, replaced way too late for Little Pepper's bum and King Robbie's crotch, especially when in adolescence he wears a lederhosen costume—it's enough to make a normal grown man cry. I may have.

For how can I begin to do justice to the injustice of it all? Viewing the cavalcade of years was as dispiriting as witnessing a child's slow death from cancer (and only a week before I'd believed nothing, but nothing, could equal that). If the first impression the "little misses" convey is the mechanical—clockwork automatons, Victorian marionettes—the lasting one is fetishism, perversion. Hard-core child pornography would be worse, I suppose. But only "differently" worse. And this was before the other tapes, the ones waiting in the black plastic toolbox.

Through the years of pageants, King Robbie kept his small size, until puberty, when he shot up to what appeared a comparatively towering five feet, becoming the husky twelve-year-old Bob Browne. After that, King Bob would make his non-competing appearances only at the end of the show, escorting the crowned Supreme Queen (invariably Little Pepper). Her Majesty and entourage of runners-up would pose, with King and Supreme Queen centring a court of increasingly pissed fidgeters.

But as the years rolled by and the featured pair entered their teens, it became clear that Bob Browne would grow no taller than five-foot-zero. He grew huskier, quite muscular, in fact, looking in his tux more and more like the bouncer at an exclusive club for Munchkins. Little Pepper, on the other hand, streaked past him like some Olive Oyle to his Popeye. They looked ludicrous and like they knew it. They continued in couples competitions, until Little Pepper was being introduced as Lady Alice Pepper-Pottersfield, a good head taller than her escort, Sir Robert Browne. Neither of them was winning anything any more, nothing but outbursts of audience laughter. "His *High*ness comes in handy for straightening Our Lady's waistband." A few times Sir Bob chased off stage after a crying Lady Alice.

Beldon and I endured a bad hour of the videotapes and paused. There was easily a week's worth of 24/7 viewing stacked and scattered about the smelly room. Somebody would have to watch it all, but not on a small TV with bleeding colours, and not in that dim and dusty cell suffused with the stink of burnt margarine. Not us. Not I.

Speechless, we began listlessly picking through the room. The promotional print material alone told a story that could make a wedding guest run to upchuck his chicken and angel food cake.

Our Little Miss was a touring show, mostly of the American southern states, with recurring locales in Texas, Georgia, Arkansas, lots of Florida, but California too (in fact, every state but Hawaii and Alaska made at least one appearance). They had local preliminaries, regional competitions, state finals, and the *Our Little Miss* International World Championship in Dallas (with four Quebec and two Mexican regional champs justifying the bombast). But a child didn't have to live in a place to compete for its title. There were multiplied possibilities for success in hundreds of shows, with the same children from a battle-hardened cohort regularly winning the prizes. One of the magazine articles estimated approximately fifty thousand participants annually. Atop it all stood CEO Alice Pottersfield (a.k.a. Auntie Alice), who hosted all state finals herself. She was Alice Pepper's aunt and later Alice Pepper-Pottersfield's stepmother. The specialized magazines tracked their stories as if they were movie stars or royalty.

Sunshine Beauty Pageants was the conglomerate whose *Our Little Miss* tour was Little Pepper and King Robbie's primary showcase. Key phrases recurred in the promotional materials.

"Let Your Little Bride (or Beau) Shine!"
(Little Bride costumes were big, bested only by cowgirls, but there were also lots of cheerleaders, schoolgirls, and even little ladies in business suits toting regular-sized briefcases, either cute feminism or anti-.)

Cash Prizes!
(Lots of pictures of brilliantly toothed kids fanning the cash.)
"What's that smell!"

"Cherubs, 0-12 months. Special Chubbiest Cherub Trophy Award Prize!"
(What, oh what, could a 0-month-old have to offer?)

"Tiny Tots, Girls and Boys 1-3 yrs"
"Not Tots, Girls and Boys 4-6"

"And Standard 11 Divisions for Girls 7-18"
(Only King Robbie survived the gender bias.)

"Couples Competition (For those who know a good thing when they see it!)"
(I have no idea about the parenthesis. Graphic icons were everywhere, overdone of course, and the above was decorated with something yellow and winking.)

"Competition In: Dancing, Singing, Western wear, Swimsuit"
(Par for a competition, with the recurrent Western wear indicating the regions of greatest fan base. The song-and-dance portions of the competitions were the most disturbing. The parents—though this seemed to be where pedophilic Dad had most influence—liked to have their tots dance to old show tunes, the kind of Let-Me-Entertain-You fare that once kept aging burlesque queens gainfully employed.)

"Our pageant team encourages self-confidence, self-esteem and healthy peer-group interaction!"
(Team.)

"Don't hide your Little Miss's pint-sized glamour under a thimble!"
"Everyone's a Winner!"
(Essentially the parents were buying one trophy or another, and there was enough hardware on display to fill a pimp museum. Show some love for Little Miss Thirteenth Runner-Up!)

"Scholarships and Fee Assistance Available"

And on and on and on it went, with lots of asterisks and daggers leading to the back of the pamphlet where microscopic text precisely gave the puny amounts available for "scholarships and fee assistance," and stipulated a means test. It was all a kickback scheme, where the money was paid to "your very own personal beauty pageant account and/or coach."

Upwards of $500 entry fees, with the moms and their daughters spending weekends travelling to an average of ten pageants per year.

The print material advertised subsidiary enterprises that would have fattened the bottom line further: *used* outfits at one thousand dollars a pop, studded chaps for the little one's Western wear, jewellery whose gem of choice was the rhinestone—earrings, crowns, tiaras, sceptres, spurs, bangles, necklaces, chokers and such. Everything "official" was emblazoned with the Sunshine Beauty Pageants' logo: a chubby-cheeked sun with eyes bugging and lips pursed as if giving an appreciative wolf-whistle. And everywhere a roll call of coaches and agents advertising their expertise in stage presence, dancing and singing, makeup, hair arranging and, of course, loan arranging.

Having scanned some of the legitimate magazine investigative reports on child pageants, I read aloud this mom's lament (in my best Blanche Dubois voice): "I know moms that spended so much they had their trailers repoed!"

Kevin laughed and that fortified us to proceed—to the black toolbox whose exploration we'd been delaying. To the other cassettes. There are always the other videos in poorly locked black plastic boxes with false bottoms. When you fall into a hole of human depravity, the ground holds for a stunned moment…then you fall farther, you free-fall in stinking darkness, till you plop at the bottom of humanity's shithouse, where fat Nazis dine Bosch-style on spitted Jewish toddlers while hungry jihadists prepare a dessert of juicy female foetuses.

This particular box had two broken clasps and a red pry bar lying inside it. Kevin pinched the bar's end and set it aside.

"Careful with evidence," he said.

Some of the contents were damaged, the old cassettes' hard plastic cracked as if they'd been attacked with the pry bar; others had their shiny tape sprawling like voracious turd-brown tapeworms. The false bottom was wedged at an angle. We chose an undamaged cassette and inserted it.

Simultaneously we sucked and held our breaths.

Now, the show has moved off the tacky stages and into neutrally coloured rooms, hotel, motel, those nondescript rooms that whisper *never tell*. We watched Little Pepper running through her fists-on-the-hips Western-wear performance, heel-and-toe and away we go! But silly Little Pepper has forgotten to don her cowgirl costume. She sports only her hat cinched tightly at the chin, underwear (which comes high above that big tummy little girls have), and her faux-snakeskin cowgirl boots. She is the only one on that video, mechanically executing her steps in front of a dead TV fixed to the wall. You blindly hope that she's simply practising her routine. But you know he's there: the man sitting on the edge of the bed, facing her, swirling vodka in a Styrofoam cup, which he rests against his rising and falling belly. You don't have to see him to believe in him.

The tapes from the black box were unlabelled and jumbled chronologically, as if time passing made no difference. In some, little no longer, pubescent Alice Pepper dances in motel rooms in the narrow alley along the bottoms of beds or in the tight spaces between them. At the end of the routine, someone will clap, loudly and slowly like considered spanking. Sometimes he whistles. Sometimes he groans. At other times, grown to resemble the Alice Pepper-Pottersfield I knew, she wears a majorette's costume of sparkling red spangles. But it's not a baton she plays with, it's a sceptre topped with an emerald ball, King Robbie's old symbol of power. Then they are little kids again, alone and waiting, as they've been trained to do. Robbie is sitting on a bed in white jockey shorts. A big hand will often come up from nowhere to block the lens.

When alone together and waiting, they have developed a routine to occupy their dead time. Alice asks, "What's that smell?" And Robbie shouts, "Shit!" The camcorder operator, always female, always snickers.

But who is recording such shows? And to what purpose? Blackmail? Personal pleasure? As a memento of the event, same as they sell overpriced at the shows? As proof of something that could never have happened? Who *was* the Leni Riefenstahl of this holocaust?... Alice Pottersfield, that was my best guess, Auntie Alice.

Before the last viewed cassette would work, I had to cram my pinkie in the tiny white spool hole and manually ratchet up its splayed tape; the nail tore right up the middle, stinging like hell, and blood dripped.

A shot dollies in along the narrow carpeted hallway as Little Pepper emerges from the motel room, quietly closing the door behind her. She notices the camera and, flushed still from a performance, melodramatically places a shushing finger to her lips. I caught my own breath. By then I could smell the hot dust of the cheap motels. Little Pepper looks momentarily confused — her Shirley Temple furrowed brow — then understands and turns back to open the door for the camera...person. The shot moves past the clinically lighted bathroom on the left, past the half-opened closet on the right, where the unzipped flap of a travelling suit bag hangs down like the butchered body in a serial killer's hidden room, and holds still.

It's olden times again. You can hear the relic zoom lens whir as the shot sneaks up on the middle-aged man in white sleeveless T-shirt, boxer shorts, and hint of gartered black socks that are mostly hidden by the near bed. It would be difficult to tell anyway, because on his knee sits that ancient ruler of the hearts of fair young damsels, the dandled King Robbie. His youthful Highness has no clothes indeed, as he's dressed in white jockey shorts only. His chin is firmly pressed between his baby-fat boy breasts, but his lower lip can be seen to protrude like a fresh wet worm. In his left hand he holds a cone of melting ice cream. The man growls soothingly at the boy. Then his fat paw covers Robbie's small hand and he pulls the cone towards his own mouth and takes a slurping lick. He says, "We're havin' some fun now, ain't we, little fella, me'n'you!"

Robbie looks up at the camera. He's crying.

The man catches the camera out the corner of his eye and his monstrous paw covers his enraged face: "Turn that *fuckin'* thing

off!"... "Sorry, but I thought you wanted it as part of the—"
"Thought nothin', you stupid cunt! Turn it off!"

Auntie Alice, camerawoman.

It didn't matter. I was in full body pain anyway. My hot head, in the sinuses especially, felt stuffed with an expanding bag of burning human shit. I just didn't want to go on living. I had nothing to live for anymore anyway.

"Kevin," I said, trying to un-house myself, dissociate, whatever. I couldn't. "Kevin."

Kevin picked up on my distress. "Listen, Lorne. In parts of the world right now, torturers are tearing the tongues out of children's mouths to make their daddies agree to avenge the family's honour. Popping out Phatma's eyeballs to make Papa see that his only hope for a quicker death for both of them is to sign his confession on the dotted line."

Satisfied that he had jolted my attention off myself—and he had—he went to the filthy window to do his gazing-out Beldon thing. Something in the stillness of his head made me know I now had to return the service and provide him distraction. I knew only one way to do that.

"Little Pepper wore enough makeup to make Lady Gaga gag, eh?" I laughed idiotically, then hurried: "Understandable, since all the blushing moms, their faces at least, looked like a cross between old Joan Rivers and that Bruce/Caitlyn Jenner character? There should have been a Super Skanky Mom trophy! But fat? Fat. Life lived off vending machines."

His left hand rose to his face. He said, "I'll bet those kids were abused in the womb already." Flat voice, none of that hackneyed *huskiness*.

I kept trying. "Chubbiest Cherub notwithstanding, I heard one of the moms scold her daughter for gaining weight. The child had to be all of three, with thighs about the thickness of your wrist!"

He looked at his left palm, then with its forefinger drew a circle in the window dirt. Shook his head.

I picked up the pace: "In one of the articles, it says a girl who lost her baby teeth just before a competition was fitted with false teeth—*false baby teeth*!" I didn't care about my dignity anymore; anyway, there was nothing I could do about the creeping hysteria. "I'll bet they were already lying about age in the zero-to-twelve-months competition! Your Honour, I put it to you: Little Missy's wrinkles were caused by amniotic fluid!"

With thumb tip he marked a spot in the centre of the dirt circle, spoke quite normally. "At first it reminded me of something, but I couldn't put my finger on it. Then it hit me: wrestling, the WWF, the garish unreality of it all, the sick agreement to believe a whopper of an ugly lie. It doesn't take Dr. Freud to see that the real action is in the parents' gallery, with the *moms*, singing and dancing along in their cheapo extensions, the enabling dads like your good neighbour Jack."

Perhaps a clinical question could distract him. "I know it's already child abuse, but do you think it always leads to sexual abuse?"

"You saw what I saw."

"But why would parents do it?"

"Mental illness, rising from the cesspool of their own childhoods. That and…well, *evil*. What else does the word mean if not this? And for money, of course, or the false hope of some." He did a fair imitation of Auntie Alice: "What's that smell?… For people who live from poor paycheque to no paycheque. They hand the kids over to some scumbag sugar daddy and tell themselves nothing bad is happening. It's just another show. And the payoff is probably no more than a tank of gas to get to the next motel."

I said, "That's what they learned as kids. Mom says we do this for the money. Now we do this. In our TCA meetings Alice Pepper-Pottersfield was the only one who supported my arguments to pay Bob Browne."

"Didn't Freud or somebody say that money to a miser is shit to a baby? Little Pepper and King Robbie hit it perfectly with their routine. What's that smell? Shit."

"I find it hard to believe that money would make a mother who wasn't starving to death pimp her own child."

"Nothing *made* them pimps, they made *themselves* pimps!" He punched the centre of the dirt circle. The pane cracked hugely and spider-webbed like breaking ice, halting with a tiny sound like a distant braking train. When he spoke again he was choked up.

"It's just, if we don't at least half-believe we make free choices and act like we believe it, then nothing is worth living for. Nothing matters. Nothing's worth saving. Nothing's worth loving. Nothing is real."

The delaying glass fell from the window in big geometric shapes — making him hop backwards — and crashed. Through the dust and dim some light shot in. He stood staring for a long while, breathing deeply. A very long while.

He turned in that shaft of dusty light and, looking down through both hands held sideways like blinkers, he lined up a cassette, took one step and with his left foot kicked the thing so well that it crashed high on the filthy pea-green wall.

I shouted, "Talk of tampering with the evidence!"

A voice came through the wall: *I'm comin' over there and tearin' you a new A-hole, you runt!*

When we turned to leave, there was a sleeveless T-shirt in the doorway, on an emaciated torso almost as white. Brown plaid slippers, grey dress pants whose cinched belt left about six inches of tongue, and the well-groomed head of a man with miles to go before the curse of holding his liquor catches him. He raised both hands and backed away, voice fading:

"I don't know nothin' about the little fella that lives here, nothin' at all, I tell ya. He an' his lady-friend visitor come and go as they please. He minds *his* business an' I…" He turned and beat it.

I said to Beldon, "You will catch Alice Pepper-Pottersfield?"

"It should be routine. I'll call this in now."

He pulled his cellphone from his pocket and pressed numbers. "I'll get a site-investigation team." He waited. Talked tersely with a "Staff Sergeant Parizeau." Waited again. Then spoke more respectfully to a "Superintendant Fortier," apologizing that his cell must have got turned off somehow. He summarily explained the connection between the abduction of Shawn and the other children, the murdered Bob Browne, and Alice Pepper-Pottersfield and the apartment site. He asked me, "Would you please give a description of Alice Pepper-Pottersfield to Superintendant Fortier."

I took the phone and without saying hello gave the description. I was thanked as "Dr. Thorpe" and told how grateful the police were to have my assistance. I returned the phone to Kevin, who said into it, "I hope to have her address in the next little while for you, uh, sir."

He scrunched a confused face that intensified to irritation. He was being reprimanded. Then his eyes widened. He listened neutrally for a while, said, "Really?" Then a longer, more welcome listening. "It will, eh? I mean, uh, thank you, Superintendent. That *is* what I want and I *have* learned a lesson about proper procedure, *and* making sure my phone's always in proper working order. I'll have that information for you ASAP."

When he finished I said, "Good news? Homicide?"

He didn't respond, just locked the door from the inside and pulled it shut behind us. Coming quickly alongside he snarled, "Bad news. Something's up at HQ, something about *more* missing children in Troutstream! The calls were coming in like hellfire as we spoke." He passed me.

I hurried, "*What? Plural?* But that's impossible! You're making a bad joke, right?"

"No joke. I don't know the details. Most likely a copycat, we're hoping. It happens all the time."

"But what copycat could have known about it, or this soon?"

"I don't know. But my immediate assignment is to get Foster to divulge his contact for Alice Pepper-Pottersfield, and relay her address. Which should be easy now. Procedure. I'll drop you off first."

Chapter 19

Veronica's Golf was not in our driveway or at the neighbour's. From the front sidewalk I spied through the Kilborns' window. All I could make out was a continual wild flurry of Jake in the front room. Where were my wife and wiry Jack that would allow such a performance?... After about five minutes I gave up looking.

The phone was ringing when I entered my house. Its red light was blinking so rapidly I couldn't count the number of missed messages being signalled. Media. I came close to not picking up and immediately wished I hadn't.

"Is one speaking with Dr. Thorpe?"

"Yes, Debbie, what can I do for you? I'm in a bit of a—"

"Well, Dr. Thorpe, perhaps I should be calling the police in lieu, because it would appear that a goodly number of my offspring have gone missing!" Her voice went up at the end. "The school phoned!"

"Wait a sec, Debbie. Didn't you drop them off at school this morning?"

"Well, no, not precisely. That's my point." The British female-impersonator accent was replaced by the flat nasal of Ontario: "I was feelin' sorta sick this morning and Alice said she could handle the route herself. I—"

"*Alice*? Alice Pepper-Pottersfield drove the bus by herself this morning? *By herself?*"

Some composure: "She doesn't have an operator's licence, true, and that's proportionately why I'm calling you instead of the police. I mean...I didn't know whom to turn to. I was taking a long morning bath with Maeve Binchy for company and the radio on, and my call display shows the police have been phoning *me* and I have all these messages! And just right now there are two police vehicles outside and I'm worried sick that an accident has hap—"

I hung up and called the direct number Kevin had given me. It took so long to get through that sweat was trickling down my sides. When I got him, the false calm in his voice didn't fool me.

"Yes, a whole busload of Troutstream kids is missing. The calls here have been screaming. We've just now got hold of the school-bus driver, your Debbie Carswell. Dr. Foster didn't hesitate — she was his first contact for getting in touch with Bob Browne."

"Listen, Kevin, I'm pretty sure Alice bullied Debbie into being sick this morning and took the school bus herself. Sounds like Debbie was ordered to shut up and hide out in her bathtub. But someone's already spotted the bus, right?"

"Wrong. I'll be right over. But first I'm going to have a word with this Carswell lunatic. Sit tight, Lorne."

I played my messages. The first was from the school, a computerized voice: "YOUR DAUGHTER — SHAWN THORPE — IN GRADE — SIX — IS ABSENT FROM SCHOOL THIS MORNING — "

On my way out I banged my hipbone on the corner of the kitchen island, then bounced off the door jamb.

I didn't knock. Jack's place was a madhouse. Jake was running circles around the bulky living room coffee table, roaring about going to see Wy. I didn't dare approach him. I found Jack at the kitchen table, which was covered with empty bottles, beer and one Canadian Club. His baggy eyes were as dark as horror makeup.

"Jack?... *Jack?*"

He was as good as asleep, trying to bring me into focus with his Goth eyes. He was speaking just an intelligible cut above Jake:

"She loves you, you know that? I love her and she loves you. Lucky bugger."

"Jack, shut up and listen. Is there any chance Shawn didn't get on the bus this... Oh, fuck it. But at least listen to Jake in there!" I pointed. He tried to focus my finger.

Jake's roaring came without letup: "*Go see Wy, go see Wy, go see Wy…*"

"Pull yourself together, Jack! This is a crisis!"

He smiled weakly and in folding his arms on the table knocked off a bottle, which didn't break. He carefully pillowed his head, face to the wall.

Where was Veronica? Why had she taken off again?… What had drunken Jack said? She loves me? Of course she loves me, you sick piece of… No: thank the gods if she still loves me. Could this mean there was nothing between the two of them? Yes! Only in Jack's drunken dreams! How *could* there have been anything?… Oh, there could have been, Dr. Thorpe. There could be.

I shouted and yanked on a fistful of Jack's greasy hair. He cranked up his head and looked at me over his right shoulder from underwater eyes. Then smiled dissolvingly, put an empty bottle in his mouth and tried to bite it. I crammed him against the wall for safekeeping, where he immediately slumped into unconsciousness, his mouth working the bottle like a baby a breast. I thought twice, but removed it.

There was nothing to do but head back home and wait for Kevin. I slowed passing the dervish Jake now windmilling arms as he beat his circle around the big golden-oak coffee table like a lacquered tree stump. To interfere would be like stepping into a rotary plough. He was reduced to emitting one sound, a screeching "*Wyyyyyyyyy…*"

I waited on our front stoop. The maroon Crown Vic pulled into the driveway, but instead of heading for me Beldon turned to the Kilborns'. He shouted, "There's no one home at your place, right? Shawn was picked up by Alice's school bus, right? Owen takes a city bus, right? Veronica saw them off, she's still at the neighbours'."

"Yes — no — wait!" I hurried after him. "You won't get any help there, Jack's passed out drunk and Jake's having a fit."

"Where's Veronica?"

"She went to bring the kids their lunches. She should be long back by now. Dear God."

"Can Jack talk?"

"No."

"What's wrong with Jake?"

"Who knows? He's been neglected. He's raving about that Wy from the TV show."

We entered and stood in the archway to the living room. Jake was no longer screeching like a stuck pig, if running even tighter circles around the coffee table, leaning dangerously inward.

Kevin said, "Watch me."

"Watch you? Oh…"

He moved within a few feet of the whirling Jake. "Jake, stop!" But Jake merely recommenced windmilling his arms. Kevin timed his foot so that Jake crashed onto the brown corduroy couch by the front window. Kevin was on him, pinning his arms to his sides and dodging attempted head butts.

I leapt in and restrained Jake's legs by lying on them — what riding a mechanical bull must feel like! Jake was now making hellacious noises and moving us both with his bucking… But his struggles subsided, though not his roaring. I glanced around Kevin. Jake's face was flaming and covered with froth and snot.

Risking a butt, I moved my head closer and shouted into his face, "Shut up, dumb-dumb!"

And Jake went limp. I distinguished something intelligible, to me anyway.

Kevin, his face streaming sweat, asked, "What'd he say?"

"He's going to tell his mother we made fun of him."

Kevin seemed to hiccup. "Can you give him something? We need to know what he knows."

I released my grip and backed off. Removing his hands from the powerful shoulders, Kevin sat Jake up. His whole head was redder than Kevin's. He huffed and he puffed…but he settled down further. He gave Kevin his broken-picket-fence grin, did his swallow-the-nose face and shouted, "That was fun!"

Kevin looked at me and I translated, adding, "There's no call for sedation. Whatever you think you can get from him, now's your window."

Kevin went blank, looked down, or inward, apparently gathering his resources. He tried to put a hand on Jake's hand, but Jake batted it away and flailed, if not as wildly. Still, we had to wait for him to settle again. Precious time.

Kevin said loudly and slowly, "Jake, listen carefully. This is very important. I'm a policeman. Where did Shawn go this morning? To see... Wy?" Big mistake.

"Go see Wy, go see Wy, go see Wy..."

We were again both lying on top of the bucking boy. I managed, "Maybe you'd better let *me* try."

"What the fuck is going on here?" Also spoken slowly and loudly. "Get off him. Shawn's whole busload of children is missing and you two are wrestling with Jake?"

Veronica. We got off. Kevin looked as sheepish as I.

"Sit still, Jake." And he did. "Where's Jack?" she asked no one in particular.

I said, "He's passed out in the kitchen."

I saw she'd not slept much in days: her hair looked in need of a wash and brush, and she was still in her baby-blue sweat suit. I had to resist a powerful urge to go and hold her, even if I was the one needed the holding. And I'm sure I looked much worse.

She watched Kevin only. "Detective Beldon, how did this happen? Every time, you assured me that things would be all right. You were going to get the *man* who abducted Shawn. Now people are dead and a whole busload of children is missing. They're going crazy over at the school. And it's that Alice Pepper *woman* who's driving the bus! The police are saying she's mad as a bat! How could you let this happen! She's the one who kidnapped Shawn, isn't she, dressed as a man?"

Kevin stepped forward and cupped both Veronica's shoulders. "Mrs. Thorpe, Veronica, I have a pretty good idea how this happened, but I was unable to prevent it. Lots of things have to go wrong for something like this to happen, and things have gone horribly wrong. But I have absolutely no time now to explain. If you can talk with Jake, I need to know what Shawn's been telling him about going to see this Wy character."

The mere mention started Jake up again: "Go see Wy, go see Wy…"

Veronica delayed on Kevin's eyes a moment, looked longer and harder at me, then sat on the couch. Without a word, she fearlessly took Jake's swinging head in both her hands, held it hard, stared into his eyes and snapped, "*Jake*." He stopped flailing and settled. She took tissues from her pocket and cleaned up his face. Then she held his hand in hers and began lightly stroking it, all the while holding him with her eyes.

"Shawn is your best friend, isn't she, Jake? And best friends share, don't they, Jake?"

Uh-huh uh-huh, Jake nodded.

Kevin and I stood in no little awe, after our shameful failure to wrestle information from him. We watched and listened as Veronica drew forth the whole story. I translated in a whisper for Kevin.

Shawn had secretly been telling Jake that a nice woman was going to be taking her and her special friends to see Wy. Jake, too, Shawn's most special friend. This nice woman lived in a big magical bus that was just for kids. She had lots of candy and toys and pets. But if any kid told his parents, all the other kids would go to live with Wy forever and ever and he would be left behind.

Jake made a big baby face, just a nanosecond from loud crying: "I'm telling Mom Shawn made fun of me now too. They wented forever without me…no friends… They had a whole bus of Oreos." He blubbered and ripped into a crying jag like a blaring train. Veronica hugged him and he settled again, whimpering only a few times, "Go see Wy, go see Wy…"

Kevin said, "Veronica, your husband and I are going back to your place. What's happened this morning could not have been anticipated and prevented. So I'm not going to keep apologizing. You have to admit, Shawn kept it from her mom and dad, as did the other Troutstream kids from their parents. I'm not making excuses. I just want us to keep this honest. I'm not going to promise you again that Shawn and the kids are safe. They're not. But we have called in the RCMP's Missing Persons Service and we'll soon have an OPP chopper in the sky, not to mention a few dozen police already out in cruisers. We're covered all the way from the St. Lawrence River to Algonquin Park. We've ordered a stop to all school bus movement. There is no way on earth one big yellow school bus full of kids can go unnoticed much longer. That I *can* promise you."

I heard Veronica exhale forcefully through her nose, a bad sign. "Even if it has so far? What has she done to them already? What *will* she do if trapped?"

"Everybody's been told to go very easy with Alice Pepper-Pottersfield. Right now —"

"I don't give a fuck about Alice!" She still hadn't turned from Jake and her vehemence evoked a whimpered *Go see Wy* like an aftershock.

Kevin compressed his lips. "I'm going next door with Lorne, where I will be in constant communication with the police. But you're right, Veronica. The fact that she's not been spotted and apprehended already is troubling. And that's why I need you to stay here and keep talking with Jake. Learn whatever else you can. But I need to talk privately with Lorne. Right now, that is our best hope."

"What? Me? No way, I'm not leaving here."

I was ignored. Kevin stepped forward and lightly placed his hand on Veronica's shoulder. "Keep the faith, Veronica. You're doing marvellously and holding up bravely. If you learn anything else from Jake, *anything*, come right over and tell me."

She said evenly, "They have obviously not gone to see…you-know-whom. Where have they gone? Not far, since they've not been spotted by all your mighty forces."

Kevin popped his eyebrows. "That's true…"

She sat back from Jake, turned and spoke across the ugly coffee table to the wall. "Lorne?"

"Yes?"

"We've gotta go," Kevin said, pushing me on the upper arm, "like right now."

"Lorne, I'm sorry about the past few days. I don't know what got into me, delayed stress or something, like you said. I'm all right here, here is where I'm needed, for now. Go with Detective Beldon, find Shawn."

"Please don't *you* apologize, dear—"

"No time now for making up, kids. I can't impress on you strongly enough that we move quickly, *now*."

I'd been pushed into the hallway and was struggling to look back. She was standing. I said, "It was all my fault, Veronica. Whatever you've done, you were driven to it by me!"

"Jesus Christ! Move!"

He had shoved me out of sight, and I called, "Is Owen okay?" I had to open the aluminum door or be crammed against it. I glanced back and caught sight of Veronica heading down the hallway to the kitchen.

"Owen's safe at school!"

Kevin kept pushing me ahead to my house and right back into the family room, where with one last shove he landed me on the small couch. What surprising strength the lanky man had.

"Sorry to be so pushy, Lorne. You understand."

"No, I don't!"

He wasn't listening. He stood flipping his lower lip with forefinger, like a distracted kid. He was looking down at me absently.

I said, "Veronica's right, how could no one have spotted a big yellow school bus packed with wild kids?"

He stared at me in a piercing kind of distraction; in fact, I didn't think he was aware of me at all. He closed his eyes and dropped his chin on his chest, breathed deeply for too long. When he finally looked at me again, his pupils were slightly dilated.

"Put on your deerstalker cap, Dr. Sherlock. After the first twenty minutes, the police search had eliminated all possible exits. Like the real Sherlock says, we now have to consider the improbable, the impossible."

"I'm sorry I—"

"The bus is still in Troutstream."

"That really is impossible, Kevin. Unless Bob Browne taught Alice to make a whole busload of kids invisible. *Wait*. I'm assuming the police have checked the community centre, where Bob had been hiding his backhoe?"

His eyes widened. He called on his cell: "Have we checked the Troutstream Community Centre?" He was staring blankly at me as he waited for the answer. "Remember, call this number first as soon as you hear anything."

He went to the patio door and stood staring out, absently holding onto a leaf of the dying fig tree. "They had checked right after talking with Carswell. But that was smart thinking, Lorne. I *am* right to rely on you. Our talking together just now made you think of the community centre. That's how I need your help."

I had nothing to say to that. He commenced rubbing a fig leaf between thumb and two fingers, like a tailor checking texture for a new suit.

"Tell me again, what was the key to your solving the arsenic-poisoning case at CHEO? Some of the boys downtown were mightily impressed at how you did that."

"What?...I... Well, like I told you, I sat down with the father and made him tell me his story over and over, till I picked up the clue about burning the treated wood. I put one and one together. I don't see how that helps here. I mean, we don't have Shawn or Bob Browne or even the Market Slasher to interview. Veronica seems to have got all Jake has to tell us. Ditto you with Art Foster. There's still Debbie, I guess."

"Forget Debbie!" he commanded, still facing the patio door.

"Frank Baum—"

"There's you, for Christ's sake!" He turned and faced me. "We've got a busload of missing children and I think you're the only way to them before real harm is done!"

"*Me*? *I* don't know where she's taken them!"

He came over and plopped down beside me on the couch. His voice went quiet:

"It's not where she's gone, Lorne. I know you don't know that. Or I'm hoping you just don't know you know. It's where she *would* go. You know Alice better than you think."

My look made him continue. "Stay with me on this, big guy. I'm already impressed by what a hard-ass you are, Lorne, so you can stop proving that to me. But Shawn's safety depends on what we're going to do here in the next ten minutes. Do you trust me?"

"Yes."

"Good. Then I want you to stop thinking of Alice as being *out there*." He tapped my temple with his finger: "She's *in here*. That's what I need you for, to get out what's in there. You're the only person in the world right now who can tell me what we need to know."

I pulled back and would have stood, and maybe even run back to Veronica, but he grabbed my arm.

"You're talking crazy!" I tried to shake him off. "Let go of me and get the fuck *out there* and find my daughter!" It was like being at the Museum of Science and Technology all over again. Was I caught forever in some mad loop?

He let go. I stood, but instantly wavered. Feeling a touch of vertigo I remembered Shawn kneeling happily by the dog, saw her coming towards me hopefully with the Styrofoam cup swinging upside down like a bell, then that cup snowballing through the darkly yellow parking lot, clean and tasteless, Kevin's coming for it with outstretched hand. I sat back down, because I had nowhere else to go for help.

"It's just that, well, you're not making sense to me, Kevin, you're —"

"Okay, listen. You saw how Veronica was with Jake over there? You saw how she got the information out of him? She held his hand and petted it. Did *that* make sense?"

"Yes."

"Good. Well, we, you and I, are going to have to do something like that. It's just remembering, like you did with the father in the arsenic-poisoning case. People could remember a helluva lot more than they ever thought they could, most of it bad, which is probably why we don't."

"I just don't know what you're talking about, Kevin, honestly."

"Leave that to me, trust me, remember."

I could only pinch my mouth and stare straight ahead. I would do whatever he thought needed to be done. Why couldn't I convey that?

"Look, Lorne, you don't have to be Wy or Bob Browne or full of shit like Foster to accept that we still know very little about how the mind works, how *we* work, that some things may be possible we'd thought impossible. I mean, look what animals can do—communicate over great distance without benefit of satellites, find their way home across whole countries, know somehow when their owner leaves work, migrate—"

"Okay, okay, already."

"You agree then?"

"Not entirely. I was going to say that you *do* have to be Art Foster to have such…faith. I'm not prepared to abandon rational thinking, especially in this crisis." I managed a smirk: "But I'm still completely at your disposal, Kevin. My daughter is in the hands of a madwoman. I do trust you. I'll do whatever you say. That's reasonable. I'm just surprised at the turn *you've* taken."

He went to the kitchen and returned with a chair. He set it directly in front of me and sat. Our knees were touching. Controlling my unease, I watched as, unsmiling, he turned up his hands in front of me.

"I want you to place your fingertips on mine."

"What? That really *is* crazy."

"You saw how Veronica held Jake's hand. Well, I'm not asking you to hold my hand, Lorne, just touch fingertips. Believe me, it will help."

"I don't like touching people, especially other men."

"You're a surgeon, for Christ's sake!"

"That's different."

"Lorne, I'll bet you think a lot about touching people—Veronica, Shawn, Owen."

"Okay, okay, get on with it." I set my fingertips on his as if lightly touching a keyboard. "What next?"

"Now we talk, that's all. Or you do. Wait." He dropped his hand to shut off his cell.

"Is that smart? Couldn't there be news? Weren't you just scolded for turning off your phone?"

"Yes. Relax, Lorne." He returned his fingertips to mine. "And remember this, *believe* it: if there's a solution, if we're to find Shawn, it's in you, not out there. You're in control, Lorne, so just relax, let it come, relive it. Start at the beginning and tell me everything you know about Alice Pepper-Pottersfield, right from the first Troutstream Committee meeting, if you like, when you walked in and Debbie Carswell introduced you and said where you worked, and Alice sent up a silent prayer of thanks to the god Fortuna for delivering a Great White Doctor into her hands."

"Just remember and talk?"

"Remember everything and start talking, as detailed as you can. But don't be afraid to guess if you have to, that's important."

"My daughter's life might depend on guesswork?"

"Much does, you'd be surprised, or I'd bet you really know so from your own work. Or call it imagination, if that helps. But Shawn's life may now depend on your memory and imagination. You have to bring Alice before us here in this room if we're to get Shawn back. Now shut up and talk."

"That makes no sense."

"Good. Go."

So I started talking, worried only for the first little while that we were wasting time. Then I couldn't stop. Kevin asked questions, made me backtrack, started me over from the beginning, kept my fingers dancing lightly on his like he was playing me. All the while he kept his eyes on mine. I felt perfectly normal, wholly conscious…when suddenly his head seemed to get bigger, then grew to fill my field of vision, the whole family room, and I had no sense of time passing…

He suddenly bounced all eight of my fingers at once and startled me out of a surprisingly pleasant reverie.

"Stop. Go back to where you said that was the only time Alice ever stood up to Debbie."

I was instantly dead tired and dying to flop over sideways and sleep; my own head was a bag of toxic playground topsoil, my lids were drooping. "Yes…?"

"Yes, back there again, tell me again about Alice's booth at the children's history fair. Close your eyes if you like, Lorne, and relax, rest, dream it, that's all it is, a pleasant dream you control, no call for concern. There, see it again, just as you remember it… Alice is touching the granny reading glasses on their red-beaded necklace, it's the nineteenth century and Blackburn Dodgson has just built a sawmill on the river. See it again, Lorne, just as you saw it. It's only a dream, you're in complete control."

I felt my arms levitate, as if by some gentle anti-gravity off his fingertips. I was back in the community centre at the children's history fair, as real as any reality. Children chimed, "Tell us the story again, *please*, Miss Pepper-Pottersfield." I was one of them for a while and it was wonderful. But someone had to do it and I was the only adult present who could.

So I gave the talk on local history and only for a short spell did I know I was doing so in Alice's voice. Then I wasn't watching myself doing Alice, I *was* Alice, and I was completely there, then, that… *earlier time far better than this time, of family fun connected to the patient rhythms of nature, a half-tamed forest world, a leisurely river, golden Troutstream, and a big yellow-and-black paddlewheel steamer, the* Troutstream Belle, *in no hurry to depart, families picnicking on the grassy slopes of Dodgson's Landing, children rolling hoops with a stick, shooting marbles, playing tag, red rover red rover come over, blind man's bluff, hide-and-seek, children with nothing to do but be children, ignored and cherished just for being children—there's the steamer's whistle! All aboard! For a safe place, a place of safety, a—*

Back in the classroom my knuckles were smacked with the pointer stick and Kevin boomed from the sky, "Wake up, Lorne! Let's go! Move it!"

I awoke to nightmare. *He* is standing and I am still sitting, in the deepest ignorant shame again. I start trembling and can't stop, I'm afraid of everything. Then somebody's crying like a big baby, just blubbering and gushing. "*Bob? Where are you, love?*" I'm so tired, dead tired, of this, the whole ugly show, and I just want it to stop, I want to go back there, to that safe place. I closed my eyes again...

"*They always make me touch their big things, and pull them. Robbie says he has to put it in his mouth too sometimes. Ee-yoo! And they won't stop touching me...there... That's where I go from, silly... No!... Please, Mister, no. Please! I'm gonna be sick! Stop! Stop! Mom-mee! Mom-mee!—*"

My head's on fire when I opened my eyes again and was looking along Kevin's forearm. He had a fistful of my hair and my head twisted up sideways. I smelled vomit.

"Aaaaaa..." That's what I said, and again: "Aaaaaa..."

He let go and said, "I'm very sorry about that, Lorne. But I had to shock you. You all right? Here, wipe your chin."

"No," I sulked. Then, cleaned up some, I set the handkerchief aside and touched my tender scalp.

"Ouch. You did the right thing, Kevin, I'm myself. I did the same to Bob Browne's flaming rug when he was dying. Those poor kids. Where the hell did all that come from?"

"Those tapes we watched, but mainly from you. Hurry, let's go."

"Go? Where?"

"The school bus is hidden in the woods down by the old steamer landing only minutes from here."

"You figured that from what I said?"

"You made me see it almost as clearly as you did yourself, as Alice saw it and felt it. I just put one and one together, Doctor."

"Shouldn't you call for, uh, backup or something?"

"I will, but we're closest. Alice sees it as a safe place, so I'm hoping she's not out to hurt anybody, but no time to lose."

"You're hoping? What's *safe* mean to Alice Pepper-Pottersfield? When are children ever safe? When they're *dead, that's* when!"

But he was out the side door, with me hurrying after. "Wait," I called, "what about Veronica? Maybe she should come with us for the children's sake."

He started the car, I hurried to get in. As we were shooting backwards he said, "Veronica's done her part, Lorne. Thanks to Veronica, we know what Alice used to lure the kids, the promise of Wy. And it was Veronica made me first realize the bus had not left Troutstream. Right now she's keeping the Kilborns from total disaster. I made her a promise and we're going to keep it right now. What's the best way down to the river?"

"River? There's no river. But north on Izaak Walton, just before St. Joseph's, cut left at the sign for the Troutstream Toboggan Hill. We'll have to walk from there. Are you sure about this, Kevin?" He didn't answer. I closed my eyes: "Of course, that's where they are."

He glanced at me. "That was some performance back there, Lorne. Some people say I have a gift. I think I know what that took. Do you even *know* what you did? You *became* another—"

"Hurry! Here! Turn in here!"

Chapter 20

I'd not run down a hill since I was a kid. And every time I'd driven past it, running down the green Troutstream Toboggan Hill had persisted as a bounding fantasy of this middle-aged man (okay, Bob: *late* middle-aged). But in the event, the hill and my legs, they let me down hard: the surface was potted, my legs were rigid poles incapable of absorbing anything and at every jolt the old knock knees felt ready to break backwards. So in the end I ratcheted down sideways like the crazy old man I was becoming.

Kevin, if dressed as inappropriately in slacks and loafers, was already waiting at the bottom. It felt immediately like there was a sun lamp on the back of my neck. Mosquitoes swarmed our heads and both of us were waving hands like dumb-dumbs signing a mad conversation. I thought of the kids, of sunstroke and West Nile virus and Lyme disease. I thought of Shawn's allergies, which instantly escalated to images of drowning, mass murder and everything from malaria to a suicide bomb!

"Where to?" Kevin called, though I was right beside him.

"I don't know. I've never been down here at the bottom, only watched the kids sledding from the top." I was breathless, heart pounding in my ears. "My guess is it's straight on and downward to the stream. In Alice's slide show the old Dodgson's Landing looked to be near where the main road crosses. It shouldn't be too…hey, the brush looks flattened over there!"

He was ploughing ahead through the drooping waist-high grass. As we neared the break, tracks appeared. We trotted along them. The grade, if not as steep as the hill's, continued downward far too dangerously for any vehicle, let alone a busload of kids driven by a madwoman. She must have come down the toboggan hill with her foot jammed on the brake—skidded down! My heart slammed.

I concentrated, switched myself into surgery mode, and only then picked up the whiff of a really bad smell. We were not far from the sewage treatment facility and the breeze was blowing from the northeast.

Out of the grass and into the brush, we were on the right path. Alice had managed somehow to avoid the more mature growth, but for how long?

We paused above the bank of the trickling Troutstream, which appeared like a brown vein in the black earth's fold. The trees grew taller there, but gloomily so, and the broad ravine that had once contained a real river opened in an immense dimness. I was sucking densely humid air. But I stayed on Kevin's heels when he ran and had to use my hands to keep from bumping into him when he halted again. His shirt was soaked.

"There it is!"

I stepped round him and immediately picked out the distant yellow-and-black bus, its red lights winking—tipped headlong into the stream! But no depth of water worth panicking about. I looked at Kevin, his pink-welted face streaming with sweat; he'd taken a lashing for me in taking the lead. He bolted, but I passed him this time. The path close to the stream was packed hard; it may even have been an ancient road to Dodgson's Landing. Still a good fifty yards from the bus, I made out some movement in the dimness…kids! We picked up the pace and arrived panting like hounds.

Kevin headed straight for the bus's open door, calling, "Is anyone in there? Come out with your hands held in front of you, Alice. Is anybody injured?"

I couldn't think till I'd found Shawn. I spotted her on the far side of the bus, apart from its eerie activity of lackadaisical children, most younger than she. She was sitting on the ground by the upturned root of what must once have been a massive willow that had fallen across the stream. I slowed my approach so as not to startle her. Her legs were drawn up and crossed at the ankles, her chin was on her knees, and her dandelion hair was a dirty-blonde clump.

"Shawn?"

She didn't look up.

"Shawn, it's Dad. Everything's going to be all right now."

She spoke in that hiccupping way of children struggling for control: "She promised we were going to meet Wy. She said he'd be here to meet us with a big-wheel boat and cake and soda and Wei. And no grown-ups, she said."

"I know, dear. Miss Pepper-Pottersfield lied to you. She's a very sick woman. Are you hurt anywhere?"

She looked up then, and her face was covered with streaks. Her voice showed some promising anger: "Stupid Jake was the smart one not to come. I knew you couldn't have a real boat here. It *stinks* here!"

She tilted her head back in that small seizure that begins a sneeze and let fly a good one. Drawing her bare forearm across her nose, she said, "I'm not crying. It's my allergies."

"I know, dear." I dipped down to touch her cheek and she swung an arm to knock my hand away.

"*You* all lied to Bob Browne about everything! Miss Pepper-Pottersfield said so."

"Sweetheart, that was diff—"

"Lorne, over here!"

Kevin was with one of Debbie's boys, who had a bad gash across the bridge of his nose, which might be broken. The boy was in shock, he'd been taking the trickling blood into his mouth and gulping.

"Here," I said, kneeling and taking his hand, "pinch your nose like this." I placed his fingers just above the cut, squeezed them there. He winced and commenced wailing, and the noise in that echoing gloom was of a tortured animal.

I said to Kevin under the noise, "I needed to snap him out of it. But he may have lost too much blood, nose might be broken, we have to get him to CHEO."

His brother, Pete, the boy whose asthma attack Bob Browne had relieved, came over and pulled a clean sweat sock from his own backpack. He placed it over his brother's nose and then replaced the hand. He set his own hand on his brother's head: "It's all right, Mickey. Everything's going to be all right now." And that settled Mickey.

I remembered Bob Browne with Pete in the community centre, the Jew's harp. Pete had learned something and something of Bob lived on in Pete. I said, "Pete, good work with the sock. But your brother's lost some blood, so I want you to stay here with him and help him keep pressure on that sock, okay?"

Pete took a deep breath. "No problem. Uh, Dr. Thorpe, is my mom, like, looking for us?"

"Yes, she's doing her best, Pete."

Remarkably, Mickey's proved to be the only obvious injury. A quick visual check of the twenty or so kids showed no physical damage, only that eerie stillness symptomatic of shock.

I cupped Pete's shoulder: "Pete, how come you're all just hanging around here? Why didn't you walk back up to the road? Big guy like you could have found the way back."

He didn't look away from his task. "Miss Pepper-Pottersfield told us to wait. She said she'd be right back, *with* Wy. She said this was the beginning of the Noble Eightfold Path and we weren't to move. But that was a big fat lie, wasn't it?"

Kevin, who'd been standing beside us, said, "It was. Which way did she go, Pete?"

"Dunno. Ask Shawn. Can we go home now?"

"I'm calling for help right now, son." Kevin picked his cell from his belt and turned away a few steps.

I looked around, only then really taking in the scene. In the fetid dimness it was like a negative of golden-lighted Shoal Park the other evening: a gloomy anti-playground. In addition to the unnatural sight of a school bus tipped into a stream, the area was littered with backpacks and lunch bags, with here a cap, there a lonely running shoe. Then my adjusting eyes picked out the strange objects, garishly coloured and sparkling: a soiled pink sash, a red cummerbund, the short sceptre topped with emerald ball, the tiny tiara like a crown of bright thorns...all like some lost child's crumb markers on a trail from no home to nowhere.

And the stink was overwhelming again. Such could come only from the vast collection of human waste nearby, a stench so eye-stingingly foul it defied nature.

Kevin finished up his call: "And Frank, cordon the bus. No one goes in before me, uh, please." And took in the scene with me.

I frowned: "There's something weirdly familiar about this. I don't mean the regression thing we just did."

He said, "Kids waiting, nowhere to go, *Our Little Miss*. It's what's left when children are cheated, abused, abandoned."

"But look at Little Pepper's tiara lying over there. Who's really to blame for this scene?"

"Alice Pepper-Pottersfield, that's who. An accessory to murder now too. Don't get all sentimental on me, Lorne. But enough talk. We have to move. Will Shawn talk to us?"

"About Alice? Alice can go to hell. Shawn's not being put through another thing. She's coming home with..."

He was already striding towards her.

"Beldon!" I called.

He crouched beside her. "Shawn, where'd Miss Pepper-Pottersfield go?"

I was happy and hurt to see her smile weakly at him.

"She said she was going to get Wy."

"Yes, dear," he said. "But where, which way did she go? Back up to the road? Along the creek? Which way? Point."

"It *stinks* down here." She made her stinky face, then tipped back her head and let fly another sneeze.

Kevin looked up at me: "What *is* that smell?"

"We're not far from the sewage treatment facility, the wind's from the north and the air would be trapped down here."

He turned back to Shawn. "Shawn, just point in the direction..."

MISSING CHILDREN

And she was crying, at last, in that childlike gulping way. She unselfconsciously wiped her nose with the bottom of her pink T-shirt with the big embossed red geranium. Done, she smoothed the shirt.

Her eyes bugged a bit, like she was remembering something horrifying. Even her face pulled forward. "She was like a *zombie* at first! Then I was, like, I want to go home 'cause it smells like shit down here! She just went *crazy* when she heard that. She started throwing our things all over. She wouldn't stop. She was, like, Wy will *never* come for us because we're *bad*! She wouldn't listen to anything. She was all—"

Kevin had slapped her lightly and her hand went to her cheek as her wide green eyes found mine. She jumped up and wrapped her arms around my waist, as she had the other night at the caterwauling in the park. I cupped her head against my chest, she didn't resist.

I nodded once at Kevin: "It's all right, sweetheart. All of you are all right now and we're going home. Detective Beldon was just helping you get control of yourself. Sometimes people have to hurt like that to help."

What heals can hurt, what hurts can heal. And I knew we were cured, just like that. The rest would be recuperation.

Her sniffling soon slowed against me. Her voice was muffled, again hiccuppy: "I screamed it stank, and she stank too. And we all cried we wanted to go home. She wouldn't listen. She tried to make us wear these kiddie costumes for some stupid parade or something. But nobody would, and she was, like, Wy will *hate* us because we're such *bad* children. And I was, like, you're full of…of *shit*, and she smelled like shit! That made her go really mental. She smashed Mickey Carswell on the nose with a stupid wand or something and the blood just spouted out of him like magic!"

I felt her hot breathing lessen on my sternum.

"Shawn, can you tell Detective Beldon which way Miss Pepper-Pottersfield went? I know she's been bad, but she's very sick and she needs help. Will you, please, love?"

She removed her left arm and pointed northward along the stream: "That way. She told everyone to wait and she'd try to convince Wy to come play with us. Then she just took off." She wrapped me again. "Did I make her sick, daddy?"

I didn't mind Beldon watching my face, but I was relieved Shawn didn't look up. My throat hurt like I imagine post-intubation must feel.

"No, love, you did nothing wrong. Miss Pepper-Pottersfield is mentally ill. She can't help herself, sort of like Jake, only bad."

She removed her head a touch, said thoughtfully, "What's wrong with her?"

Even in that mucky atmosphere I felt a chill where her face had pressed my centre. "I don't... Somebody hurt her, really badly, and a lot, starting when she was a very little girl."

She pulled back farther and looked up at me: "Was it a *no-feeling* thing?"

Her school's code for sexual abuse.

"Yes."

She wrinkled her nose at me: "You smell all pukey."

Kevin said, "We have to go, Lorne."

"What? Me? No way. You go. I'm staying right where I am. We're going home. We can't leave these kids alone again. Are you out of your f—...mind?"

"No, Lorne. I need you with me. Listen... Hear those sirens? They'll be here in a minute. The children are all right for a while with big kids like Shawn and Pete here. Come with me. That's a police order, and I'm not joking."

I heard the sirens, which suddenly *booped* to silence.

He said, "I told them to cut the sirens when they turned off Walton. Frank Thu's leading them, no one better. Now, let's go!"

I still wouldn't move. Shawn detached and stood away from me, looked at my face and sputtered a small laugh. She said, "It's okay, Dad. I'm okay. Pete an' me'll look after the little kids till the police get here."

I cupped her head and quickly kissed her right cheek, where Kevin and I had slapped her. "I love you, sweetheart." She smiled at me, the way her mother does, indulgently.

Kevin was gone ahead of me already, jogging now to conserve energy.

I came alongside: "What the hell do you need *me* for *again*? Are you that hopeless?"

Unaffected, he picked up the pace. "I don't know what condition we'll find her in, but I suspect she's going to have to be talked to, and you can help there. She knows you and you *are* a doctor, Lorne. Good God, if this smell gets any worse, *I'm* gonna puke!"

I breathed through my mouth, hustling to keep up. He was right about the stink, but at least I was no longer bothered by the bit of vomit on my chest.

The remains of the old river road narrowed to a path crowded on the right by scrub growth and on the left by the diminished stream. Troutstream had shrunk to a couple of yards as it trickled over tree roots and rocks, past a shiny shopping cart, the remains of corrugated cardboard beer cases, one turned-down rubber boot, and a toilet with tank and seat intact, gleaming white in the dimness like a Halloween prank.

The path suddenly narrowed further, Kevin stopped dead, and I bumped into him. He reached to the ground and turned with a pink cardigan hanging from his forefinger like some gentle pelt.

"Alice's," I said.

His face was soaked. "She's been living in that bus in the community centre, you know."

Panting, I tasted salt. "*How* did she get that bus down there without killing everybody?"

"It's not the first time either, those tracks weren't worn today."

It hit me: "The allergic reaction, this is where she took Shawn Sunday! Ragweed up top and all sorts of mould down here." And more: "That's the school bus I'd parked beside at the museum! What were we thinking? A school bus on a Sunday! Remember your sniffer dog refusing to leave the spot?"

That spurred him and he was off again.

The woods thinned and opened up and he arrived at the St. Joseph's Boulevard overpass just ahead of me. It was unnoticeable as a bridge when crossed above and only a five-foot-diameter concrete tunnel below. Two scuffed black shoes, pumps, were set neatly at the passage's entrance.

He moved to take off but I grabbed a fistful of his shirt. "Why is Alice accessory to Bob Browne's murder?"

"She must have convinced the Slasher that she was in love with him and he was in love with her."

He tried to pull away but I held tightly. "Yeah, I know that, but *that* doesn't make her accessory to murder."

"Okay, *quickly*. Mad Alice didn't want Bob around any longer, no doubt because he knew about the child abductions and was threatening to inform us. So she used the Slasher, was likely riling him up with stories about Bob being her lover — I think we know her talents for deception and turning people against each other — and the stupid bugger cut Bob Browne's throat in a jealous rage. But for now, this is all guesswork. Who was the real Alice? Who knows? The woman was all actress, all alters. The real Alice died as a toddler in those bad movies we sat through. But, Lorne, I need you to forget your feelings for Bob Browne and talk *sympathetically* to the Alice we find. Can you do that?"

"I doubt it. I hate her."

"We gotta go!"

He pulled away from me and scooted through the concrete tunnel, crouching low and zigzagging up and down its sides to avoid the small stream of water. I followed, out the other side into blinding brightness, then through more tapering brush, until we broke into an open field.

The stinking wind was now freer from the north, and rotten though the air was, it was at least cooler. The sky was darkened now by funereal grey clouds, while distantly a solid black line of storm advanced southeast like a sliding lid to inter the summer's last heat wave.

We took off running through a badly rutted field like desert (my ankles would pay the price in swollen pain). Our destination was the grey-and-maroon complex of the low-lying sewage treatment facility about a half-kilometre away, which waited like the epicentre of a stinking world, drawing us on.

We met no security at the first shed, of course: who would want to break into a sewage treatment plant? We just walked in the first exit door we found at the back corner—and into a blinding environment of near-suffocating stench. The air was a gritty miasma and we stood and stared and blinked strenuously till our pupils adjusted to the crepuscular atmosphere.

What emerged looked like hell's own Olympic-size swimming pool. A huge open tank of chocolate sludge appeared to be lying still. Then it shifted where we stood, swelling, rising and rearing the width of the pool, cresting aloft to become an undulation that snaked towards the opposite end. From that far end a loud burping noise came intermittently, like monstrous gulping as the sludge was moved along to the next pool. While back of it all high-pitched machinery buzzed like a holocaust of insects.

Kevin raised his left arm and, already moving, pointed high into the distant corner. I widened my eyes—they stung worse—so squinted and made out the figure up on what looked like a catwalk near the ceiling. As I followed Kevin along the right side of the pool, he continued pointing across with a commanding arm.

"Do not move another step, Miss Pepper-Pottersfield. This is the police and you are under arrest. *Stop now!*"

He'd startled her out of a downward-peering reverie. As we rounded the far end of the pool, she sped up inching sideways along the catwalk that ended in right angle to a trestle-like structure extending out over the pool a ways. On that side of the room, the pool came right up to the wall. Kevin scurried and skidded to a stop on the slick floor.

I was right behind him on the iron-rung ladder up to the catwalk. My right foot slipped in the sludge that seemed to coat everything and my hands slid down—ploughing the stuff below them—before my grip braked me and I regained footing. I flung the goo from my hands, climbed and helped myself up onto the catwalk by its shaky wire guardrail.

And came up short yet again behind Kevin, who had paused near the end of the narrow catwalk. The six-inch sheet-metal tube it met reached some two metres out over the pool and was cradled in thin metal strips attached to the ceiling the same distance above; ventilation seemed non-existent, so the tube must have been for exhaust. Alice, in her smudged plaid slacks and once-white blouse, was already sliding along the juddering tube. She reached its end and lightly held the metal strips, leaned out and gazed down. The nape of her pale neck looked as frail as Shawn's. I needed no other encouragement to talk to her gently.

Kevin had paused to breathe, which he did laboriously, like a climber in thinned oxygen. Except this air was toxin-thick. I felt my own dizziness.

But I sucked it up and spoke loudly: "Alice, it's me, Lorne Thorpe. Bob Browne still loved you. With his dying words he asked me to tell you that."

The magic name had its effect and she turned her head to the left, looking back at us from unblinking vacant eyes. She was only a short distance away on the diagonal, but there was no way for Kevin to reach her without turning at the end of the catwalk and going out along the thin tube, which could only be disastrous.

Alice smiled so weakly that it could well have been a passing shadow. She held up a black object and frowned at it, as if she too were seeing the old VHS cassette for the first time. Opening her hand, she let it fall from her fingertips and we all watched it drop. There was no splash, more a cushioning and swallow, then a darker smudge where it had momentarily parted the frothy ooze, which again closed over.

Kevin said, "Okay, Alice, that's the worst of it, gone forever. You've done what you came here to do. Now come back to us."

She was still staring after the cassette. She managed somehow to inch farther outward. The end of the metal tube would be overstepped with another such inching. Her bare feet made her look yet more childishly vulnerable.

Kevin said, "Don't, Alice, please." And when she didn't respond, he looked intently back at me.

I said clearly, "Come back, Alice. We know what was done to you and Bob as children, how you suffered more than any child should ever suffer. But, please, Alice, don't do this to yourself, you don't deserve it. Alice?..."

With only one hand lightly holding a metal guy-strip, she again turned her head. She whispered in the clipped schoolmarmish tone I'd heard her use at the children's history fair: "You do not know what you're talking about, Dr. Thorpe. *You* don't deserve *them*." Then turned away and gazed downward again.

"Who, Alice? Who don't I deserve? I don't know what we're talking about. Tell me, please."

Seeing I had her attention, Kevin slid to the very tip of the catwalk. He waited.

Her head whipped up and she screeched at me, "The children! That's who. None of you does! And you especially, Dr. Lorne Thorpe! *You* don't deserve the children!... And neither do I." She dropped her head and seemed to be sniffling into her chest. "That's why I had to leave them back there."

Kevin merely shifted forward and the iron catwalk made the metal tube whine.

Alice flinched, sucked air. Somehow she found space farther out, causing the flimsy cylinder to tip and vibrate and screech in its cradle of metal strips never intended to hold a body's weight.

Kevin looked back at me again, eyebrows rising and eyeballs bugging.

I closed my eyes, searching inside for something of the spell or trance he'd earlier induced in me. I wanted so to speak to Alice from that imaginary place where I knew her best, instead of from my rational self to her mad self. But nothing came. All I could do was open my eyes and look at her standing there wanting to die. Who could blame her? I opened my mouth:

"Alice, listen, please." She again looked back over her left shoulder, with the whole room rocking and crying. "You're right about us *and* about me especially. But I'm trying, I'm learning, I hope. I can do better. We all can. We need to stop interfering with children, in every sense, and in every waking moment of their lives. We need some humility, love that isn't only about us. Bob Browne helped me see that. And so have you. You have so much more to teach us."

But she looked downwards and shook her head *no*. I think she smiled small, mouthed *Bob*.

I said, "Yes, Alice. *Bob*."

She leered at that shit pool. "*Bob*, it's a pun, dumb-dumb. Do you think Gary Lewis would slap a table for me, Dr. Thorpe? Poor Bob, poor silly old buoyant Bob had to...bob off!" She made a noise like a kid snorting up much mucus.

And I knew the powerful presence of crackling madness, of a child made mad, of a human being made evil by evil. It was the detention centre visiting room times a hundred, it was Michael transforming into the Market Slasher. I didn't know what to do. Instead of speaking strategically I asked, "Why, Alice? Why did Bob have to die?"

"Don't be dumb-dumb... The bleeding-heart runt was about to close my whole...show..."

"But why that way, why use the Market Slasher that way?"

When she spoke she continued staring downward, holding two guy-strips like a reluctant girl standing on a tree swing, or a doubtful trapeze artist. "Oh, almighty Dr. Lorne Thorpe, judge and jury. Poor Michael was raped every night of his life by his mother and stepfather." She actually spat ahead of herself. "War was a vacation for him. Just another part of the same old show."

My stomach turned like a rolled-over rotting corpse. A good soldier peering into a pit at Auschwitz might have felt as I felt: not wanting to know any more anymore, helpless, hopeless. It really was time to close the whole show.

Kevin stepped out onto the thin metal tube, it screeched and wobbled. Reaching behind to hold the slack wire of the catwalk with his right hand, he slid another step and extended his left arm toward Alice, stretching himself to the limit. There was only a couple of feet between them. He said with remarkable calm, "Alice?" She didn't budge. "Alice, I agree too, we don't deserve the children. You taught us grown-up dumb-dumbs a lesson. You were just trying to make it better for the children."

No deal.

Then in a remarkable take on Auntie Alice he snapped, "Get back here this very instant, Little Pepper!"

At last she twisted her head to face him and with a small smile said, "Nice try, Mr. Police. But Little Pepper was never permitted to return, only pushed out again and again and again." She let go of the metal guy-strips and, with her back to the pool, was balancing on the front half of her feet like a diver on the end of that nothing metal tube.

"Don't, please, Alice," Kevin pleaded in his own voice. Barely in touch with the wire rail of the catwalk he risked a farther inch along the tube—reaching, stretching—it swung and screeched like some straining jaws of death. Alice instinctively grabbed one cradling metal strip, tilting toward us on her toes. Kevin miraculously found yet another inch forward.

Realizing how far ahead of me he'd got, I slid to the end of the catwalk, gripped its flimsy wire rail and leaned as far out along the metal tube as I could, flailing a bit to get hold of his shirt, fearful of dislodging his anchoring fingertips.

I shouted past him, "Think of the children, Alice! Bob would hate you for what you're doing!"

She said, "I've lived my whole life in shit, I may as well die in shit." She smiled peacefully, an Alice I'd never seen before, sweet, resigned. "At last, one thing's worked out for me. I'm sorry."

I shouted, "Bob's life was shit too, Alice, and he never gave up! Children have to grow up in this shitty world. You can still help them!"

She spoke calmly: "I only ever belonged with Bob, once upon a time, and that's where I'm returning now."

She let go, raised both arms straight out from the shoulders, and went over backwards, whispering upwards, "What's that smell, my love?"

Kevin lunged and the metal tube gave way with a noise like a garbage truck compacting a metal swing set. But I was ahead of him for once. I caught his collar and yanked him back just as the tube fell away at its open end and, with that sudden strength in crises, lifted him with one hand to perch on the end of the catwalk; his feet dangled above the tube which, holding at its wall connection, screeched to a stop. It slanted like a playground slide into that massive vat of human waste.

In that same instant we looked downward after the slapping splat, only to see Alice disappear. Her body left a dark star-splayed outline. I thought of a snow angel. Then a shit angel. Holy shit. Another perfectly paradoxical caduceus. Then it too was gone.

Kevin twisted to get up, his ass slipped off the catwalk and he caught the iron walkway with his hands behind, his body bowing and his feet pedalling the air for purchase. Again I caught his shirt collar and hoisted him back. I turned sideways to hurry down after Alice, slipped on the slick catwalk and plunged backwards feet first, taking an iron uppercut on the chin and passing into unconsciousness.

Chapter 21

In high school I was a fair distance runner. But always just when my modest talent was beginning to make me friends, my diplomat father would be reassigned. I remember best a school in Dublin that had only a cinder track. No team, including our own, would run anymore on the ankle-twisting surface. My ankles were killing me. But I loved that old cinder track, its textured blackness, its heavy cellophane sound, its wet-ashes odour in the daily misty rain. So I ran my laps alone, lap after lap, under occasional blazing sun and in downpour, even in the rare Irish snow, while at home my parents prepared our next move. Lap after lap, going nowhere, the track sliding under me like black diamonds, I would run like this forever, alone and doing something I was good at. For whole days and long after sunset I ran. I'd never done anything else but run like this… And then I noticed someone in the centre of the infield, or not so much somebody as just a lighter spot in the green field, out the corner of my eye, and I plodded on, hoping it would leave me alone and go away. Leave me alone! But it — or he rather — seemed to come closer to me, or I was somehow spiralling nearer my god to him, that white-clad man, or the track was shrinking, day by day, hour by hour, then lap by lap, till I was running tight Jake circles around that squatting figure, on a cinder track the size of a kids' wading pool. The rain was a downpour and night had fallen, yet I was dying of thirst, and the darkness had thickened so that he was all I could see. He persisted holding out his filthy red tumbler of water, mumbling something, a somehow familiar phrase, over and over. I always knew it would come to this. I forced my gaze downward and saw he was shitting, a brown snake of a turd extruding like some living thing, curling underneath him forever, world without end, amen. Dying of embarrassment, I shouted, Get away from me, you fucking loser! *Then quietly,* What? What are you saying? *He raised his face to me, the Tanzanian Marathoner, but gap-toothed and haggard as an old Bedouin now, and said insistently,* Can you see us? Can you see us?... *I clued in:* Caduceus! Caduceus! Jesus Christ! *I accepted his offer, put the filthy glass to my lips and as it cracked and shattered straight away the world was drenched in light...*

My eyes hurt like hell, so I kept them closed. I swallowed and my throat hurt like hell. My chest hurt like hell. I tried to move my mouth and my jaw hurt like hell. In the painful haze there were faces I believed I recognized but couldn't put names to. My brain hurt like hell. Then the faces of Veronica — Owen — Shawn, more composite than individual. I tried to smile, which hurt like hell, and fell asleep, which etc. etc.

I came clear at last, with my whole hell hurting like hell. I flopped my head sideways to find Kevin Beldon sitting beside me and smiling weakly. I squinted.

He said, "Where are you, Lorne?"

I mouthed more than whispered, "Hell."

"Close. You're in your own hospital. The only adult patient ever in CHEO. You're safe here."

He watched me. After what seemed forever, I nodded, which etc.

He continued: "You've been in a coma, Lorne. But deeply only for the first night, Thursday night. Mostly just unconscious these past two days, Friday and Saturday. You've been coming out of it slowly. It's early Sunday morning. They say you're going to be all right."

He paused and looked at me closely. "Take it easy, though. You've had a pumping tube down your throat." He nodded at the far side of the bed. "Those other tubes in your arms, one's for antibiotics and the other's just a solution of stuff. But I'm sure you know all that."

I dozed. I woke painfully. He was still there.

I touched my swollen throat, my tender chin, swallowed saliva that was shards of shell. I thought I was saying something but only a moan came out. Water sluiced my throat and I coughed and sputtered onto my chest.

"Easy does it, big guy. I'll call Veronica."

"Wait," I managed hoarsely.

He sluiced me again and left the plastic bottle on my chest.

"What..." I moved and reached and used my hand as if for the first time ever, squeezed off some water, amazed that I'd ever taken this miracle drink for granted. If anyone tried to take it away, I would start a world war.

"What...happened?"

He placed his hand on the bottle on my chest, rested it there briefly. "You don't remember anything?"

I didn't have to think for long, painful though it was. "I remember everything, right up to...falling."

"I saw your chin hit that iron catwalk and you go straight down like a body buried at sea. The doctors believe you were knocked cold. In fact, they think that may have saved your life. But a quantity of the crap got into your lungs. They say you've been in toxic shock as much as a coma. How do you feel?"

I held the long spout in my mouth and squeezed the bottle. The water was lukewarm, perfect. I took a deeper breath. It felt normal. I clenched my fists and wiggled my toes. My ankles hurt like hell. I winced and let my head sink back on the pillow. I'd come out alive after all. His chair scraped.

"Wait. I'm okay. You saved my life, Kevin, didn't you?"

He stood by the bed. "Buddy, you saved mine twice up there. It was the least I could do."

"Alice?"

He pinched his mouth and dropped his chin, shook his head once. "I got you out first. You looked dead. I cleared your airways and did some quick mouth-to-mouth. Not to worry though, we won't be running off to Niagara Falls any time soon."

Laughing was like spiked fists on my head and chest.

"Sorry," he said. "For a while I thought *I* was about to pass out. It took too long to fight off the disgust. But miraculously my cell still worked after the shit bath and I called the emergency unit that was with the kids at the bus. That was done in nothing flat. But it was only then that I went back in after Alice. I've also been told by your colleagues that she was long gone after the first seconds anyway. They say it looks like she just gulped the stuff when she hit the pool."

After a while he said, "I should call Veronica. Shawn wouldn't leave this morning unless her mom went home with her." But he made no motion to go.

I looked out the window: slate-grey sky, lowering, beautiful.

"You saved my life, Kevin. You went out on that flimsy tube then back into that pool of shit to save Alice. You're the real thing, Kevin. Thank you."

"Like I said, you'd already saved me—"

"I'm a born coward. Thank you. Why me?"

"What?... Well, like I said, it was sort of a mini-triage situ—"

"Why me?"

When he didn't answer after a while, I turned from the window to check if he was still there. His ginger knob was bowed and it made me think again of a small earth-trapped sun. He was contemplating his steepled fingertips, which were doing a springing little dance for him. He was the real thing, all right. Like many men, I suspect, I'd often wished I was, but I'm definitely not, and I'm not so sure anymore that I'd want to be. It must get awfully lonely out there.

I said, "Putting yourself in a trance, Detective Mesmer?"

He squinted a smile at me: "You're your old self again all right, Thorpe."

"I hope not."

He looked puzzled, then broke his steepled hands and performed all his tics: pinching the bridge of his nose and sliding his fingers down, rubbing his ginger dome from forehead to crown, then back from nape to brow. He pursed his mouth and nodded his head once at me.

"Who knows *why you*, Lorne Thorpe. Or why any of it, really. You know as much as I do, or almost. You stepped into it when you joined that Troutstream Community Association. Like I said before, you walked into Alice's life at the right time, or the wrong time, as she must've been stressed to the point of cracking by then, if she'd not already cracked. You had gift horse written all over you: the middle-aged white man of power, ideal opportunity for her mad revenge. Then, in her eyes, you became part of the TCA crew cheating Bob of the money owed him, and she and Bob *had* to have that money. She'd been working only as a crossing guard and as the school-bus assistant, minimum wage for few hours. She volunteered a lot of time to local children's agencies and charities and was always in hock for promised donations, including to all those places she'd brought to the children's history fair. So money again. She needed the money Bob Browne had been promised by your TCA. *She needed money to give to charity.*"

He paused and shook his head. Proceeded: "So Alice decided in her warped way to teach you and the TCA a lesson, but especially you, Dr. Lorne Thorpe, by taking Shawn and the other children. On top of that, you probably made her jealous, because you and Bob became friends. He was her great love since childhood, as those sick videos showed us. She went crazy over time—I think we know why—and Bob loved her to the end, as you told her up there on the shit diving board. Some love story. Think again, Lorne, what were Bob's last words? *Willie Pep?* The boxer?"

"Of course. Little Pep. Save the children. Save Little Pepper."

"She'd lost it, whatever of *it* she had left by then. I mean, she even turned against Bob. Maybe it was her jealousy of Bob's friendship with you inspired her to use jealousy with the Slasher against Bob. But I won't lie to you. It also happened to you because you *are* you, Dr. Lorne Thorpe. You rubbed her the wrong way, like you rub a lot of people the wrong way. That's *why you*. Really, though, we may as well ask, why *not* you?"

"Wy Knots?"

He chuckled. "Don't be dumb-dumb, ask again!"

In my sore head I zoomed back to beginnings. "Alice fits the physical profile of the man with the dog at the museum. But how did she know Shawn and I would *be* at the Museum of Science and Technology last Sunday?"

"You must have told her."

"No."

"Who else knew?"

"Veronica, Owen…"

"You told Bob Browne?"

"No, I'd not seen Bob— Wait, I'd complained to Foster in a text Saturday night, because he'd had my Caddy since Friday, about having to drive Veronica's car to the museum next day."

"That's it then. Foster could have mentioned it to Debbie—his first friend of a friend—who was always at CHEO with one of her kids, as you know. That was the routine: Foster calls Debbie, who contacts Alice Pepper-Pottersfield with a request for Alice's special friend, Bob Browne, to visit a problem child at CHEO. All done anonymously, and Debbie must never have been allowed to meet him at CHEO, so she couldn't match him to the Bob Browne you brought in to do the playground work. Or Foster could have mentioned it to Bob himself, jealously making fun of your fixation on your Caddy, since you and Bob were already friends by then."

"Alice *set* Bob on me, told him to make my acquaintance, become my friend, and to say that he needed work badly. She prepped him and counted on me getting him for the playground job to solve their money problems."

"Most likely. But Alice didn't need Debbie and Foster and Bob to know what you were up to, Lorne. Soon as you walked into that first meeting of the TCA, she knew everything about you. She already knew how to manipulate men like you, like us. Call it a gift or a curse. She'd learned it the hardest way.

"I've done some more checking, talked with all your TCA friends again. Debbie is *still* scared shitless of Alice Pepper-Pottersfield. How could you have sat through recent TCA meetings and not noticed *that*, Dr. Sherlock? Frank Baumhauser, too, *and* the Lewises, they were all scared to death of her, did what she told them to do, believed what she told them to believe. Not at first, but I suspect that not long after you joined, all she had to do was raise an eyebrow and the rest kowtowed. It probably began with that children's history fair. Baumhauser claims she'd been working on him for weeks. All you've gotta do is say *Alice* to any of your committee friends and it's like saying *boo* from behind—even now when she's dead!"

I squirmed. "Did you ever find out where they came from?"

"The info was still in their phones and a server's cloud site. Alice and Bob showed up in Ottawa about a year ago. They'd been activists in Germany for a couple of years. Alice went to a G20 summit in London to protest child-labour sweatshops and joined a group there, or took it over actually. They were apart for a few months, then she emailed Bob in Munich that she was moving to Ottawa because the Canadian prime minister had promised to make child poverty a priority."

"Oh, yeah? Whatever happened to that promise?"

"Same as all the other bullshit you hear in Ottawa, fresh and fuming only until the next election's over."

I sipped and thought. "Okay, say a lot of it was my bad luck, even just me being me and being in the wrong place at the wrong time. I can accept that. But why did Bob Browne survive it all and Alice didn't?"

"Bob survived?"

I took another drink. "How come, after the exact same childhoods, Alice goes psycho and Bob turns out...well, weird, sure, but such a great guy too? And more than that, his own little miracle worker?"

He steepled his fingers again, placed them over his nose and spoke between his hands, like someone megaphoning quietly: "That's a mystery, Lorne, bottomless, one that no Dr. Sherlock is ever going to explain and tie up neatly in some lousy movie's reveal scene. Maybe the difference between Alice and Bob was in their infancies, from their parents, the quality or quantity of their mothers' love, say. But going from what we do know so far of their identically perverse childhoods—Little Pepper's and King Robbie's—I'd have to say that earlier upbringing can't account for the big difference either, or not alone. For some reason — say, as a toddler, Alice saw a cat kill a bird, something that insignificant — Alice turned inward. Then she was horribly abused and filled with self-loathing. Alice disappeared, got lost inside somewhere, and a number of other Alices — more powerful, in control of things — got pushed out onto life's stage. Nowadays that's pretty well textbook multiple-personality disorder."

I extended his line of thought: "And Bob — who could have witnessed the very same cat kill the same bird — became altruistic, with Alice as his chief charge, his responsibility, and the love of his life. Still, you're right, that hardly explains the gigantic difference between them."

He blew air. "No, it doesn't. Maybe it's just testament to the value of teaching and learning and practising — *believing* in the Golden Rule. But like I said, these are not questions we two dumb-dumbs are going to answer. We'll just have to live in some bafflement. You need to rest up and I really better call Veronica."

"Tell no one else I'm awake."

"Gotcha."

He was at the door when he turned back with a drawled, "Oh, yeah…" Looking uncharacteristically sheepish, he returned to bedside, undid the top button of his polo shirt and lifted a necklace over his ginger knob. "A little get-well gift."

With some effort I moved and rotated my hand, and he placed the Jew's harp in my palm. Blankly I stared.

"Don't worry," he said, "it's been cleaned."

"Too bad."

My inability to continue made him nervous. "You also might like to know that I arranged for Bob and Alice to be buried side-by-side."

"Good." I plucked the trigger with my forefinger. It made a barely audible tone, a forlorn note. My eyelids weighed on me. "Aren't you messing with evidence here, Detective Beldon? I mean, this *was* a murder weapon."

Fading fast I just caught what he said.

"*Some* prized evidence, I had a helluva time locating it. The murderer himself is dead and so's his accomplice. Who are they gonna prosecute? But better keep it under cover all the same or I'll get…busted back to…Missing Persons."

I held it under the covers, squeezing till its point dug into my flesh. Self-surgery. What hurts can heal, what heals can… And sank deeply into welcome, dreamless sleep.

When I next awoke, Veronica and Shawn were waiting by the bed. Veronica leaned down and kissed my desiccated lips.

She smiled an old smile and said, "How are you feeling, dear?"

"Much better *now*."

I raised myself up on my elbows and was soon fairly propped on pillows by the nervously bustling two of them. One of the tubes was gone and I fingered the other. "Do I still need this?"

She looked towards the door, where Art Foster had quietly been standing. He came to the other side of the bed.

"No, you don't need that. You can finish the course of antibiotics orally at home — *the whole course*, Doctor. Keep sipping this water, though, you need the glucose and electrolytes. Eat a banana when you get home."

As he was removing the IV and dabbing the puncture, he whispered, "Lorne, I can't tell you how sorry I am about all this." He kept his head bent overlong to the simple task of applying a Band-Aid.

I whispered, "Don't worry yourself on my account, Art. If you need my forgiveness, you're forgiven. But you don't need it. How come you're not suspended?"

Straightening, he grinned, and I recognized my devious old friend from long ago and far away. "I may be yet. I've been legally cleared, but the board's still contemplating some form of reprimand for moral turpitude." He turned to leave.

"Art, I want to testify for you."

"Thanks, old buddy." He was already at the door.

"Art, what's happening with the Caddy?"

He glanced first at Veronica and Shawn, then quizzically at me. "I don't know. It's no longer impounded, thanks to Detective Beldon, if that's what you mean. I'll see about getting it, uh, fixed up and returned pronto."

"It's yours."

He startled. "Mine? I don't... What would I do with...? Besides, well..." He briefly shifted his eyes to Shawn.

"Will you do me a favour then? Arrange to have it sold and the money donated to the Children's Wish Foundation."

"With pleasure. It should fetch a price." And he was gone.

I looked at Veronica. "Who made Art my doctor?"

She put her arm around Shawn's waist and brought her close to the bed. "He did. He took right over. He's broken a ton of rules to get you in here and protected from everyone."

We were making strange. It was in the stiffer way she held her head, the lack of eye contact, the tone echoing her Jake-voice, the way she was positioning Shawn. Hollowness bubbled in my chest, a nudging panic.

She moved behind the uncharacteristically shy Shawn. "Shawn and I have made a deal that she's going to visit with you alone first. I'll be back." She held Shawn's shoulders and smiled around our growing daughter. "Are you sure you're strong enough for this now?"

"I am."

Without a backward glance, she left.

I felt pain when Shawn hopped up and perched on the edge of the high bed, but I smiled. She leaned across me — *ouch* — and touched the Band-Aid.

"Are you really all better, Dad?"

"I am, sweetheart, better than ever."

And without further preliminary she just lay easily on my chest and cried and cried like the world could never get enough of her tears. I stroked her dandelion head and waited. Hurting like hell. I never felt better.

She sucked it up, but didn't sit up. "It's all my fault. I don't care what Mom says. If I'd never gone with that crazy Alice and the dog she stole, none of this ever would have happened. But right away when I came out with the water for the dog she told me she liked playing dress-up as a man and started talking about knowing Wy and how she would bring me to him for helping with the dog. I shoulda told you and Mom and Detective Beldon the truth. If I'd not made that Alice mad down by the stream, she wouldn't have gone to the sewage building and be dead and you'd not have been nearly killed!"

"It's not your fault, Shawn. Your mom's right and I think you're old enough to know that."

"*Sure*... Then whose fault is it?"

"Don't be dumb-dumb, ask again?"

Lovely laughter before she asked, "Was it Bob Browne's fault?" She sat back and looked at me as directly as any adult.

"Sweetheart, it *was* Bob's fault, but not much. My fault and Dr. Foster's fault too, and a lot of other people's fault, including you a little. Do you remember what I said to you down by the bus?"

She reflected. "You said she was mental because grown-ups sexually abused her when she was a little girl. And I'll bet because nobody loved her enough, either."

"Smart girl, you."

"How can you love anything if nobody ever loved you enough? It's like what Wy says about all animals."

God bless Wy. "But still, even after all her pain and suffering, Miss Pepper-Pottersfield did love someone and very much—Bob Browne."

She made her scrunched face: "Hmm... I guess I can see that. I'm glad."

I rewarded myself with a hit of the sweet warm water.

She grinned mischievously: "I'll bet you didn't know I saw you last Tuesday!"

"What?" I steadied myself. "But how could that be?"

"I got Miss Pepper-Pottersfield to drive the school bus past our house. She made it like a game and got all disguised like a man in sunglasses and a cap and I crouched down behind her. It was real fun, you looked like you were kneeling in the driveway beside Jake and washing his legs! I said that to her and we laughed and laughed and, well, like, hmm… I guess she was okay too sometimes. She let me out later by the community centre. She drove the bus right in and I just walked home."

"You know, I actually remember that bus, and I'm glad it wasn't all bad for you and Miss Pepper-Pottersfield. But how're all the other kids from the bus?"

She couldn't get it out fast enough: "Mrs. Kilborn's home again and she's trying to organize the parents to sue everybody and *she's* suing the school board because Jake was left out of our *adventure*, she keeps calling it! Can you be-*lieve* it! But we're all okay. A lot of us met in the busted-up playground yesterday, *after* we heard you were going to be all right, I mean. Anyways, we started a club and all the other kids who missed out are *so* jealous. And we got the grief people to get us some time off school for secret meetings in the playground and Jake's mom told Mrs. Carswell her lawyer friend says Pete had better shut up saying he's all right—"

"All right, you two, break it up. My turn."

I could have listened to Shawn forever, or at least till I saw Veronica again. She came forward and Shawn said, "Oh, all right." She stood away from the bed and grinned.

"Well," she continued, "I guess I have to leave you two old lovebirds alone now." She passed behind her mother and backed out making mock-kissing noises. The door closed quietly.

We laughed uneasily. We looked away. How could *we* be uneasy alone with one another? Yet there we were.

I smirked. "Old lovebirds."

She looked at me and didn't blink. "Well, are we?" She awkwardly sat on the edge of the high bed.

"To tell you the truth, I don't know why you put up with me. But *I* certainly hope Shawn's right, that we *are* a pair of old lovers."

When I looked up she was just watching me with those deep brown eyes that had been saving me from myself since we'd met. Saying nothing, she made me suppress a conniption of pain by collapsing lightly on my chest, resting her left cheek over my heart.

It had been our first long walk to the beach at Mooney's Bay, in early summer, our third date, the perfect evening of a wonderful day. We had rested together in this very pose on still-warm sand. She'd joked: Uh-oh, I don't hear anything. My heart. *I'd been about to tell her for the first time that I loved her. Instead I'd breathed deeply her tickling wind-freshened hair as her head lifted on my breathing in gentle waves...and let the moment extend comfortably, as I watched the stars prick infinite darkness with the eternal mystery of light. She'd actually fallen asleep. She snored. I'd fallen forever in love, for the first time. I was forty. A miracle. Yes.*

Now I broke the silence, whispering: "First I'm saved by my mother's love, then by yours. There must be something wrong in that?"

She eased up and sat back in a very controlled kind of way. "Not by my lights. You do your job, we do ours."

"You're way better than me at multitasking." I laughed weakly.

I sensed her selecting her words, in the same way she examined a bin of Granny Smiths or remainders at a bookstore, with doubtful eyes and tongue tip just parting her lips.

"I never went to *be* with Jack Kilborn, Lorne, sexually speaking. Nothing so exciting. Or desperate. It was Jake I worried about. But I *did* leave you for a while, I won't lie."

She gazed at me in a way that made me feel lost. I must have looked a sight because she hurried, "It was all part of the craziness of this whole business."

Deal. *Crazy* would be our explanation then, same as Kevin explained mad Alice at bottom. As the poem has it (the one Veronica recited to me once over a campfire in Algonquin Park, with Owen sleeping in his car seat between us, and which instantly burned itself into my poor memory for such): *When we are old and grey and full of sleep, and nodding by the fire...together we will remember these crazy days, this crazy story.*

"Let's forget it then," I said.

She patted my chest—*ouch*—and stood. "We'd better not. But I will for now if you'll just crack an old smile for me."

It hurt, but I cracked one.

"You call that a smile?" But she was light-hearted and moving off.

"It's this." And like a magic trick I produced the Jew's harp from underneath the covers, where it had been pricking me like hell.

She gawked, then squinted recognition. "I won't ask where you pulled that out of." She was turning to the door.

"Hey, wait a second. I was just thinking, we should get that gas fireplace you've lusted after for years."

"*That's* what you've been thinking?" Her steely look could have riveted me to that sick bed forever.

"*When you are old and grey and full of sleep, and nodding by the fire, take down this book, and slowly read, and dream of the soft look your eyes had once, and of their shadows deep*... I remember. I love you."

She stood still and stared. Her look softened, she smiled. Turning away, with some difficulty: "I have to get back home to —"

"Owen! How's Owen? Where's Owen?" I alarmed myself that I'd not asked after my son till then.

With her hand on the door handle she looked back, smirking lightly, tipped back her head: "I thought you'd never ask, Dr. Thorpe... That's some memory you've got there."

"It's just that...well, I..."

"I was referring to the Yeats, dear. Owen's been up here a lot. He's been worried sick. But you know Owen, he just doesn't show it. Or he has his own way of showing what he feels, like someone else I know *and* love. Once we knew you were out of danger yesterday, he went out and got a tattoo."

"*He what?*" That really hurt.

"Don't look so pained, he's the last of his friends to get one, even the young girls. I wasn't to tell, it's a homecoming surprise for you, so act surprised."

"A surprise for me? I don't get it? Wait, don't go!"

"You'll see," she sang. "And *don't* be critical."

"C'mon, you can't just leave me like —"

"I've left your clothes on the dresser, overnight bag in the bathroom. Rest. We'll be back to pick you up later this afternoon. Art said we can have you back at five-thirty."

"But—"

She raised her right hand and gave me the Stan Laurel wave, and left.

Chapter 22

I awoke alone. Outside was dim and inside dimmer, though it was only five. I made it to the bathroom like some old tar negotiating the deck of a tossing ship. I tried water without the straw, my hand trembling as I brought the glass tumbler to my mouth. I splashed my face, brushed my teeth twice and rinsed repeatedly. I still tasted something rotten.

I looked a shocker: a blue-and-green badge on my cheekbone where Kevin had belted me, and my chin bruised black, with a raw strip like fiery gills laddering my Adam's apple. I needed a shave badly, but flinched at the thought of anything harder than water touching my face. How had Shawn and Veronica kept themselves from screaming? Must be they'd had time to adjust while I was unconscious.

My body was still a coherent pain. I shucked off the hospital gown and dressed, which hurt. I sniffed my armpit: deodorant? Had Veronica washed my body?... Yes. I checked the room and found nothing else of mine. Were my dirty clothes police evidence?... No: Veronica had collected them.

I moved about gingerly, shuffling and pacing the floor for exercise, needing to rest less and less on the edge of the bed. But I would not leave the room till I could walk from wall to wall five times without looking like a doddering old man.

At 5:20 I looked into the hallway, saw no one. I recognized the top floor of CHEO, where the executive administrative offices were protected from the real business of the hospital. My room was not for patients but for the sleep of late-working execs (which explains the dangerous glass tumblers). I moved into the hallway and headed for the elevator, whose doors whooshed open before I could turn away. A blue pinstriped suit pulled up short. I recognized him but didn't know his name.

He stood still, his face following me like a searchlight as I stepped into the elevator. "Dr. Thorpe, good to see you're up and about! Wow, that's some…"

He had to call through the closing doors: "Hey, great work on helping crack those crimes connected to the Market Slasher case! First the arsenic poisoning and now this! I trust we're not going to lose you to the police!"

I smiled to myself and it hurt like hell: so that's how the twisted tale's being spun by CHEO's crack PR team.

Tamara discharged me. For once neither of us wisecracked and for the first time her ebony sheen didn't strike me as strange, but familiar and welcome. We just looked at each other and I knew she knew everything. It surprised me only mildly that I didn't mind.

Still no Owen, only Shawn accompanied Veronica. Excited Shawn kept badgering me about coming to her school to give a talk on playground safety and—wink wink—meet with her new club. She was shushed by Veronica and sat back glumly in the rear seat with her arms crossed tightly on her chest. Veronica drove with a smile on her face that made the Mona Lisa look like Oprah. I couldn't smile normally yet. It hurt too much. *What* had I been doing with my face when I'd thought I was smiling at them from my hospital bed?

When we pulled into our driveway, Jack and Trixie were standing in theirs and pretending to be messing around with Jake. To their credit, they merely called hello and welcome home. I thought, *Welcome home to you too, Trixie.* But that was Jack's bed of nails to lie on.

Jake broke away and came scuttling across the patch of yard between us, with neither parent moving to stop him, of course (they could well have nudged him). Veronica intercepted him, running interference not for me but for Shawn.

I said, "Just a minute," and stepped around her to meet Jake. I slipped the Jew's harp from my pocket and handed it to him.

Without a word Jake inserted it correctly and struck the trigger. His eyes widened. He struck again and varied the tone, struck again and again. He commenced a kind of rocking jig and danced towards his parents, who were smiling widely. Veronica laughed and Shawn chimed in, me too, laughing together for the first time in a long time. Jack and Trixie each put arms on Jake and turned towards their home.

So the old wives' tale has truth: some Down's kids do have musical aptitude. And Bob's Jew's harp had served again as the perfect distraction. What more did Doubting Lorne need to see and be touched by? There was music and magic in that Jew's harp!

We turned into our house, our never-so-welcome home sweet home, as welcoming as when we'd brought our babies into it. Veronica and Shawn moved a couple of steps along the front hall and, most strangely, turned back to me, smiling in weird expectation.

Owen's bedroom door opened and I watched his hairy legs descend the stairs. When he reached the bottom, I stepped forward with arms spread to hug him, as I'd hugged Shawn, though I'd not hugged Owen in a long time.

With his dark face open but unsmiling he stuck out his hand and said in an affected baritone, "Welcome home, Father."

We all laughed nervously.

I took his hand and looked at him with what I hoped was radiant paternal love. His eyes widened as he took in my face: "It's really great…to see…ya. Wow!"

Veronica said, "Oh come on, Owen. Give your dad a hug."

He gave her a smirk and swung back to me with a bemused frown. I was still holding his hand, so I pulled him forward and hugged him, patting his back like I was giving comfort. He remained stiff as a tree trunk.

"Ow," he said. "Watch the upper arm, you're not the only injured party here, you know."

"Show him!" Shawn squealed.

I stood back and acted my curious best: "Show me what?"

"Owen got a tattoo yesterday even when you told him he never could!"

He snapped at her — "You be quiet!" — suddenly losing about five years. Which he reclaimed as he turned back to me.

"He did, did he?" I drawled. "Taking advantage of the old man's incapacity, eh? Let's have a look. What is it, a pierced heart with *Dad* on it?"

He wasn't moving. I never knew what it was with him. And me with him, I guess.

Veronica stepped fussily between us and turned Owen a full quarter clockwise. He was like a passive runaway brought before the judge. She pushed up the left sleeve of his black T-shirt.

And there it was, executed in sky blue, earthen black and blood red: the caduceus.

I was knocked back. I leaned forward, brought my face closer, raised a finger and touched it lightly. It still looked a painful, raw wound.

Veronica beamed at me: "Isn't it a beauty?"

It was, and it wasn't, of course.

Still turned aside, he spoke to the wall opposite: "Uh, you kept mumbling it when you were, like, passed out the second night. I'd thought you were, like, raving. *Can you see us? Can you see us?* But one time Dr. Foster came in, he told me what it meant. Like, how it started with the Olympics and the god Hermes and all that. Dr. Foster thought it was a great idea for me to get one as a tattoo. He said it would, like, send positive energy to you, wherever you were, like."

For Owen, that was a Speech from the Throne. I found my voice, if a wholly wrong voice. "Right, only that's what the Maharishi told the Beatles when Brian Epstein died, *like*, half a century ago."

He frowned hard at the wall: "*What? Who?* The *Beatles* again?" He reached for his sleeve, shaking his head: "I knew you'd say something like that." He turned, stuck his face in mine: "But it worked, didn't it, you're home and alive?"

Veronica held him back from going upstairs. He didn't struggle and she made an imploring face at me. So I hurried: "Okay, okay, sorry. Where'd you copy it from?"

Wearing his stoic face, he was talking to the stairway wall this time: "They had a bunch of pictures at the tattoo parlour."

"*Parlour?*" I just couldn't help myself.

He twisted his sore arm from Veronica's light hold and pushed down the sleeve, was turning to the stairs.

I caught his forearm, he winced, and I hurried again: "No wait, that was just my usual stupid joke. I like it, I really do. Let's have another look."

I pulled him toward me, he resisted lightly. I pushed up the sleeve and, cupping his upper arm so high that my hand was lodged in his hot and hairy pit, took a really good look. The winged standard always made me think of a fallen angel more than something hermetic. In Owen's version, two red-and-black diamond-patterned snakes twine a dark pole beneath two blue wings to flick tongues at each other. The caduceus had centred a lot of my "big" thinking, what I would call my philosophy, for most of my mature life. I loved that it was the symbol of my profession and that its full meaning would remain as mysterious as the eternal dance of yin and yang. Although I'd explicitly forbidden Owen many times from disfiguring himself with tattoos, I found myself fine with the idea that the caduceus now branded my son.

I said as best I could, "No joke, it's a…well, I think it's a beauty. Maybe we should all, the whole family, get one."

Veronica chimed in two syllables, "Lo-orne?"

"I'm serious." The joking father who cried serious, or half-serious anyway.

"Like I care." He was climbing the stairs, but turned after only two: "Hey, was it you snuck that *Abbey Road* into my player?"

"Guilty, son, I apologize."

He was higher up now, if sounding closer: "When they all, like, jam out at the end, it's like they're talking to each other in a whole new language. That really *the Beatles*?"

I called, "What about 'Oh! Darling'?"

Nearing his room he loudly and ironically sang the opening of "Octopus's Garden."

I smiled at smiling Veronica: "He was smiling heading up, you couldn't see."

She smile-frowned: "To tell you the truth, I think the tattoo looks awful. Does it look infected to you?"

I gazed up the dim stairs: "Probably still too soon to tell. I'll keep an eye on it."

I'd not noticed Shawn leave for the family room, though I recognized the gong and tinkling bells that began *Wy Knots*. Veronica looked up the empty stairway after Owen, then gave me her oh-well smirk. I was suddenly dead tired.

She saw my weariness, kissed my tender cheek: "Go lie down for a spell. I'll keep your supper for whenever you come down. Chicken soup!" She laughed as lightly as Wy's tinkling bells.

I obeyed. I didn't drift off right away, perhaps because I'd slept so much lately or from the nervous excitement of being home and Owen's tattoo and all. I stared at the stippled ceiling and thought about the brief visit I'd made at CHEO before meeting Veronica outside the Discharge pod. More a reconnoitring than a visit.

The Catholic privacy room had been empty. In the wall mural I could detect no crack running up from the little girl's proffered lily through Jesus' robe and on up through the ceiling. Maybe the crack had opened only briefly and closed, the concrete shifting in cooling temperatures as wood breathes? I would *not* check my parking spot in the underground garage where I'd first hit the wall with Veronica's Golf. Anyway, I couldn't remember whether I'd actually seen a crack down there or envisioned it later. I was fine with that too.

Previously I'd paid no attention to the mural's title, which scrolled above in a Gothic script banner held in the beaks of bluebirds:

Jesus Suffers the Little Children

An odd use of the word, that "suffers." No suffering the big grown-ups for Jesus when he's taking a break. He preferred children and whores and thieves, and losers for apostles. But give us a break too, suffering J, suffer us successful middle-class, middle-aged men and women of Troutstream. (Okay: *late* middle-aged.) We're dying out here in the 'burbs...if slowly.

L'Envoi:
The SUV to Troutstream

We are returning from Place D'Orleans Mall in our spanking new Ford Escape, with an unsecured big mirror in the back seat partially blocking the rear view. We've had a gas fireplace installed in the family room and it needed something above it. We agreed on the traditional golden-framed mirror. As we make the tricky left turn onto Izaak Walton Road against heavy traffic, Veronica reaches into the back seat as if calming a dog or soothing a child. We are soon slowed behind Mann Quarry's regular convoy of dump trucks, even on a Sunday, and by families streaming to the Sharks Tank soccer fields, themselves driving slowly or strolling the road's gravel shoulders from distant parking spots.

On this way into Troutstream the tendency is to keep eyes right, away from the pandemonium of the quarry with its gigantic racket, low clouds of stone dust and growing cones of gravel. We approach the entrance to the Troutstream Toboggan Hill, and we both look glum but say nothing. Until reaching the soccer fields, the area on the right is wooded with umpteenth-generation maple and poplar and spindly birch. Now, at this season, the cool end of a hot September after a tropical summer, the woods appears weary of its green leaves, as if dreaming of earth tones and the deep sleep of winter.

Veronica catches me looking and says, "Keep your eyes on the road, dear. There're lots of soccer kids around."

She returns to the view. "As it slides past, it's like a Monet painting. Did you know he would paint the same haystack over and over in different lights?"

She's showing off. Once, mere weeks ago, I'd have made some crack to ridicule her affectation. *Did you forget your contacts?* Or perhaps a groaner in a Maurice Chevalier accent: *Sairtannly zee painteengs would be worth bo-coo de moe-nee.*

Now I say, "The very same haystack? But I don't think you *can* look at the same haystack twice."

"That's the point. And that's Heraclitus, who said you can't step into the same stream twice."

"Or drive into the same Troutstream?"

She laughs the unreserved laugh that makes me love her. And says, "But you're right, of course. Haystack, stream, Troutstream. Everything is changing always and forever, and thank God it is."

God. Singular. *There's* a sea change.

I risk it. "Ever notice in first-blush spring, the whole woods radiates a green nimbus just above the actual trees? It looks like the feel of a newborn's skin, more the *idea* of green than the thing itself."

"Gotcha, Shakespeare. Shit. Sorry, that was uncalled for. That's actually pretty good. Maybe you've been a poet all along pretending to be a scientist."

I keep my face to the road: "Sometimes I don't know what I am anymore."

"You'll get over it." She turns again to her side window and says more quietly, "We will."

"We will," I echo.

"And happy belated birthday, darling."

With a sigh she turns and this time reaches her left hand to the nape of my neck. Nice. I was feeling a chill there. I'd turned sixty in the middle of it all, though no one celebrated, understandably. I was on the threshold of old age, the "new fifty" or forty or whatever be damned. Bob Browne was right: I'd missed my time-lapsed middle age still thinking I was young. I imagine many do. The Age of Delusion, if that's not already been every age for us deluded boomers, from the decade of the '50s onwards. *We* would never be dying slowly, no, not us, babbling our protests all the way to the grave, as though life was just another talk show, a rehearsal for some "revolution." *We* would be Nature's conquerors—the very first immortals! The cosmos would just have to make an exception for us.

Dear God, have I latently been mourning my lost youth? Is that, then, what this has been all about?... Okay, why not? I'll be mourning for the Lorne Thorpes that were and never were till the day I die. Poor multiple Alice, she never got the chance.

I say to the road ahead, "It always helps to know you're only a decade behind me." Which at forty-seven she's as good as.

"No regrets. I was thirty when I...when we had Owen. It took us seven years to know that one wasn't enough, then a whole year for this old lady to get pregnant again. Remember that rigmarole? We were like breeding livestock."

"I've suffered worse, old girl."

Before she removes her hand, we smile briefly at each other, unsentimentally, no moist eyes. Just a mutual hope for what lies ahead. Soon we will regularly be hearing about the deaths of friends. Already two acquaintances of mine have died recently, one of late-detected prostate cancer in his early fifties and the other of a brain tumour at fifty-six. Both ugly deaths. I could be next. I will be, of course, eventually. Again, as Bob Browne (deceased) said.

We pass from the weary green of the desiccated woods to the wide open space of the soccer fields. A new cream-coloured field house with a big stained-glass window in the image of a soccer ball sits in the middle of some dozen pitches. It looks like a modest little church where the soccer moms go to pray, not for victory but that everyone has fun and no one gets hurt. If their prayers are answered, soccer will become *the* children's sport of North America.

I slow for the thickening crowd and reduce further to a funereal pace. Veronica lowers her window to the sounds of children shouting and their parents shouting at them, urging them on only to do their best. She smiles to herself and I can't read her like I used to. I think I like that.

She says, "Soccer moms compete like mad to appear non-competitive, competition being *such* a bad thing. But children read hypocrisy quicker than they text."

My dear. "Not child beauty pageant moms. They're like fucking gladiators."

Things will never be the same again. But then, things never are. A daily sky can shift continuously, dramatically, and nothing has changed but the changeable weather. The night sky looks the same for thousands of years, yet it's an explosion at a fireworks factory out there. Shawn was returned to us this time, but in no time she and Owen will be gone for good. Or we'll be leaving them.

For a moment I wish like a shooting-star-wishing child that, old as we are, we could have another baby. I feel such a heaviness of heart knowing we cannot, as I do at those sudden weird reminders that my mother has been dead for years. Life can so easily seem just one bad cosmic joke. Some distracting fun. Then the fun's over, thank you, Kevin.

For the present, though, climbing the same old hill into Troutstream, to entertain my wife I sing: "I don't know why you say hello, Troutstream, I say good…bye…"

Just ahead on the left, where the curving road rises most steeply, I spot the Tanzanian Marathoner shuffling along, doing his falling forever forward bit. I lower the window, sip the cool air and hold it. A joke is always risky, a gamble that fewer and fewer are willing to make in these grim times… Fuck that. I exhale. What's the point in living at all if you haven't the conviction of your own experiences? Otherwise, just find another hole in another wasted playground, pack it in this time.

"Hey, you look like you could use a lift!"

Without slowing (he jogs so slowly as it is, he could hardly slow further without coming to a stop), he brushes me off with a flapping right hand.

"C'mon, friend," I persist, "that left knee of yours has been waving the white flag for years!"

He squints angrily as I continue to pace him. The car behind honks. I glance in the rear-view but see only the new mirror. Veronica is pinching the dashboard with both hands, as she does on winter roads. She says my name in a hush, but not insistently.

The Tanzanian Marathoner—Ben Singh Cahir is his name, as I was reminded by Shawn, a retired computer engineer originally from Cork, Ireland (of all places), as I'd learned long ago from Jack Kilborn—Ben smiles a smile of recognition only a lifetime of North American dental care can deliver.

"No, no thanks, Dr. Thorpe." No Peter Sellers East Indian accent, as I always did him for our family dinner theatre, knowing full well that he wasn't an Indian immigrant; if anything, I now detected a lovely Irish lilt. "I think I can just make it to your place under my own steam. You might open a beer for me!" Huffing and puffing away, he's not kidding about the effort, but joking nonetheless. Good man, Ben!

"It's Lorne. And consider it done, Ben. Seriously now, I'll have two cold ones open and waiting at our front stoop! You've earned it, old man!"

In my excitement I hit the accelerator—the car jumps, there's a thump behind followed by a groaning from Veronica. I drive off glancing in the rear-view to see simultaneously the back of her head and startled eyes in the new mirror with its silvery stretch mark.

"Guess what cra-acked?" she sings.

"*Shit*... Ah well, all the better, we're still hanging it."

"*What*? No way... Oh, you're joking."

"Me, joking?"

"You are."

"Like shit I am!"

About the Author

Gerald Lynch was born in Ireland and grew up in Canada. *Missing Children* is his fifth book of fiction, the third set in the Ottawa suburb of Troutstream, and preceded by the acclaimed novels *Troutstream* (1995) and *Exotic Dancers* (2001). He has also authored two books of non-fiction, edited a number of books, and published many short stories and essays and reviews. He has been the recipient of a number of awards for his writing, including the gold award for short fiction in Canada's National Magazine Awards. He teaches at the University of Ottawa.

Eco-Audit
Printing this book using Rolland Enviro 100 Book instead of virgin fibres paper saved the following resources:

Trees	Solid Waste	Water	Air Emissions
4	173 kg	14,092 L	567 kg